A
DEWDROP
AWAY

by C.A. Allen

Dedication:
To my grandmother, Agnes Allen, with whom I first
shared the idea years ago.
To my mother, Julia Allen, who would also have loved to
see these words in print.
To my father, Tony Allen, for his support, constant
encouragement, and infinite knowledge of computers.
To all of the friends, family, and professors who have
supported my writing over the years.
And to you, the reader. Thanks for stopping by,
incidentally.
I hope you enjoy the journey.

ARBORAND

Table of Contents

BOOK I: *The Golden Chestnut*

Prologue

"Rupert, listen closely now. I love you above all else in this world. As long as you stay true to your own heart, it will remain my dwelling place until you join me in spirit."

Rupert brushed his matted gray fur out of his eyes as a tear trickled down his nose onto his paw, clasped in that of his mother.

"Please, mother. Everything will be all right. I'll send word to Zirreo. We'll get you better. You'll see." He strained to speak through his tears, voice a choking whisper. The young mother squirrel smiled weakly up at him as he began tenderly stroking her shoulder, where the scars from years of cruel labor stood out boldly.

"Rupert, there is but one thing I have left to tell you, something you must never forget. I want you to remember this the way you would remember a prayer. Rupert, no matter where you go, who you meet, or what fortune awaits you in this world, you must remember that though the creatures in it can be vastly different, our hearts beat as one, and our souls are naught but a dewdrop away. If everyone only understood what I just told you...then maybe...they...could...reunite as...one...Goodbye, Rupert."

"Mother," the young squirrel pleaded desperately, "don't just leave me here...I don't understand! I can't..." Rupert's voice trailed off into a sob. The chill of realization had come, leaving his chest cold and constricted. The icy paw of death had visited his home and left him alone in this death camp. A wave of exhaustion came over the orphaned gray as he collapsed on the cold straw next to where his mother laid, her words echoing through his head.

"Our souls are naught but a dewdrop away..."

Rupert woke in the stifling silence of his lean-to. All the dried, dead grasses he used for his bed had been kicked out from underneath him. For a moment, Rupert only stared, blinking, at the sight immediately around him and at the rising sun up to his right. The morning was cold. And as if this mild realization were some sort of door through which understanding moved, he remembered.

He'd dreamed about her again, about it. It had been a full ten seasons since Rupert's mother had died, fully succumbing to the chill of a particularly bad winter combined with the wall-work the blacks had them do day in and day out. It was natural; it was horrible. But it was so, so long ago. Why now, the gray squirrel wondered, sitting up and feeling dizzy from the emotion the night had drained from him. It was so long ago, so why should it come back in its full power now? He couldn't remember any of the little details—the room they were in (that particular lean-to had been destroyed after Enevah's death, and anyhow, they all looked the same) or even whether it had been winter (it might have been fall, a voice whispered in his mind). He wasn't even sure that all of the words his dream-mother said to him were indeed the same that she had whispered on her death bed. All except for that last…that part had been real. He still remembered the way her paw turned out again as it finally lost all movement, the way her chest hitched once, twice, before she spoke. Our souls are naught but a dewdrop away. It was a nice sentiment, he supposed, and it had always sounded pretty to his young ears, especially in her voice, when he let it echo in his head. It meant little, though, and only served to make him sad.

Why now?

BOOM. BOOM. BOOM.

The sounds of the drums reverberating through the distance towards him snatched him from his painful reverie. So. It was that time again. Going as slowly as he thought he might be able to get away with, Rupert dragged himself to the 'door' side of his lean-to and peered out. Sure enough, beyond the few other lean-tos in his immediate area, he could see the grays coming back across from the wall. Rupert's shift was not until later, so he'd been getting his sleep in at a fairly decent hour, but this certainly wasn't the luck of most of the grays imprisoned here. Some of them had been forced to work building the great rock walls that surrounded the compound nearly all the way through the night without breaks. Rupert dreaded that shift. It was tiring and dangerous in equal amounts. The walls that the black squirrels had them build were gargantuan, rising about a hundred squirrels in height, but it was the bits of stone, sharpened to deadly points sticking out everywhere that made the job a nightmare. It was not unheard of for a gray to lose his footing or even to be pushed by one of Emperor Venul's chickarees, and end up impaled. Rupert himself had almost suffered a similar fate, but he had ended up saved by Oliven, his friend, the smoothest and most agile squirrel that Rupert knew. He could have sworn sometimes that his friend hadn't grown up in the Firwood compound, as comfortable with climbing as he seemed.

BOOM. BOOM. With only a couple more beats, the sound of the drums echoed off into silence and Rupert propelled himself from his lean-to with a sudden start. It would be no good to show up late. After a time, the fierce red chickarees started closing in around the gatherings, and they wouldn't let him in without a fight.

Luckily, there was a gap in the crowd settling in around the great tree when Rupert arrived, and he was able to slide into the mass of bodies undetected. Being jostled this way and that, Rupert stared up at the great tree where it rose starkly into the sky, the only tree he'd ever seen in his life, a powerful thing, black as the squirrels within and pumping with magic and strange life. The crowd began to settle and they waited.

They did not have long to wait. At the base of the Great Tree there stood a platform, about half as tall as the tree itself. It was from this elevated height that the black squirrels usually gave their orders and their messages and…their warnings.

Today was one such day. As usual, the black squirrels spoke through their chickarees. It was rare for any of the grays in the compound to catch sight of one of the immortal and dangerous blacks, and many never had for all the years since their birth into slavery. Some said that the blacks didn't really exist, but Rupert knew otherwise. He had seen one once, cutting his way through a crowd so that he'd had to look twice, and it wasn't something he was like to forget.

"Attention, all yew grays!" shrilled one of the chickarees, now perched atop the platform. The black bark made the red squirrel's coat appear to be on fire as he raised his arms and the crowd came to a hush. The chickaree paused, his greedy little eyes focused elsewhere, and then, as though his next words had come from somewhere beyond himself, he zeroed in on them again with fiendish delight. "Emperor Venul would like to call yer attention to a fellow gray of yer aq-ac- quentince-whatever." Parts of the crowd tittered softly at the red's struggle over the word, something he didn't fail to notice. Glaring at them and then appearing to argue softly with someone no one else could see, the red continued after a break. "He wishes to make an example of a squirrel who broke the law."

The sea of grays was silent now; every smirk had been wiped from any face that had dared crack a smile. Once more, they waited. The chickaree reached downward now, beckoning for someone to come join him on the platform. The squirrel that stepped into sight made Rupert's insides seize up.

Anyone would have been bad, anyone, but this—

Rupert tried to convince himself of useless things in his mind, things that did not change who the figure was on the platform. It was Oliven.

As he watched, Oliven climbed the platform easily, though Rupert thought he saw a faint tremble in the other gray's step. When he reached the top, Oliven faced the crowd and gave a shaky smile. Rupert knew he was only trying to be brave, but it seemed the smile was directed at him. Other squirrels around him seemed to have the same feeling; they shifted about uncomfortably until the chickaree called them to attention once more, looking slightly peeved.

"This fine day," the chickaree crowed, "we will see what it means to try to *escape*," he put stress on the word, "as this squirrelly thought he could." He sniggered and smacked Oliven on the back, reaching around to grope at one of his pockets as he did so. Oliven pulled back, refusing to play the game of fright, and the chickaree frowned. "Well then," he said, "we'll be taking this ikkle one to be hung."

Everyone's eyes were drawn to the one thing they'd been trying to avoid the whole time: the noose hanging from the gallows that the platform really was.

Afterward, all Rupert could think of was Oliven's quivering smile, the way even toward the end, his friend had been brave. He didn't think of the noises of horror or the way it had taken Oliven so long to die. There was no other way. His friend was— had been a survivor.

It was different this time, though, this time above all others, because even as he went to walk away, even as he went to take his shift building the walls that imprisoned him, Rupert thought of the dream, of the memory. Oliven had died trying to escape the compound. What would his mother have wanted of him, had she been alive? He had a hard time thinking she would have wanted for him to die here...but what other choice was there? The wall holding the grays inside of their imprisonment rose up in front of Rupert like a warning, but Rupert wasn't paying attention, not really. Even when a chickaree came within two feet of him, whip in paw, he barely flinched as he bent to scavenge for stone in the rocky earth. There was a reason for everything, as Enevah had been fond of telling him. As he'd gotten older and increasingly more jaded, Rupert had dismissed this reminder, assuming that it was only created for the comfort of youth. But perhaps the problem was not that the words weren't true, but that he hadn't believed them until now.

For years of oppression, Rupert had dealt quite well; it was all he knew after all. It was only now that he allowed the anger to come.

Chapter One

He could see them clearly now, the black squirrels were coming closer. He didn't know if they could see him behind the veil the waterfall created, but he hoped not. He edged further to the right and felt something touch his foot. A small, round leather case was wedged in between two rocks next to him. With a strange lack of hesitation he picked it up, opened it, and looked at what was inside.

It was the prettiest thing he had ever seen, a shiny chestnut crafted of a smooth golden glass. Hesitantly, he took it out of its case and felt its warmth on his paws. He felt a magical tremor within him. A high-pitched gust of wind came and went, and when he looked around for the black squirrels, they were gone, all but a few who seemed afraid of him. He heard wind blowing underneath his feet, though the rock remained solid as ever. "Southwest under the falls," it whispered in a gust that sounded like breath. The glowing chestnut got brighter and brighter until…

Rupert woke again with a start. It was about the first hour of the morning, and he couldn't tell what had caused him to wake this time. Earlier in the night, he had awoke twice to nightmares, one concerning Oliven coming toward Rupert with a smile on his face, a smile that faltered as Rupert watched him slowly strangle to death on the air around him, no rope in evidence, calling for Rupert, asking why, why would he not help him…then it had switched to the image of his mother once again, saying her dying words.

But this dream…this dream had been different.

He closed his eyes and slowly it drifted back to him. "Southwest under the falls", the golden chestnut, the disappearing black squirrels. It seemed so real that he could not just brush it off. It stuck in his head, nagging him unbearably. Rupert had rarely, if ever, dreamed at all before now, and the strange succession of dreams, growing more disturbing each night, was really putting him off kilter. He needed answers, especially pertaining to this last, newest dream—he couldn't shake it from his head no matter how he tried.

Rupert forced himself to rise from the straw he was lying on. It was uncomfortable and smelly, but he was used to it. He must go see Zirreo. If anyone knew what his dream meant, it would be the wise old squirrel. It was still night, so he had hours until his day shift at the wall. The biggest problem would be not getting caught. He crawled to the entrance to his lean-to, and checked for guards. Visitations were not allowed at night. The three guards on the far wall of the compound were quarreling, something red squirrels did often. Too often, Rupert thought. He darted out quickly, knowing that if he were caught both he and Zirreo would be sentenced to death. He made it to Zirreo's just in the nick of time.

Zirreo was a mystical figure. Though he appeared to have been trapped in the compound like everyone else, he was different from the others, first of all because he was a white squirrel, perhaps the only white squirrel in Firwood. White squirrels were said to be magic, the reason most other feared them. Even the black squirrels knew enough not to bother Zirreo. Though they were immortal, this was apparently not enough to keep them from fearing magic. Emperor Venul would sometimes call on him to solve little problems he had. Rupert didn't think Venul knew about Zirreo's alliance with his family, or he would have done something about it by now.

The inside of Zirreo's living space was a tad larger than the living spaces of any of the other squirrels, and pitch black due to the fact that Zirreo's place had four walls and a roof of bark. The entrance was a leaf flap. Considering that most squirrels liked to keep neat, Zirreo was on the messy side. However, most of the mess was paper, and Zirreo always seemed to be fussing over tidying it up. It was this very activity that Rupert found Zirreo engaged in as he entered the old squirrel's makeshift home. Rupert smiled as he watched Zirreo curse under his breath as he let a paper slip from his paw. "Messy as a chickaree," he laughed.

"Rupert, you know better than to go around insulting others," Zirreo scolded him without looking up. "Why are you up this late anyway? Sleeping problems?"

"I had a, uhm." Rupert felt lame speaking the problem aloud, but he pushed on. "A disturbing dream."

"Strange."

Rupert stared at Zirreo confusedly. He felt like a newborn every time he was around him.

"What's strange?"

The light from the firefly cans on Zirreo's desk illuminated his face in a mysterious and somehow dangerous way. "Nothing, Rupert. What was your dream like?"

So Rupert went through his most recent dream again for Zirreo. He figured he could exclude anything about the numerous dreams of his mother. They seemed more emotional things than anything else, and he didn't want to seem overly paranoid. Rupert kept from looking at Zirreo as he was talking, but after he had finished he had no other choice. Zirreo seemed greatly worried. It was not what Rupert expected.

"My," the old white squirrel whispered, "this is too much. But it fits. It fits."

Rupert couldn't contain himself. "What, Zirreo? What's the matter? What does it mean?"

Zirreo turned to Rupert and smiled in a warm but serious manner. His pink eyes twinkled with some hidden excitement. Rupert was mystified. "I'm glad you came to me tonight, Rupert, very glad. What you have dreamt is a series of things to come."

Rupert felt a chill go down his spine. "You mean it's the future?"

"Don't be silly Rupert, no one can tell the future for sure. Do you know why the black squirrels are immortal?"

The question caught him by surprise. He had always been told that the black squirrels were "the chosen race" to reign over Firwood, and eventually all of Arborand. He had been taught that about sixty seasons ago, the heavens above, along with the squirrel goddess Astrippa herself, made the black squirrels, her own kind, immortal. Rupert told Zirreo exactly that, proud that he knew something of history. To his astonishment, Zirreo only laughed at him.

"And why would Astrippa do that, I wonder?"

"She's a black squirrel and she wanted her race superior," Rupert answered without hesitation, surprised at Zirreo's apparent ignorance.

Zirreo's expression shifted quickly to one of outrage.

"How could you say that? No one knows what color Astrippa is and she is certainly not pleased at what you've learned. The black squirrels were only made immortal by a very special object. Some say it was made by Astrippa herself, but that's all rumor and in any case it's about all that you could pin on a god. The black squirrels just happened to find it first."

Rupert felt his face get hot, but he noticed that Zirreo was watching him closely, and then he understood what should have been obvious sooner.

"The golden chestnut in my dream."

Zirreo smiled, but Rupert was still confused. If the black squirrels had the golden chestnut to make them immortal, why had he found it under a waterfall in the dream? It seemed utter nonsense.

Zirreo seemed to read his thoughts.

"Do you know what I think, Rupert?" He paused and then carried on without waiting for an answer. "I think the golden chestnut has disappeared."

"Disappeared? How?"

"There are many ways it could have happened. The black squirrels, however, are still immortal, so no other must have touched it yet."

"Was it magic?" Rupert's brain hurt. If such a great possession as this chestnut was supposed to be was stolen, wouldn't the thief want to touch it?

Instead of scoffing at Rupert's confused suggestion, Zirreo brightened. "Good thinking, Rupert! You possess an amazing amount of insight for one so young!" Then his expression grew serious once more. "Do you know what this dream truly means, Rupert? Astrippa herself has called on you to retrieve the chestnut. You are to be the one to change the lives of grays in Firwood."

"But you said Astrippa—

"Astrippa has nothing to do with anything evil, such as the corruption of the black squirrels; they brought that upon themselves when they found the chestnut. But that doesn't mean that Astrippa can't intervene for the correction of the folly we commit."

"So the black squirrels, they weren't…they weren't always like this?"

It was hard for Rupert to imagine the black squirrels as anything but mysterious, sinister figures who dictated every misfortune of his life, but Zirreo was nodding.

"Yes. You see, in the beginning Firwood was gray land, and the blacks kept to Oakwood, on the border. Everything went along fine and they traded peacefully…until the golden chestnut was found. At first, the black squirrels had everything they wanted. But then they grew jealous of the land the grays had, and easily used their immortality to take over Firwood. Now they own both lands, enslaving the inhabitants of the latter and treating them cruelly. Venul has taught the grays a false history so no one will know of the chestnut."

"How do *you* know, then?" Rupert asked.

"I have ways of finding out," Zirreo replied, "I have convinced Emperor Venul that I am trustworthy. You must go, Rupert. Don't you see? Once the cause of their immortality is taken away from them, those who have lived past their time will fade away. Venul is one such squirrel."

Zirreo seemed to sense that Rupert did not appear sure of himself. "Rupert, it may help you to know that it was your own grandfather who led the defense against the blacks when they stormed into Firwood."

Rupert's eyes widened. It was absolutely too much to take in. He knew nothing of his family, aside from his mother of course. His father, Floridem, had been sentenced to death on mere unproven suspicion of trying to rise against the crown. Rupert had been a mere three seasons then, and remembered only his smile.

"I--I'll do it of course," he said, "In fact, I'll go tomorrow night."

"No, no my boy, it must be tonight." Rupert could not escape hearing the urgency in Zirreo's tone. "You see, once a thing of magic strays from its owner, the owner feels a sort of emptiness. Venul feels that emptiness. He came to me about it. Of course, I didn't tell him, but it will only be a matter of time before he figures it out, and finds it gone. You must leave now."

Rupert wanted to know so much more, but the look Zirreo was giving him told him in the kindest way possible that there was no time. He turned to leave and then turned back. Something was still niggling at him, and it was more than a suspicion.

"Zirreo?"

"Yes?"

"Once I touch this chestnut, the grays will be immortal, won't they?"

"Yes. And Rupert...because of your paw in their freedom, they may count on you for guidance. It is hard to pick up one's life after it has been so fettered with terror. They will need...someone to lead them."

Rupert stared at Zirreo, who was giving him a sly sidelong look out of the corner of his eye, calculating. It was still too much for him to take, still too much...and yet, he remembered well the anger from yesterday, the first time he'd properly felt the need not just to lay low, but to do something. Zirreo was giving him a perfect opportunity. He could not afford to look back.

"I'll be a good ruler, if need be. I promise."

Zirreo smiled, but the intensity in his eyes never once faded. "I'm glad you will Rupert. But just remember, countless things can go wrong when holding an object of magic."

Chapter Two

Rupert wished that the night he began his quest was warmer. The chill air felt numbing on his skin. He curled his tail over his back in an attempt to keep warmer. He had made it to the gallows so far without being seen. Did chickarees ever quit quarreling? In any case, he was thankful for it. He couldn't even imagine what the feisty little reds could possibly be nagging about, but at least it distracted them.

Right now, Rupert had a bigger problem. He needed a way to get out of the camp. And fast, before dawn broke. He looked around and his eyes caught on the place where he knew the trap door must lie below the noose dangling from the gallows. It was worth a try. He looked over at the chickarees. It looked like there would be blood between the three of them that night. And to think they always did this! Rupert ran up the steps carved in the side of the platform—yes, it was there, he could see it!— and pulled on the door. No use! Feeling panicked out in the open, Rupert turned to go back to his hiding place and slipped in his haste. Suddenly, there was nothing under him but air, and he was falling!

Rupert landed with a bump on solid ground. He reached up groggily and found his nose was bleeding from the impact. Rupert looked up at the swatch of night sky above, like cool velvet encrusted with diamonds, and realized he had fallen through the trapdoor! It was so dark down underground that he couldn't see anything. This made him fairly nervous, as squirrels are none too fond of the subterranean world. He reached out to either side of him and immediately felt the dirt walls. Feeling slightly better, he started groping his way along the narrow passageway. At about two points, he felt openings like doorways, but went past them into the continuing darkness beyond. Perhaps this tunnel did not feel so sinister in the daytime.

Rupert got the sudden sensation that he was being watched. Slowly, he turned around. He thought he caught a bit of movement behind him, but he couldn't be sure. The sensation had left however, as quickly as it had come, and Rupert continued on. He began to feel a draft of air, and shortly afterward the tunnel began slanting up.

Before he knew it, Rupert was outside in the cool night air, a few inches from the enormous tree the ruling black squirrels lived in. Startled, he put on a burst of speed and got farther away from the cursed tree just for safety's sake. Finally he could let his feelings take free reign, now that he was out of immediate danger. In doing so, Rupert found that he felt overwhelmed and excited by what he had to do. Rupert turned and looked back at the labor camp in the distance. A blood red mist seemed to settle over it with the dawn of day.

"Goodbye," he said, unsure whether the words heralded a blessing or a curse. It was only for one squirrel now, after all. With that one word, he turned and didn't look back. He knew his quest, and he knew where his destination lay. *Southwest under the falls."* He kept the North Star in his field of vision, and with the wind at his back, Rupert finally understood the tingling feeling inside him. For the first time in his life, Rupert felt free.

Emperor Venul paced his throne room in a fit of rage and panic. His life was at stake. The golden chestnut was gone-vanished along with the case he had left it in, into thin air. He flicked his tail in a disgusted manner.

Zirreo had to have known this had taken place. Venul was almost certain Zirreo possessed magic, and that made him a very possible suspect. Venul spat at the picture of Goddess Astrippa hanging at a lopsided angle on his wall. In it, the goddess had been depicted as a beauteous black squirrel floating on a bit of cloud.

"Bet it's just fine with you, staring out at that wall like nothing's wrong. What kind of a goddess are you anyway? Neglect your chosen ones once more, and I'll do for you!"

Having blown off some of his steam, Venul straightened his crown and tried to think. Perhaps it had been stolen. A knock sounded at the door. Venul fingered the blood red diamonds around his neck. "Come in."

The door swung open at the curt order, and in came a young chickaree. She would have been pretty, were it not for her grim expression and stone cold eyes.

It was Kyan, his head officer. If there was a greedier squirrel in all of Arborand, Venul had not yet recruited her. Kyan entered the room coolly, and performed the required bow. She did not over-exaggerate or grovel at his feet. Instead, she looked as if not at all fazed to be in the close vicinity of the emperor. "Officer Kyan," he snarled. She acquiesced and gave him another bow.

"Good health to the emp'ror."

"Kyan, you don't really wish that, do you?"

But Kyan was eying the diamond necklace around the emperor's neck with a lust in her eyes. He decided to get right to the report. Chickarees were so rude!

"So, what have you come to tell me about, Officer? Make it quick."

"A gray has escaped. He used the trap door. I followed him a ways down the tunnel myself. 'Parintly,

Beesom and Laggo forgot to lock the door," she sneered, "They must also have extremely lousy guard bisnis."

Venul couldn't believe this. "I'll have them sentenced to death," he growled. Then he thought of something. It all seemed rather fishy. If Zirreo had in fact moved the chestnut, he could have sent the gray one after it, because he was too old and lazy to be bothered with such menial tasks himself, perhaps. Venul tried to keep the thought from stinging, but it didn't help.

"I have a task for you. A very important one. You may have noticed that I have had a shiny gold chestnut hanging around."

"Gold?" Kyan said with interest.

"Gold colored glass."

"Oh. Haven't noticed."

Venul feigned surprise. "That chestnut is a special family heirloom, and it's been taken. I have a hunch that the gray squirrel who escaped is after it. I want you to follow him to it. It is very important that you get to it first. Whatever you do, I do not want you to take it out of the case I had it in. I don't want you fingering my prized possession. If I spot one paw print, and you know I have eyes like a hawk…if you touch it, you're dead. Understood?"

Kyan understood perfectly. "What's in it fer me?"

Venul chuckled. "If you're not dead, then you will be handsomely rewarded." He paused, then added, "I swear on my immortality," and waited for the reaction.

Kyan looked as if she were trying hard to hold in her excitement.

"What—er—what exactly is 'handsome' in this case? Just so I get the idea, like."

Venul's eyes roved to the ceiling. Only Kyan.

"Let me make this clearer for you. If you carry out the task I have assigned you, *to the letter*, then you will receive *all* of my jewels. No exceptions. If you fail, however…the price will be *severe*."

Kyan didn't seem even to have heard the last part. She gulped, her eyes widening with unmistakable greed. When she spoke again, her voice was dry and raspy.

"Right, oh emperor. You get the chessnut, back untouched, and I get all the treasure. Deal!"

She saluted cockily, and left in pursuit of the gray.

Venul smiled craftily. He hadn't had another black go on this mission for the simple reason that they were all immortal, and would demand the position of emperor in return. Chickarees however, were useful for this sort of thing. He could, unlike with the blacks, simply go back on his promise and give Kyan the reward of death. So much for his vow on the treasure. He would have thought that chickarees would be smarter about this sort of thing, seeing as they never kept their own promises—they were too used to having every other squirrel be leagues more honorable than them. Venul sat back in his throne smugly. Things were getting better by the minute. After a moment, he walked over to his door and opened it. The chickaree guarding it had been taking a nap. He snapped awake immediately at the noise.

"Emperor." They always forgot to bow.

But his thoughts at the moment were much more of much more importance than self-centered chickarees.

"Go to the compound and bring me the white squirrel. It's time we had a little talk."

Chapter Three

It was a bright, sunny day out. Rupert awoke from the pile of pine needles he had used to hide under. After clearing a couple of miles the previous night to get far enough from the labor compound, Rupert had reached the edge of Aspen Forest, a mix of aspen and pine trees. He had been so exhausted from all the excitement and suspense last night that he had overslept. Rupert guessed it to be about noon. He got up, stretched, and nibbled on a pinecone to satisfy his hunger. He wished there was a pond or river somewhere nearby, as he felt a bit thirsty. *Oh well* he thought. Things had gone well so far, he couldn't ask for much more.

As he turned southwest, away from the forest, he felt the fur on the nape of his neck rise as a chill crept down his back. Rupert felt like he was being watched, the same sensation he had felt the night before in the tunnel. His eyes wandered up to the trees above him, but there were so many shadows up there that he couldn't tell if one of them was the watcher. Rupert told himself to stay calm. It was probably no more than his mind playing tricks on him. Besides, he had an urgent quest to go on. If Venul found out…well, he wasn't sure he wanted to think about that right now. He checked the position of the sun and set off away from the forest.

Rupert had always imagined that Firwood outside of the compound must be exciting, full of fascinating landmarks and even more fascinating squirrels living under this thing called freedom. The trail ahead of him, however, was mostly grassland with a couple dozen trees scattered about every mile. Every so often, he would climb one of these trees and check the horizon, but all he could see was the same view for what seemed to be miles and miles. By the end of the day, Rupert was starting to wonder if he would ever find water. His mouth was parched and he was growing weary. Though it was growing dark, he knew he could not just fall asleep on the spot, where his coat of gray would give him away easily to any unfriendly squirrels living nearby. Stumbling along, his eyelids starting to drop, Rupert felt the ground beneath him giving way. Too late he realized that there was a small hole right underneath him, and then he was falling.

It was only a split second before he hit a hard surface of clay-like soil, and then, before he could get his bearings, he was off again, sliding, sliding further down the tunnel. He feared what was waiting for him at the end. All of a sudden, the tunnel took a sharp turn and Rupert was flung head over tail into a brightly lit underground dwelling. Then, before he could gain his bearings everything went black, as if someone had turned off the lights upon his arrival.

A great deal of whispering from somewhere else in the room ensued. Rupert listened, unsure whether it was okay to breathe yet.

"Must've knocked over the lamp, Nim."

"Might've been the newcomer. There was more than one lamp, sir."

"Someone's in here Nim. I can sense it."

"That's what I said, sir."

"Oh no…"

"Yes, sir? What is it?"

"Nim, what if it's them?"

"B-but they wouldn't…they can't."

"They could have found me."

"What do you suggest, sir?"

"Talk to them while they're still in the dark. Scare them off when they can't take a shot at us."

Rupert was still trying to figure out whether these creatures were hostile or not, when one of them pressed a sudden, threateningly toned inquiry on him.

"Hey you! You be warned that there are a lot of us here, and if you mean no good, this is not the place to be causing trouble!"

Lots of them, Rupert thought. He had only heard two voices…and the chamber had looked rather small before the lights went out. When the voice spoke to him again, it was shaking slightly. "Go ahead; state your name and species. And be warned, if the lights come on and we find you to be some ruffian chickaree of Venul's…"

That got Rupert talking. "N-no! I'm a-a gray, but please don't turn me in, I was escaping, I didn't mean to- Rupert cut himself off as he heard a low hiss come from someone in the room. Gathering up his courage, he took one step forward into the darkness and said boldly, "I don't mean any harm, but I'm not afraid of you either."

Immediately, the light was restored to the room. It was a very simple dwelling with a grass bed, a table, one chair, and four firefly lamps scattered about, lighting up the place. Rupert, however, took no notice of his surroundings, and continued to stare at the figure across the room from him. He was a sturdy looking gray fellow with a jagged, fleshy scar under his right eye. He looked to be a bit past his prime, and some of his fur was turning white. A slightly crazed look of defiance was gleaming in his eyes, seeming to have been fixed there permanently by events long past.

"Floridem?" the squirrel asked, breaking the silence. His jaw trembled slightly. "Flor, is that you?"

Rupert blinked in surprise. "Floridem is-was my father's name," he said slowly. "But how did you--?"

"Your father, eh?" A smile spread over his face, "Well…what did you say your name was?"

"I didn't. I'm Rupert, sir."

It was then that Rupert took notice of the smaller creature standing by the other squirrel. It looked just like a red squirrel, only with black and white stripes on its sides, which were heaving up and down rather excitably.

"Sir, may I ask you why you have some sort of chickaree next to you?" Rupert asked, trying and failing to hide the disgust in his voice.

The other only laughed. "Oh, him? He's just a chipmunk. Haven't you ever seen one before? Harmless as dust, but good servant material. Mine here's named Nim." He turned to the chipmunk, who stepped forward and dipped his head in a polite bow.

"Pleased to make your acquaintance sir," he said with reverence.

Rupert turned back to the gray. "But—who are you and how do you know about my father?" he asked cautiously.

"Oh I'm so sorry," the other apologized, flushing a bit and turning his wild eyes to the side briefly. "After being stuck down here with only Nim for company for who knows how long, I've grown a little rusty in the art of introducing myself. My name is Talkin, and I have been dying to meet you."

On these last words, his eyes met Rupert's once more and steadied themselves there.

Rupert was thoroughly confused.

"Wait a minute here, how did you even know I existed?" he asked.

Talkin snapped his fingers and Nim pulled up a chair. "Please sit down," he told Rupert, "and I will explain."

Rupert sat.

"Your father was a very brave squirrel, and a good friend, Rupert. Floridem was the best friend I ever had, and the most valiant. Ironically, it was his boldness that got him killed. You see, in the back of his mind, Flor knew his beloved wife and tiny son were in danger under the rule of slavery we were living under, and nothing on earth could have stopped him from protecting them to his last breath. So it was that Flor tried to organize a secret revolt against the blacks. We found places in the walls, attempting to get through. We might have even made it with the numbers we got, but someone must have betrayed us at the last moment, because they were waiting outside, a whole group of them.'

I remember exactly what happened, remember turning around and screaming for all I was worth for your father to retreat, there was nothing he could do. For a brief moment he turned towards me, and I saw a black squirrel come up behind him. He was an evil half-breed type like I'd never seen before, with a white streak of fur across one side of his face. I've never seen a squirrel of mixed blood before, and it made my own blood chill at the cruel delight shining in his eyes as he raised a stone spear above his head. I started running towards them, but I reached them a second too late. As I lunged, hoping to take him off balance, the half-breed brought his spear whistling down. Halfway through its travel, it sliced my face open just under the eye. In the midst of my agony, I heard Flor scream his last and felt something small and cold hit me. I searched around for it, but in the blinding wall of snow, I couldn't see much. When my paws finally found what they were looking for, and clasped around it, I looked up to find myself facing about twenty black squirrels. I did the only sensible thing left to do. I ran. I ran far into the night. Even though I knew they had long since stopped following me, I would not stop running. If I stopped, I would have to admit I was lost and face the truth that I would slowly fade away, alone in the blizzard. I was running out of breath though, and soon I would have no choice. I silently prayed to Astrippa to give me a miracle, and- Talkin paused to take a sip of the birch beer Nim held out to him. "Lo and behold, I got one. All at once my paws went out from under me as I was nearing the border of Ashwood, and I found myself in this very hole. Nim's hole it was. Instead of forcing him out as some might have done, I gave him the honor of becoming my servant."

"Still the deepest honor sir," Nim commented, bowing yet again.

Rupert felt greatly saddened upon hearing of his father's demise. When he could find his voice again, he told Talkin of the quest he had been sent on. Talkin listened eagerly, his eyes widening when he heard the part about the chestnut's power.

"You are a very special squirrel, Rupert," Talkin finally said after digesting the news. "I have little doubt that Astrippa herself has chosen you. Though having known your father, I'd be inclined to say it's no surprise." The expression on Talkin's face was reverent.

Rupert knew it must be getting dark out by now, and no matter how he would have liked to stay for the night, he might be endangering his father's old friend, if he was in fact being followed. When he told Talkin about this, the older squirrel looked a bit disappointed, and

Rupert thought he could imagine how lonely he must be. Then, Talkin spoke.

"I see the sense in what you are saying, Rupert," he agreed, "I know of a hollow not far from here, right outside the border of Ashwood, where you could spend the night. I will show you to it in a minute. First, however-he paused to go over to his bed and took something out of the straw where it seemed to have been hidden. He walked the short distance back to Rupert. In his paws, he held a delicate silver chain from which hung a small acorn, silver to match. On it was engraved the letter "F." *F for Floridem,* Rupert thought as Talkin handed it to him.

"I would like to give you this before you leave. It was your father's. He would have wished it to be yours someday. Who knows, maybe Astrippa saved my life so I could carry out this task. It's kind of funny how much luck falling into a hole can bring." He and Rupert shared a little laugh at that, and Rupert found himself smiling wistfully. He didn't think he would have found another friendly face so close after losing Oliven and it made him sad to have to leave so quickly. Talkin broke into his thoughts once more.

"Well, Rupert, if someone *was* watching you, and I always like to trust my instincts, then they saw you go into this hole. They mustn't see you come out with me; your enemies are mine as well, and it would cause too much trouble. Nim, you'll have to show Rupert the place. It looks a little strange to see two squirrels coming up from underground anyways, as most of us are blessed with a good limb on which to make a home." He said this in a wistful tone of voice, and Rupert understood that living aboveground would make Talkin too easy to find so close to the Firwood compound. He was intrigued by this tree business. He was always hearing it was how squirrels were meant to be, and what sort of squirrel did that make him?

Nim got up and went to the entrance, beckoning for Rupert to follow. And follow he did, but not before saying goodbye to Talkin, who said his parting words.

"Your father was a great squirrel, Rupert. You are very much like him. In your eyes I can see his spirit and it lifts my own a great deal. I believe that someday we will have the chance to avenge him. If it is the will of Astrippa, Rupert, it would be an honor to Firwood to have you as our ruler."

Rupert smiled grimly to himself as he followed the tiny figure of Nim out across the hard ground. They had only gone a few yards when they came to another tree much like the one near Talkin's hole, only this tree was hollowed out near the base. Nim gestured towards it. "A snug sleeping place for you sir," he said.

"Thanks." Rupert yawned, exhausted.

Nim bowed and took off, and Rupert crawled into the base of the tree. Silently, he agreed with Talkin. He was tempted to try sleeping up in the tree itself, but there he risked greater chance of being seen. However, despite his discomfort, he was fast asleep within seconds, the lovely silver chain clasped in one paw.

From up above, in the leafy branches of the very same tree Rupert was abiding under, Officer Kyan watched him sleep. Although she knew she should stay out of sight lest the gray wake up, the chickaree was in a trance, gazing at something enclosed in his paw. It gave off a rare glint indeed.

"What has the filthy gray one got there?" she muttered to herself, pacing back and forth on a middling branch. "The emp'ror said nothing about this thing; he did not say 'Kyan, you mustn't touch this.'" She snickered gleefully. "So I will."

Kyan glided down from the tree with a single bound and soundlessly crept towards the sleeping Rupert.

"So shiny, so beautiful," she whispered, edging closer, her eyes shining with greed. "It's silver, it is. Sweeter than gold and silky in my paws," she murmured, moving her paws slowly up Rupert's body to where the little silver acorn glimmered in the rising sun. The breath she had been holding in thus far came out in one harsh sounding breath.

"Mine!"

Chapter Four

Emperor Venul stared wrathfully into the misty pink-red eyes of the white squirrel he had formerly trusted as a sort of personal advisor. No, not only a personal advisor. There was a time Venul might have thought him a friend, but being immortal didn't really allow any time for such things, and he'd made the trade so long ago he could barely remember it.

Two chickarees flanked the old squirrel, one on either side, spears at the ready lest he dare make an attempt to move from his uncomfortable position, slumped on the floor of the throne room, back against the wall.

Zirreo stared back at Venul calmly, without blinking. The latter spat to the side and ground his impressively sharp teeth angrily before speaking.

"So!" he snarled, "how clever you must think yourself, Zirreo, mighty clever to have outwitted an emperor like myself. But just how did you do it I wonder? Yes, that is what I would like to know. Tell me how you did it!"

Zirreo gave no sign of hearing him. Venul was becoming incensed. Somehow he realized it must have been his fault, letting Zirreo go so long unquestioned. That other revolt, the one they'd crushed, he'd suspected Zirreo all those seasons ago, Zirreo in addition to Ritorren's abhorrent son, *Floridem*, they were really close after all, but he hadn't wanted to believe it. But now...

"This is the last time I'm going to tell you, Whitey-interesting how you seem to go deaf whenever it suits you. Now answer me!"

Two spears instantly appeared at Zirreo's neck as he raised his head. "Well Venul, what is it you want me to tell you?"

Finally.

"Don't mess with me Whitey. You know what I'm talking about." Venul leaned over, so that Zirreo's nose and his own were almost touching. He spoke each word individually, through gritted teeth. "Where…is…my…chestnut?!!"

The two chickarees on either side of Zirreo exchanged glances. Zirreo raised an eyebrow, suggesting mild surprise. "I do not know why you would think I would know where the chestnut has gone, Venul, but I assure you that no one has taken it from you."

"What's that supposed to mean?!" Venul had had it with Zirreo's riddles. From day one, it seemed all the white squirrel was able to do, and after nearly a hundred seasons it was too much to take. "If you're trying to fool me, it's not working. I know what types of things you white types can do. Even a blind chipmunk could tell there's magic involved."

Zirreo's eyes twinkled. "Do you really think so?"

Venul paused for a moment, and then posed another question, this time with a sly edge to his voice. "Do you wish to explain to me the escape of a certain young gray squirrel just a couple nights back?"

No response. Zirreo was one of those who had the useful art of keeping his face devoid of emotion mastered.

Venul smiled. He had caught the older squirrel off guard, and he knew it. "Weren't expecting that, were you, old one? And just what would you do if I sent someone after him?" he paused to let the effect of his words sink in before saying, "a thing which I have already done, of course."

Venul knew the gray squirrel in question. Indeed, he wondered why he hadn't kept more of a close eye on him until now. He'd only seen him face to face once, when coming through a crowd of grays, threatening them to kill him, to try to mark his immortality. They had all been too afraid, of course. He remembered his eyes meeting those of one among their number, and holding. He'd known, then. It was Floridem's son. Floridem's son meant Ritorren's grandson. They were all the same. They were all trouble.

Zirreo let out a small, tired sigh. "Who'd you send after him, Venul?"

Venul scowled, and then decided no harm would come of answering the question.

"Kyan."

Zirreo's eyes widened slightly. He had met a few of Venul's chickarees in his time, none of whom he would have been proud to admit the acquaintance of.

"Kyan? What do you trust her for?"

In answer, Venul fingered his diamonds lazily and gave him a crafty smile. The chickarees on either side of Zirreo were staring at their emperor's necklace. Venul almost expected them to start drooling.

"Venul," Zirreo began, "I have no idea what the gray has to do with anything, but I do know where the chestnut is."

Venul, who had been pacing the room in thought, spun around immediately. "So?!"

"I told you I knew about the chestnut," Zirreo said simply.

"Where is it? Tell me!"

"No."

"Why?!" Venul was so angry he might as well have been spitting flames.

"You are far too corrupted, Venul. Whatever you did with the information I gave you would not be for the good of all. Therefore, I cannot give it to you. I am through, Venul."

Venul spun about. "What?" he asked, for once without any venom.

"You heard me. Anything you do from now on has to be without my guidance."

Venul began to shake, his motions quickly becoming those of cold fury.

"Take him away," he hissed, his eyes narrowed into tiny slits, "Take him away and lock him up in an empty room for two days. If he does not tell me everything, and I mean everything, then on the third day, he *dies* if he does not satisfy me. And he will," Venul added, as the two chickaree guards dragged the white squirrel out of the throne room.

When the great wooden door had closed with a dull thud, Venul let out a great breath of air. He sat back in his grand oaken throne and wiped his brow, just under his crown of emeralds. It was then that he realized something that made him feel very uneasy, something that made his blood chill.

Emperor Venul had been sweating.

Rupert came awake with a start. He knew at once that he wasn't alone. Something had been breathing on him. In a frightened panic, he scrambled to his feet, almost hitting his head on the low overhang of the tree he was under. Clawing his eyes, he searched wildly about for any signs of life.

The pale pink light of dawn was just beginning to visit the sky, and Rupert wished he hadn't come awake so suddenly. But he could've sworn on his life that some other presence was nearby.

Cautiously, he stuck his head out of the hollow and looked around.

All of a sudden, a rust red streak came out of nowhere and something hit him hard in the chest, knocking the wind out of him. Before he could so much as regain his senses, he felt himself being brutally choked, and pinned firmly against the ground. As the dust created by the scuffle cleared, Rupert found himself looking up into the face of a female chickaree, around his own age he would have guessed. She had the most wild, fierce expression in her eyes that Rupert had ever seen. As they stared into each other's faces, she slowly loosened her grip on his neck, got up from the ground, and continued to look at him.

Kyan's mind was ticking frantically. That wretched, stupid gray! How was she to know he'd wake up so suddenly? He'd cheated her of her lovely silver prize, he had. It was his fault, totally his fault she had attacked him, his fault she was angry. Kyan clicked her teeth and flicked her tail in frustration. She needed to think of something quick, something to douse his obvious suspicions. Luckily, Kyan had a clever mind, one in which a plan was already beginning to form.

Meanwhile, Rupert had gotten up off the ground, and was slowly dusting himself off without taking his eyes from the chickaree, lest she seize him again. Chickarees were never to be trusted. She must be one of Venul's, he knew it. All at once, a burning urge rose up inside of him, an urge to strangle the smaller squirrel standing in front of him, as memories from his early childhood came flowing back to him. His mother being beaten-by chickarees, his friend being hung-by chickarees, feeling his broken body being whipped by the bloodthirsty little creatures and not being able to fight back. Now he was alone with one, and actually finding it hard to decide what to do about it. The thought was shameful.

Kyan was growing impatient; the gray was taking too long, she must make the first move.

"Ehhem!" she coughed, "'scuse me whatsurname, but I thought you was-was someone else."

The gray looked at her, startled. Her plan was working.

"Lissen, er, I didn't mean to do that to yew back there, but I was skerred, see, thought I was being follered, I wuz growin' tired and weary and thinkin' I wuz gonna die o' thirst whin I came to this likkle place under this here tree, and it's around dawn, and I'm thinking to meself, 'Kyan, this 'un looks a better place th'in none.' So I come into here, and all of a sudden I realize I 'ent alone. Yew comed outta nowhere, see, an' just started thrashing around, so I goes an hides myself and then dives on you when the time's right. Thought you was a bad 'un all right. But then the dust clears, and yore just some stup-I mean, er, *friendly* looking gray fellow or other. So glad you're not them, I am." She concluded her tale, her expression silently smug with satisfaction.

The gray appeared totally nonplussed. He looked at her hard for a moment, and then his expression turned to one of curiosity tinged with suspicion. "Who's this 'them' you keep talking about?" he asked.

"The black squirrels o' course," she grunted, "Emp'ror Venul hisself sentenced me to death just cause I didn't wanna whip no grays." Kyan reflected on what she had just said. She could have patted herself on the back and hugged herself twice for the wonderful pack of lies that had just come out of her mouth. Kyan was a mistress of deception, and she knew it. She used her tongue like a weapon, a deadly weapon on some occasions. Something she had said had obviously perked the gray's interests, because just then he spoke.

"What did you say your name was again?"

"Didn' say. M'name's Kyan."

"Kyan," Rupert said aloud to himself. In spite of himself, he was beginning to rather like the blunt mannerism she portrayed. Still, there was something about her, something he didn't like. 'Never trust a chickaree, he'll leave you empty pawed' he thought, remembering a favorite saying of Zirreo's. Rupert thought a while. With his mind finally made up, he turned back to Kyan and said, "My names' Rupert. I am also escaped from the black squirrels."

Suddenly, his voice became hard and cold once more as he remembered something else. "Oh, and Kyan? I would like to know why you were following me."

Kyan's mind went blank and she cursed under her breath. This gray was smarter than he looked. She hated squirrels like that. Once, another chickaree had beaten her at a game of chessnuts. She had torn one of his eyes out in the resulting fight.

Kyan feigned a surprised look of innocence.

"Follerin' yew?" Whya think that? I 'ent never set eyes upon yew until this morning, and you're sayin' I'm follerin' yew?! That's inj'istice if I ever heard of it!"

Rupert looked a little unsure after this sudden outburst. "Well," he said, deciding he would treat her civilly until he gained further confidence in what to do, "I saw something-I mean no, I didn't, I heard-I heard sounds-sounds behind me." He cut himself short, realizing how lame he must have sounded. All he had for proof were *sounds* after all. Sounds and a *feeling* that there was something nearby. None of that was good enough to say for certain that someone had in fact been following him.

The poor blundering fool, Kyan thought, watching the somewhat embarrassed gray trail off into silence. An undisguised smirk crept across her features, which quickly turned itself into a pitiful frown as she remembered the rest of her sneaky plan. But the gray was not looking her way. His eyes were focused on the ground, and he seemed again to be in deep thought. Those grays and their thoughts! She became sorely tempted to say something nasty and facetious to snap him out of his little contemplation session, and had to focus on a nearby twig in order for the urge to pass.

Rupert looked up from the ground to where the rusty coated squirrel stood across from him, and noticed that her head was turned to the side, her eyes downcast so he had no way of telling what she could possibly be thinking. Could she really be telling the truth? He had the most difficult time discerning what was genuine, and he supposed he was rather naïve in his young age, certainly not as wise as Zirreo was, though he had the distinct impression that that certain wisdom was reserved for white squirrels alone. He felt he should know very well what chickarees were like from his experiences: greedy and always craving something, with little regard or understanding of the concept of 'others.' Yet could this chickaree be different? Could she really be upset over the thought of whipping grays like himself? The thought of whips made his blood boil, and he was reminded of the blood red scourge from his dream.

Thinking that it would be only appropriate to say something at this point, Rupert spoke out.

"Um…Kyan, did you say? Listen, I'm sorry if I startled you, but you did the same to me. I was taking a rest for the night, and didn't realize that someone else might stumble in upon me."

Rupert was not totally convinced that the chickaree was telling the truth. Chickarees were liars, which he knew well enough. But he had come upon the realization that if he let Kyan continue on her way, and she was, in fact, spying on him, which was perfectly possible, his lenience would maybe cost him his life. Who's to say she would leave him alone? Chickarees were not squirrels of their word. However, Rupert's sense of justice would just not allow him to kill anything that had any slight chance of being innocent. And so it was that he came to the only other conclusion left, though he didn't like it much at all.

"Kyan," he said, "As I have no reason to believe you guilty of following me," *Except my instincts*, "I have-well, that is, how would you like to be able to get back at the blacks? For all they've done to you, don't you think they deserve punishment?"

Kyan blinked, careful not to let the surprise she felt show itself on her face. Get back at the blacks? What in the name of rotten acorns did the thieving gray mean? He had robbed her of her beautiful silver treasure, and that was about the only thought that occupied her mind right then.

"I s'pose so," she snapped, then saw her mistake. "I mean, of cirse I would. How would yew be gittin back at 'em, I wonder?"

"Well…" Rupert started, stopping when he realized he obviously couldn't tell her about his mission.

"Let's just say that I'm on a type of quest to find a weapon which will make all the blacks go away, or so I'm told. I'm sorry I can't be more clear about it, but it's a secret mission, and I really don't know what exactly the weapon is. Someone sent me-

Rupert stopped short, his eyes widening a little. He had just let slip something which he shouldn't have, and he knew it, if nothing else by the way the chickaree female's eyes widened at this last.

Kyan had never felt so triumphant since the time she had gotten away with stealing her Aunt Gretchen's silver collection. So the gray was sent by the old white one, just like the Emperor said!

Rupert sat in stunned worriment. There was no way he could trust this chickaree so openly. For a moment, he even thought of putting her on a lead of some kind, then was disgusted with himself. Perhaps it was what her kind deserved, but his natural, inborn chivalry would not allow him to.

"Right...Kyan. I--we should probably get a move on, as the sun's already up. I want you in front of me, where I can see you."

"Oh, mighty suspicious are we?" Kyan sulked. She seemed about to issue another complaint, but her voice trailed off as she watched Rupert take the silver acorn on its chain, and hang it about his neck. Rupert looked at her questioningly.

"But then...I do want to get back at them black ones. So I'll ignore jist how mean yew are to me, yes I will, p'tend I don't notice at all, that's what I'll do. Because we got common ends, don't we oh gray one?"

"That's right," said Rupert heavily, shouldering his pack and moving off.

There was little conviction in his tone.

Chapter Five

A dragonfly glided past Rupert's ear, coming to land on a nearby leaf. He smiled at the creature, glad for some company other than that of his less than amiable companion. Whatever else Rupert was preoccupied with, he did take the time to notice what a stunning place Ashwood really was. Sure, it had its balmy, down-south type downsides, but he wasn't about to complain. For the first time in his life, Rupert was experiencing the freedom of traveling en route through the forest. The view from here was amazing, and the sunlight dappling through the trees, reflecting off of itself and casting it's warm glow on his fur caused a peacefulness to descend over him. Why, he could go to sleep right here and now...

"Cripes! Will you getta move on!"

The relaxing atmosphere did not seem to be having any effect on his companion. Kyan was hopping about impatiently at the end of the branch.

"Sorry," Rupert said, shaking out of his reverie. "I'm just happy to see the forest, you know. It's not every day I get to do this." He said this last bit pointedly, but Kyan ignored him.

"C'mon then, whilst you was napping all slowlike, I went ahead a bits and guess what I saw?"

Rupert was startled. Had he really taken a nap? He couldn't be so careless; for all he knew, he could have awaked at the end of a dagger. He trusted Kyan about as far as he could throw her.

"I saw others, and they en't like us," Kyan went on impatiently. "They're huge things, they are."

Rupert was jolted out of his suspicions. "Other squirrels, you mean?"

Kyan rolled her eyes. "No, other half-witted lumps like yerself. Of cirse they're other squirrels."

Rupert ignored the insult, following her as she leapt over two trees to a large, mossy oak. Peering down from the end of a branch, he could see nothing at first.

"Yer looking in the wrong spot," Kyan hissed, nudging him. He followed her gaze up into the dark shadows of a clump of ash trees, and still his eyes could discern no movement. Was this some trick the foul mouthed chickaree was playing on him?

"I can't see anything."

Kyan didn't answer for a full minute, peering off into the darkness, searching. Then she darted to the side so quickly that Rupert barely had time to register the movement.

Then three things happened at once. Rupert turned to see where Kyan had gone, heard the scratching sounds of claws shifting their grip on wood, and jumped out of his skin…and off of the tree.

Falling from a tree is not such a perilous thing to a squirrel, for they land in a fashion reminiscent of a cat, lightly and on all fours. Rupert was prepared for a landing such as this, but he never got one. Instead, what felt like a mass of vines began to twist itself around his plummeting form, catching him none too gently in the air.

Rupert hung suspended, the imprisoning net he found himself in swinging from side to side, slowly losing momentum. Rupert's heart set to work doing the exact opposite, going into total overdrive. He was sure this was the doing of the black squirrels. Kyan had lured him into a trap, and now they would take him back to the gray enslavement camp. Take him back and hang him, or worse, torture him into saying what he knew about the chestnut and its whereabouts.

Rupert felt a sharp yank on the net he was in, and he began to move upwards once again to the trees above. He steeled himself, getting ready to face his captors, resolving not to go down without a fight.

Soon Rupert was up over the edge of a branch, and his paws quickly found purchase on the wood, between the slats in the vine crafted net. He turned his head slowly to the right, and found himself staring into the tawny eyes of his captor.

It wasn't a black squirrel.

This squirrel was bigger than any black squirrel Rupert had ever seen, with odd, long, tufted ears and strange, reddish brown fur that appeared coarse and wiry. Strangely enough, the squirrel's eyes told a different story than his imposing body. He looked almost scared.

The squirrel jabbed a stone-tipped spear into the net, holding it at Rupert's throat.

"Who are you and why do you come here?" he asked gruffly, and this time, there was no doubt about it. Rupert could *smell* the fear. This guy may be big, but he wasn't as tough as he was trying to appear. Rupert spotted two other large squirrels behind the first, hanging back. Their eyes held the same trepidation. He didn't understand, but he didn't dare say anything with the cold stone point so close to his vitals. He heard a rustle from close by, and saw that Kyan was trapped in a similar net. She was busying herself with trying to chew through the vines, but they looked as though they were holding.

Rupert's captor shifted his attention to Kyan, jabbing his spear at her instead.

"Stop that, you," he said in what Rupert could tell he hoped was a menacing voice.

Kyan bared her small, pointy teeth at him. "Shiddup, yew big gnarly lug," she snarled, obviously in a temper. She dodged his spear, spitting a piece of chewed up vine at him. It hit its mark. Ten points. She snickered.

Rupert, taking responsibility as the more decent of the two, decided it was high time to negotiate.

"Look here," he began. All three huge squirrels shifted their attention to him. Rupert cleared his throat.

"You have no business to be imprisoning us, we haven't done anything wrong. I'm sorry if we've offended or scared you in any way, but that's no reason to lash out like this."

The lead squirrel started toward him with the spear.

"Oh stop waving that thing around, we know you're not going to hurt us," Rupert snapped, impatient to be getting on with his quest. He was losing time like this, and it was clear to him now that these squirrels, big as they were, were no killers.

The lead squirrel blinked at Rupert. "As far as *we* know, you're not intending harm for us," he answered, eyes narrowing suspiciously.

Rupert predictably began to regret his harsh tone. "Please just let us pass by, we're peaceful enough."

The other squirrel cast half a glance over to Kyan. Rupert sighed.

"Well, I am at least."

"Take them out of their cages," the lead squirrel ordered, and the other two complied, using their identical stone-tipped spears to cut a few key vines in the caging. Rupert gingerly stepped out, and was immediately seized by the squirrel who had opened his cage. The creature's grip was too much to fight, leaving Rupert to fume inwardly as he was flung unceremoniously over her back.

One cannot imagine how uncomfortable it is to ride on the back of someone else, whilst that someone else leaps from one tree to the next. Suffice to say that Rupert found himself concentrating a lot less on escaping and a lot more on holding on for dear life. Even Kyan was still for the moment, though Rupert guessed that wouldn't last long.

They passed from tree to tree, trying to hold whatever food their stomachs contained and not look down at the same time. Finally, the burly female squirrel Rupert was riding came to an immediate halt. Rupert looked around him, expecting to be let down, but the massive squirrels continued to stand in place on their hind legs, keeping a firm grip on their captives. Rupert strained to look around his captor's head, and found himself staring at something incredible.

Perhaps it came from being born in an enslavement camp and never having seen any squirrel communities at all, but the sight that met his eyes took his breath away despite his current situation.

They were standing facing an ash tree of staggering size, and a shape that could only be described as truly weird. Shooting upwards from the barely-distinguishable ground for several feet, then curving, almost curling in on itself in a strange stunt of growth, it traveled halfway back to the ground again. At the highest point, where the tree curved, was a grotesque looking knot in which a single, shaded window was placed, looking out over them like an admonitory judge.

The three large squirrels seemed to be waiting for something. Sure enough, out of a single knothole in the impressive tree, parallel to the branch they were standing on, came another squirrel, this one looking stern and nervous at once.

The new squirrel walked carefully, haltingly, coming up to the others in his own good time, and circling around them to get a good look at Rupert and Kyan, the latter of whom was now looking very sullen, bordering on murderous. Motioning to the other foreign squirrels, he led them into the knothole from whence he had come without speaking. Rupert was beginning to feel uneasy.

"Hold a second, what's this here?" he asked indignantly. "We're posing no harm to you, and we'd like to pass through this region, if that's okay."

The large squirrel leading them turned around swiftly, taking Rupert by surprise. Squinting into the other's eyes, he spoke at last.

"What exactly are you objecting to?"

Kyan watched the goings-on with renewed interest. Maybe the bigger squirrel would eat the gray.

"I'm objecting to you treating us like captives. Prisoners."

"I know what a captive is," the larger squirrel said gruffly, but his expression was easing up.

"Let them walk on their own," he told the others. Rupert and Kyan were placed gently on the ground once more, sandwiched between the four strangers. Kyan made a move to go back up out of the tree, but two of the other squirrels barred her passage forbiddingly. Rupert turned around indignantly, and the squirrel who had ordered their release held up a paw, silencing him.

"We would request that you spend a night with us, first. We will use this time to check that you do not have others with you, hiding about the forest, and then you will be free to be on your way."

Rupert was about to argue, when he realized how he and Kyan must look traveling together. Grays weren't known to get along with chickarees, and chickarees weren't known to get along with anyone. Slumping a bit, he resigned himself to the fact with an unhappy nod.

"As long as we can leave tomorrow."

There was a long pause, before the lead squirrel said

"My name is Glimrod."

"Rupert, and this is Kyan." He indicated the red squirrel, who looked testy.

"I can intraduce myself," she muttered.

Glimrod cast a last, questioning glance over the two of them, before leading them up along a wide, dark passageway. This was the first of several strange things Rupert began to notice in the fox squirrel (for this, he would learn, was what they were called) community. It was very dark. So dark, in fact, that Rupert was beginning to think that the window he had seen earlier was the *only* window this dwelling possessed.

Perhaps even more disturbing than the lack of light were the squirrels they passed along the way. There were very few of these, but those they did come across gave purely frightened looks in their direction before scampering away. Finally, Rupert couldn't take the paranoid glances anymore.

"Glimrod?" he asked politely.

The fox squirrel cocked an ear to show he was listening.

"Why is everything so silent?"

"Most of us are eating dinner now," Glimrod answered. Rupert couldn't have found his response any more ludicrous, but he didn't press any farther. Glimrod led them through so many twists and passages that Rupert began to feel sure he must've underestimated the size of the tree, hard as that was to stomach. Then all at once they had arrived at their destination.

A very officious looking door arose in front of them, and they looked up at it in awe. Glimrod knocked, and stood back respectfully. The door opened to reveal a wizened squirrel with small, watery black eyes. The old squirrel stared first at Glimrod, then at Rupert and Kyan, before stepping back to allow entrance. Rupert moved forward, but as soon as Glimrod crossed the threshold, the door was shut again, practically in his face. He started forward again, intending to knock, but he was held back by the same burly female who had been carrying him earlier. Feeling thoroughly disgruntled, Rupert fingered the silver acorn on the chain around his neck, and waited.

Kyan was feeling severely wronged, and the stupid gray hadn't made matters better by bickering constantly with the big fat squirrel. Again, she was reminded of her mission. Did it all fall to her to get them out of this place? And now some sort of conference was going on, and they were wasting precious time. Kyan strained to hear the muffled voices on the other side of the thick door, edging forward with silent purpose. One of the large squirrels with them twitched in her direction, but she was ultimately successful in securing the opportune position.

"Do you think that…?"

"I have told you several…it is important that they do not…" Here the elder's voice rose and then fell. Kyan waited for more, but instead footsteps sounded up to the door, and it was opened again. Glimrod came out into the hallway and stood among them silently for a moment. There was no sign of the older squirrel, though Kyan strained to look back into the room from whence he had come.

The gray was fidgeting with his precious, pretty piece of silver, which really ought to be hers. It would be hers. In the end.

Glimrod came out of the sort of daze he had been in moments earlier and sprung into action.

"If you two will just follow me, I will lead you around." With a wave of his paw, he dismissed the three others, who obeyed. Rupert felt relieved to see them go. Turning back the way they had come, Glimrod led them down the main hall a ways, before breaking off into a cavernous, arched chamber. Even here, it was dark and dim, giving the oppressive feeling of constant night. A few firefly lamps were lit on raised tables down the length of the room, and the walls were padded with books, literally thousands of them. Rupert, who had never seen one book in his lifetime, could only stare in wonder, momentarily at a loss for words. The bookshelves were covered with ladders at intervals, upon which several chipmunks appeared, hard at work organizing several more volumes. Rupert could make out a sort of insignia that he guessed represented the colony as a whole branded on their flanks in the same place in which Talkin had branded his chipmunk, Nim.

"Brilliant, isn't it?"

Glimrod had turned to face them, a contented smile on his tawny face. Rupert looked to him with a sort of question in his eye. The larger squirrel looked down, for a moment, almost ashamed.

"Well…I'm sorry if I was a bit…tense…before. But the fox squirrels of Ashwood have always had a certain way of doing things, and…"

Rupert gave him a half-smile. "I suppose I can understand," he said slowly, forcing the slight frown off of his face. Rupert didn't like the situation, but he couldn't figure out why he felt so uneasy. Glimrod and the other fox squirrels hadn't seemed malicious to him at all, and he found it hard to imagine that they wanted to inflict harm on he and Kyan. On the thought of her, Rupert turned to look at Kyan. She appeared simultaneously bored and sullen, not pausing to appreciate the astounding, beautifully bound quantities of books on the walls, but stifling a yawn instead. He wasn't too fond of her either.

Glimrod noticed Rupert's appreciation of the books, and grinned.

"Literature of the old world is very popular with us," he explained. Then, with a note of pride in his voice, "These books, some of them are thousands of years old," He paused to let the effect sink in. "We preserve them here, for we are the most studious of the races. And believe me, the others just don't appreciate this anymore. It is normally kept a secret, a very solemn one indeed."

He gave Rupert a between-you-and-me glance.

Rupert couldn't understand exactly why Glimrod would share something supposedly so secretive with a random gray and chickaree, but once again didn't comment on it. His mind was in overdrive, partially set back by the wonder of the room they were walking through. He just couldn't seem to find a suitable explanation for any of this.

But Rupert was preoccupied as he and Kyan followed Glimrod through several chambers, some interesting, but none anything like the first. Everywhere it was dark, and there were several chipmunks hurrying discreetly past them at intervals, assumingly carrying out some demand or other of their respective masters. In minutes, Glimrod had come to a set of stairs carved simply into the thick wood of the tree, and Rupert realized almost unconsciously that this must be near the trunk. Opening one of several doors coming off of the room at the bottom of these stairs, the fox squirrel waved them in.

The room beyond was rather Spartan in appearance, but comfortable enough, judging by the look of the beds.

"Our leader normally keeps this room closed, but he doesn't mind you using it for a bit," Glimrod told them genially. A second later, he had closed the door, and the two were left alone in the room.

Kyan went over to a bed and sat on the edge looking sullen. Rupert turned to her, and their eyes connected for an instant. It may have been destined to be the only time their minds were seen to run on a similar track. Rupert voiced the thought first.

"We need a plan."

Chapter Six

Rupert had known it as soon as they had been guided to their quarters, the source of his unease growing climatically until he finally realized it. And even when it had been realized, it didn't make much sense. But whether sense it made, Rupert could feel it to be true.

The fox squirrels weren't planning on letting them go. Letting them out. Ever. It was chilling and confusing at once, and for a while all Rupert could do was stare at Kyan, lost in the fact of it.

"Right," Kyan muttered, "So we need a plan. Of cirse we do. I can't spend the rest of my nat'rul life here, and you got a mission to destroy the blacks. So let's have it."

Rupert blinked; Kyan smiled craftily.

"No plan, eh? Well, I'm good at 'em. I'll get us a plan." As she spoke, Kyan moved around the bed and small bedside table, poking and prodding at everything in the vicinity.

"Hey now, I haven't even had time to think properly," Rupert protested. On sudden inspiration, he moved to the door and tried it. It inched open a crack, and he was staring into darkness. Good. So at least they weren't *locked* in. But Rupert was fairly sure they wouldn't let him go the next morning, and that there were guards posted all around a tree of this size.

Kyan, groping around under the mattress of one of the beds, felt her paw connect with something cool and hard. Pulse speeding dramatically, she froze, whiskers tense.

"Eh..." The sound died on her lips.

"Hmm?" Rupert murmured.

Kyan wrapped her paw around the object. Cold. Hard. Rather large. Her eyes widened and she struggled to breathe.

Rupert turned to her, and she slipped the object into the pouch around her waist deftly. One for the treasure hunt. Maybe this wasn't such a bad place after all. Searching the other mattresses, more careful now, she found something that felt like a coin. Once again, she pocketed it, making sure the gray did not see.

Rupert frowned at her.

"What *do* you reckon we do?"

Kyan looked taken aback.

"Never mind, I've just had a thought. I don't know much about chipmunks at all…in fact, I didn't know they existed until recently, but…"

Just in time, Rupert caught himself from mentioning Talkin.

"But I heard they live underground, normally, don't they?"

Kyan stared at him, then smiled slightly. She was impressed.

"…Yes. The chipmunkies' quarters. Is that what yer suggesting?"

"If it'll work. Uh…do they *have* quarters?"

"Of cirse they do. They got to. Chipmunkies is afraid of being up inna trees too long, they're afeared—

Footsteps sounded, and faded. Kyan lowered her voice.

"—afeared because they haven't got nat'rul talent like squirrels. There's got to be an opening to above ground too, somewheres not too noticeable or grand, maybe not guarded even…"

Rupert, who was beginning to doubt his own idea, asked, "But how do you know that?"

Kyan brushed the question off impatiently. "D'you really think, even if the chipmunkies would like one-a those high up entrances, the squirrels would give it to 'em?"

Rupert had caught on. "Oh...a servants' passage doubling as an escape route which no one but the inhabitants know of? But how would we get to it without being seen?"

"Don't ask me, I en't official answerer."

"Kyan, I'm thinking out loud...okay?" Despite the tone of his voice, Rupert was too engaged to be exasperated. They were on to something here. "And, well, listen."

He crossed over to one of the beds and sat on it. He leaned toward Kyan, and for a moment she looked curious despite herself.

"Did you see the way the squirrels here were acting? They're so paranoid they won't let us go, they're acting as if we're prisoners of a sort, even if they say we're not, and the looks we've received in the halls...which, by the way, are the darkest halls I've *ever* seen."

"Haven't you never seen any halls before?" Kyan asked impudently. Rupert gave her a swift, angry look.

"Sorry. No, it en't normal. Only one window, and they've covered it too." She turned to him. "What do yew think they're hiding?"

Rupert turned into himself, his face drawing closed as he pondered.

"I don't know," he said. "Maybe it's themselves."

There was a short bout of silence in which neither squirrel could hear much but the occasional tap of an insistent foot on the ceiling above them.

"We should go tonight," Kyan said, snapping back into a semblance of her old familiar impatience.

Rupert felt fear constrict his chest, but he nodded in agreement, knowing she was right. There was nothing for it. Time was of the essence in this quest. The safe way would have been to wait a few days, to find the location of this other exit, and to find the right time to make an escape. But the safe way was also the more risky way, in a sense. What if Venul found out the chestnut was missing tonight? What if he already had? What then? No, waiting would not do.

Kyan had gone over to the door, and pressed her ear up against it. Nodding to Rupert, she opened it silently, just a crack, and peered out. Rupert waited apprehensively.

"Nothing," she mouthed to him, and slipped out and to the left. Rupert followed, the darkness enveloping him immediately. If afternoon had seemed dark in this beast of a tree, it was nothing to what evening looked like. Rupert found that his eyes could barely adjust to the shifting darkness in front of him, and became very uneasy.

Judging only from the faint shape of the walls around them, the two started down the hallway nearest them, the only way to go other than the way they had been led earlier by Glimrod, hoping against hope it was the right way. Only a moment later, something shifted behind them, and Rupert froze. Kyan's paw grabbed at him, pushing him to the wall beside her. They waited.

Something passed them by, something small and hurrying with nervous energy. Not a fox squirrel. Rupert looked over at Kyan. Though he couldn't see her eyes, he could swear she was exchanging the same glance with him. It appeared their room had been in the opportune position.

When they were certain the passerby was far enough away, and that no one else was coming their way, they peeled out from the wall and started off again, Rupert reaching out for Kyan's tail in times of dizziness, when the dark began to get to him and he couldn't tell which way was straight.

When Kyan stopped suddenly, Rupert almost bumped into her.

"What is it?" he whispered. Kyan made a quick motion at him to be silent. Rupert edged around her, and almost fell out into space. A stairwell stood before them. That was when he noticed that the ground under his feet felt unusually solid. Compact.

They were going underground. This would be the way out! But how would they get past the chipmunks? The stairs were cold, damp and winding, becoming earthier and less tended to the further down they went. Rupert led the way this time, though his vision was a bit worse than Kyan's, and he kept a paw on the wall for fear of the steps giving way beneath him.

When they reached the bottom, they were greeted with an unwelcome sight. Rupert didn't know a thing about what chipmunk's quarters normally looked like, but he did not expect what he saw. There were a mere couple of firefly lamps set atop two roughly hewn wood tables, the dim light they cast illuminating the shapes of about ten chipmunks on either side of the narrow chamber. A few roots came down ominously from the ceiling, the vestiges of the large tree above, reaching as if the tunnel had almost escaped their hungry, sucking grasp. Rupert felt odd, and from the way Kyan swayed momentarily as if having a spell of dizziness, he could tell she felt the same. Even though they were not that far underground, it still instilled a feeling of dread in him. He would have much preferred to be up in a tree somewhere, the wind playing with his tail, the feel of the rough, dependable bark underneath him. Most of the chipmunks appeared to be asleep, though it was hard to tell from where Rupert and Kyan stood, in plain view of whoever might look their way.

Soon, someone did just that. One of the chipmunks, possibly the one they had followed down here, came over to them, giving them a guarded, curious look. Reaching them, she bowed deeply.

"What service do you require, sir and miss?"

Rupert felt pressured into doing some quick thinking.

"We're guests of…the colony," he said lamely. The chipmunk didn't look like she bought it. He didn't really blame her. Kyan cut in.

"They're offering us somewheres to stay for the night, and we was wondering where to git a drink. We're mighty parched, and our room's a bit up from this."

Rupert was surprised, and then a bit uncomfortable about how easily it came to her.

"It's very late, miss. Most of the chilled drinks will be put away."

"Are you saying we can't git any?" There was a layer of threat in Kyan's tone. "All we want is water, 'sides."

The chipmunk looked nervously at her.

"Of course you can, miss…sir…" she said, bowing to each of them in turn, and left quickly. Kyan immediately started toward the other side of the chamber, past the sleeping chipmunks, and Rupert followed her cautiously.

Mercifully, the other chipmunks were either sleeping, or didn't pay them much mind, and they made it to the other end without much event where the expected tunnel greeted them, the first sign of its presence being the cold night air they felt ruffling their fur. The tunnel was built much larger than any chipmunk, from which Rupert gathered he must be correct in assuming it was also used as an alternative doorway in case of ambush. It turned out to be extremely lucky that this was so; if the door had been made for chipmunks, Rupert would stand no chance of getting through. Even Kyan would have had to work in that case.

Quickly, making as little noise as possible, Rupert scrambled up and out, Kyan close behind.

Rupert only had a split second to breathe in the chill night air before he heard a sound behind him, and turned lightning quick. But he was not quick enough to stop what came next.

A chipmunk had emerged out of the hole behind them. Rupert got the sense it may have been awake and following them out all along—he hadn't had the sense to look back. The chipmunk came up over the top of the hole, pivoted its small, furry body in their direction and opened its mouth to say something, to exclaim.

Quick as a flash, Kyan, who had let out a hiss of breath upon seeing their follower, picked up a good sized rock. Before Rupert could speak, she cracked it down on the unarmed chipmunk's head. A sickening crunch was heard, and the chipmunk collapsed where he stood.

Tossing the rock away, Kyan turned to go on, waiting for Rupert, who stood transfixed, staring at the unconscious creature. When he regained his senses, he rushed forward, feeling for a pulse on the motionless chipmunk.

"Get off it," Kyan said nervously, edging into the darkness.

"But…" Rupert felt anger coursing through him. "He could be dead! We can't just leave him here!"

"Shouldn't've come out then, shouldy?" she argued, stepping back farther. Voices could now be heard from down the mouth of the tunnel, but Rupert held firm until he detected life in the chipmunk. Its head was bleeding profusely, however, and Rupert knew it needed treatment, and quick. It was not something he could provide.

He was considering calling for help, lowering the fellow down into the tunnel, and making a quick getaway, when he felt small paws grip his arm and pull with a vengeance. The voices were getting closer, and Rupert could tell someone was coming outside. He fought Kyan savagely for a minute, but she was surprisingly wiry for a squirrel of her size. In the end, he let himself be taken, convincing himself that the fallen servant would find help from whoever was coming. It was likely, but his insides wobbled, and he pulled away from Kyan once they had put a considerable distance between themselves and the great ash tree.

They had escaped the fox squirrel community, at least for now. Everything should have been all right, but the telling space between the two squirrels and the biting silence which cut the night, with its waxing gibbous moon drifting between clouds, grinning madly, was less than comforting.

They walked on in silence, the wrongness spread out between them, waiting for the next day to be confronted.

The sun rose like melted butter in the sky, spreading across the clear blue. The day was beautiful, but the sun ray that tumbled graciously through the window hole of Emperor Venul's chambers found itself the only warmth existing there.

Venul, a dark shadow on one side of the room, faced two other figures with a cold fury etched in the lines of his face. One of those he faced was the white squirrel, Zirreo, looking pale and drawn, the other another black squirrel, this one pacing and rubbing his paws together, murmuring under his breath.

"One chance," Venul breathed, his eyes boring into the pale red of the albino's. His voice was harsh and grating, and he knew it to be intimidating to most any squirrel he had come across. Except Zirreo. It figured.

Through the past day, he had asked the chickaree guards Farcel and Jann to keep watch for signs of weakness, of breaking, from this one, and he had been met with nothing. Past prisoners had been smart enough to realize things were hopeless in a position like this. No matter, it was the old squirrel's fault if he couldn't figure it out. Venul would win. He always did.

"One more chance. Then you're dead, imbecile. I hope you're hearing me."

Zirreo merely stared back at him impassively.

With a flick of his paw, Venul dismissed the other squirrel in the room, the black one who had escorted the old white one in. Callisto. Crazy. An ugly brute of a half-breed too. Venul had placed him in charge of keeping the old one captive, a job he hoped the fool wouldn't bungle. You never could tell with Callisto; always lurking around, talking to himself, usually about fighting, and about some lady squirrel Venul had never met, and never wanted to due to the number of times "she" was brought up.

Callisto stood by the doorway, lingering after he had walked through the archway. The streak of white fur to one side of his face twisted down by his mouth and made him look a bit crazed as he grinned at Venul, looking right through him all the same.

"Why do I have to leave, then?" he asked, unable to escape the brutal glare sent his way by the elder squirrel. "I haven't done anything, have I?"

Venul intensified his glare and rigidly pointed to the door, an emerald ring glinting in the sunlight.

"She wouldn't make me leave, would she?" Callisto said, a pout in his voice. "She trusts—

"Go now, Callisto," Venul hissed, leaving no room for argument. Callisto shambled off, muttering under his breath worse than ever. Venul turned to Zirreo, a crafty smile on his lips. He had decided he was going to enjoy this.

"You know," he began, pausing delicately, then drew his voice down to a murmur. "My chickaree will have caught up with your gray by now. What say you to that?"

Zirreo looked up at the black squirrel as if he had just heard him speak. A look of mild surprise was evident on his face.

"Rupert is his own squirrel."

"What's that supposed to—hang on. Rupert. That's his name, is it? Bad move on your part, whitey. You never know when a name could be useful. But, I digress. He is 'his own?' Do you like this young one? Is he...*important*...to you?"

Zirreo's shoulders sagged.

"He is very important."

"I bet he is. That's why you filled his head with lies, isn't it? I know you told him I was at the head of that invasion, that the black squirrels turned on the gray. Well. it looks like you're a bit of a liar, too. Perhaps you've forgotten that these were *always my lands*. It was he who kicked me out first, he who decided he couldn't stand it if more and more of his own wanted to join me, he who attacked."

"I said what was necessary, Venul."

"I bet you did. Where is he going?"

Silence.

"I will ask you again, whitey. *Where is he going?*" Venul's tone was laden with threat.

The room went still upon the death of his harsh tones, and the silence held itself tangibly between them before breaking to pieces softly with Zirreo's next words.

"Are you scared, Venul?"

"You are not answering my question, old one." Venul tried to reason himself out of the cold sweat that had come to his forehead. "And unfortunately, you have tried my patience for today. You will have one more chance. And after that—

"Are you afraid?"

"…After…you will be dead, do you understand?" Venul's paws tightened on the arms of his chair, willing away the single bead of sweat trickling down his face. "Guards! Take this squirrel away, I am done with him!"

"Are you scared?"

"You will regret this, old one. Everything. You just wait and see."

"Are you?"

"GUARDS!!"

The massive door slammed open on its hinges, and in came two surly chickarees, looking like they had just been fighting amongst themselves. They were followed a bit too closely by Callisto, whom Venul gave a withering glance.

"Eavesdropping?"

The younger squirrel snapped out of a seeming daze. "I don't need to," he muttered, seizing Zirreo's shoulder. The white squirrel was still staring at him, the intent of the stare nothing Venul could read. Once again the white squirrel was dragged forcefully from the room, and once again he put up no resistance to his antagonists.

The door shut with a firm thud, and Venul basked in the warm glow of the sun filtering through his window, trying hard to ignore the fluttering at the back of his mind.

Are you scared?

Chapter Seven

Kyan spat on the ground distastefully. She and Rupert had been traveling too far, too long, the silence between them so gaping that she felt she must fill it with something, be it cursing, or spitting, or one of the hundred other less than desirable traits that come with being a chickaree.

Rupert turned around once, gauging the distance and where they were now, looking at and past Kyan at the same time, his face impassive. Kyan looked at him resentfully, knowing full well she would only be ignored. They had been escaping, she had saved both their tails, and now not so much a word of thanks from Rupert. The dratted gray. They were all the same. Full of confused ideas of valor and sacrifice, both of which were ridiculous notions to begin with. They didn't understand self preservation, the fear a tyrant could bring…

Kyan stopped in mid-thought, stricken. Venul. The Emperor. Would he truly give her all his treasure? He had sworn on his immortality, but wasn't there something supremely fishy about all of this? Didn't Kyan have a right to know more? She had been risking her neck to track the gray, and he hadn't thought to tell her anything more than to stay on his tail. And the chestnut. Don't touch the chestnut. Kyan hated her job. Couldn't get as much as the silver necklace around Rupert's neck, could she? What *was* she getting out of this? Here and now…nothing. And the impatience that was inherent in her kind smoldered.

The chipmunk had been pesky. Nosy, irritating. It had got what was coming to it. Kyan didn't see why Rupert was upset. Her own mother had clunked her some good ones, and she wasn't any the worse for it. Oversensitive, grays. They all were. Didn't see the best.

Why do I care so much?

Rupert had made the decision to keep to the trees early on, trying to stick to those with the most leaves present as protection from those they had just left in case anyone was looking for them. Stuck in a brooding trance, Rupert tried to keep the task at hand in mind. The sooner he could get to the chestnut, the better. Then he could come back to Zirreo.

Zirreo. Rupert wondered if he was okay. Had he managed to hide what he had shown Rupert from the black squirrels, or had Venul found him out? He hadn't cast much concern on the subject until now. Zirreo to Rupert seemed indestructible, an unwavering and constant source of calm to which others weaker in spirit came to feed.

But the black squirrels were immortal. And they could do things…

Unconsciously, he quickened his pace, taking long, strident leaps from branch to branch, his fear of falling slowly fading. Though Rupert had spent all of his life before on ground, there was a seemingly inborn ability in him to climb, to move freely through the air on nothing but a maze of rough, unyielding wood. It seemed to him ironic that this should be the best part of his life so far. He was in danger, they all were, but he was *doing.* And freely. The dismal gray compound back in Firwood flashed through his mind, and he nearly lost his grip on the wet bark of a hickory tree.

Oliven, you will be avenged. I promised.

The day wore on. Closer and closer. Southwest. Freedom.

Once or twice in their endless flight, Rupert thought he caught Kyan glancing at him out of the corner of his eye.

Kyan, who could have murdered.

He would speed up on the thought, trying to put space between them for the seconds that screamed

Wrong about you

No, he corrected himself. Not wrong exactly. He hadn't honestly trusted the foul chickaree, had he?

She had done it to get away, to save them both, he told himself, knowing the excuse wasn't anything.

Could have killed before.

Southwest. It was starting to rain again. Together, silence maintained, the two continued into the afternoon.

It was growing foggy, drizzly, and plainly speaking, miserable, by the time Rupert stopped for a much-needed breather. It was hard to see in front of him, and hearing nothing from Kyan, he wondered for the first time whether she was still following or not.

Why do you care?

Rupert paused, struck by the thought, before a ungodly odor hit his nose, nearly making him gag. Drifting up lazily from beneath him, the smell was one he had never encountered before, one that smelled of musk and dead things, and waste.

"Swamp, that is," a voice declared softly, so close to him that he jumped a mile in surprise. Kyan was behind him now, looking thoroughly displeased with the world in general. "Just our luck, eh?"

"I suppose," Rupert said haltingly. His feelings weren't so warm toward the chickaree now, but he really had no idea as to what a swamp was. All of a sudden, it came to him how ridiculous it was that he had been selected to do this, to go on this sort of quest, when he hadn't known the world beyond his front door, figuratively speaking. Grays weren't allowed to have doors back where he came from. In a grudging way, he supposed he needed Kyan, even if she had no sense of civility. She had experience.

Rupert fidgeted with the silver acorn on its chain.

"What…?" he asked, then stopped himself, loathe to get advice from the red squirrel. Kyan seemed to know what he was saying.

"Oh, now you want help, do you?" She peered out into the fog. "Trees are far apart from each other here, relatively speaking. They'll be all wet from the fumes, yew can bet. There's nothing fer it but to go through an' stick to the dry patches and rocks. Careful fer the rocks, though."

Looking rather smug at the sight of Rupert's discomfort, Kyan skittered down the tree some ways without looking back. Rupert followed, the foul smell getting continually worse as he descended. He could hear the sound of water bubbling, slowly, and the croak of something unknown. Dearly hoping it would remain that way, Rupert noticed that the ground had become clearer, easier to see beneath the fog. A mound of a rock loomed below them, large and wet and black. Without warning, Kyan leapt from tree to rock in a heartbeat. His own heartbeat accelerating, Rupert followed her lead, and they made their way through the fog.

The low, ominous murmur of the sludge around them, and the unidentifiable sounds coming from a new direction each time drove Rupert insane with fear and the urge to find his way up to the safety of the treetops once again. Time and again, he thought of asking Kyan what sort of things lived here, but the tension between them was not gone, and Rupert rather thought it might attract undesirable attention to them anyway. So they continued in silence.

Every once in a while, Rupert would feel himself slip, and he would fall fast before catching hold, his heart pounding in his ears and against the rock that had betrayed him, hearing his foot hit the water with a *plish* sound. Kyan seemed to have better balance than he did, and once he could have sworn he saw her grin at his difficulties. More than anything, he hated the fact that he was being made to follow her through this, when it was he who was the leader, the one who knew their goal.

My goal, Rupert corrected quickly.

He took another leap to the nearest rock, felt his feet fly every which way, and his heart leaped into his mouth as he attempted to keep hold, scrabbling on air and hard places interchangeably until he fell.

The water was thick and grimy with sand and mud, sucking him down. His mouth was open, he realized in the panic of his brain, and he could feel the thoroughly unpleasant sensation of his lungs being strained to bursting. He thought of calling something, anything, and a garbled screech rose out of his mouth. The hard, cold weight of his acorn pendant connected with his face, hard, and he began to lose consciousness.

Zirreo was on trial again, this time for the last time. Venul sat in his high throne of a chair, not bothering to suppress his delight in antagonizing the older squirrel. Things were simple, after all. The old one would give him his answers, or he would personally deliver his untimely and deeply unfortunate fate to him. He would look forward to it. He-

-would not be afraid this time-

"So, white one," he smiled wickedly. "Are you ready to give me the answers to the questions that I ask?"

The half-breed Callisto giggled darkly in the corner closest the door. Venul turned his chilling gaze to the younger squirrel and waited. The laughing subsided, and the other fell into a sulk.

Zirreo shook his head slowly, serenely in answer to Venul's question.

"Venul, let us not kid ourselves," he said softly. "You are too self-centered to get an answer, to get a chance at any of this. Rupert knows this."

Venul stiffened.

"Would he—this Rupert—would he have me dead, now?" he was unable to escape the trepidation that lent his voice a hollow sound. "Would he?"

The room was layered with a breath's silence, and Venul realized he was not alone with his captive. Motioning Callisto from the room impatiently, he locked his gaze on that of Zirreo as soon as the door shut.

"Is that what he would have happen? Did you *tell* him?"

No answer came from the old squirrel, and Venul's voice rose in an odd sort of hysteria. "Where is it? I need it, where did you send him?"

"It's death then," Zirreo breathed after some time. There was an odd expression on his face that gave even Venul pause, one of a sort of curious wonder bordering on admiration. "Interesting."

Venul blinked, but came back to his senses quickly.

"Fine then," he snarled. "I will not bring you out again. In a day's time, you will die, and then you can see how interesting it is for yourself. Guards, take him away!"

Immediately, Callisto and a chickaree, looking drunk on hickory ale, entered the room and dragged the old squirrel off. No resistance. Again. No fear, either. It infuriated him.

Once Zirreo was back in his cold, dark cell, the guards having departed, he stood, his white form given a ghostly glow from the dim light coming through the small, barred window. Walking slowly to the corner of his prison, he bent, rising with something clasped in his paw. Zirreo went to the window, squinting out with his admittedly poor sighted gaze at the world beyond.

A low sigh expressed the only resignation he had shown in a time, a time which might be gauged 'long' by other squirrels, but which was nothing to the mind that had seen time beyond length. He would not help right now. Only Rupert could do what was necessary. The young squirrel was brave, and Zirreo knew he would triumph. But he must give him some warning. Zirreo took the brittle ladybug shell out of his paw, and sent it spinning on the air, out through the bars. Watching it go, he felt a trace of unusual sadness for the young gray squirrel.

When Rupert came back, he would not be here.

Something was grabbing, clutching at him, and Rupert struggled to pull free through the murk of his barely tangible consciousness, but the grasp it had on him was too strong. Relenting to its pull, Rupert felt himself tugged sharply upwards before he blacked out completely.

Only a moment later, it seemed, he was being shaken roughly awake. The rough touch was accompanied by an unpleasantly familiar voice.

"C'mon then, have no stamina at all, do yew? Taken forever for yew to wake, an' I hafta sit here, sit here and carry yew and…"

Kyan trailed off when she noticed that Rupert was awake, and staring at her through half-lidded eyes.

"Ugh?" he muttered, trying to move, to sit up.

"About time," she breathed, pushing back her relief for comfortable scorn.

Rupert regained himself enough to sit up. Ignoring the derision in his companion's voice, he attempted to speak.

"What—what happened to me? Did I drown? I thought I drowned…and the swamp! Shouldn't we be getting through the swamp? We can't be in the middle of it all when night falls…"

Rupert felt dizziness wash over him, and lay down quickly again to avoid throwing up. Kyan stared at him, exasperated, before answering.

"Yew hit yer head, yew big lump, yew were panicking so much. I laid yew on a rock and tried to wake yew, but yew wouldn't wake, so…so I had to carry yew. Mind, it weren't easy, yer too fat," she added, sounding almost in defense of herself.

Ignoring this last insult, Rupert sat up, staring at her. Kyan avoided his glance, staring off to one side as if she were supremely embarrassed.

"Kyan…" he said.

"Yeah, what?"

"You saved me."

"Yeah, so what?"

"Why?"

Kyan blinked. Somehow she didn't think *Because I have to follow you to some stupid chestnut so I can get a lump of treasure* was going to get a good response. Anyway, was it just that? Of course, lumps of treasure were better than anything else, but Kyan sometimes had moments, she supposed, where she was stuck in a void of *doing,* forgetting why she was doing and only knowing she was. She was sick of this adventure. She wanted things she could touch, silver and gold and rubies, and nothing stupid like honor and loyalty, or to think of new motives when lumps of glorious treasure were all that mattered anyway.

So once again, Kyan pulled out her "mistress of lies and deception" guise, and said, "Because I want revenge on the black squirrels too, remember? We got a common end…and yew *still* won't tell me what yer doing. Don't yew think that's a tad unfair?"

Kyan stopped, realizing she really *did* want to know. It was a surprise that made her doubt her good sense.

Rupert's mind was numb. Kyan had saved him, dragged him from the water when she could have just let him drown. Who knew how much effort that had taken? They hadn't been on the best of terms beforehand, and after what the chickaree had done to the chipmunk, he had been sure he had the measure of her. But Kyan had saved him.

"Kyan…I just wanted to say…thank you. Really. We do have to get out of—

Then he stopped, realizing that they were situated a ways away from the edge of the swamp, the fog not nearly so blinding here, though the day had now graduated into night. She had carried him out completely. Rupert couldn't help feeling bad over his former treatment of the smaller squirrel, much as he told himself she had deserved it.

Kyan didn't say anything, and Rupert continued speaking before he could think longer or better of it. He couldn't have the matter of what had happened on his chest this whole time, and perhaps there *were* things Kyan deserved to know.

"Look…that night at the fox squirrel community…I was scared, we both were," Rupert plucked a leaf from the ground and began to dry himself as best he could while he spoke. "At least I think we both were. It's hard for me to trust…anyone, really. But especially squirrels like you chickarees. You know. But you saved me, and I suppose maybe I have something to learn from this." He set the leaf aside.

"There's a thing…that my mother told me, before she died…"

Kyan waited impatiently, but Rupert didn't look like he'd continue. Rupert looked up, and he must've sensed something of her impatience, or her insincerity, because he never finished his sentence.

"Never mind. It's late, we should probably sleep. You're probably tired from carrying me…" Then, with a touch of a smile, "Am I really fat?"

Silence.

"No."

Rupert thought he meant to say something else, or that he had meant to *mean* something else, and he could still smell the swamp air, and held on to it. But finally he drifted into sleep as the night melted on. His dreams were of blood red scourges and a shape, not unlike the one that hung around his neck, glowing as he neared it, only to shatter into pieces and dissolve when he reached to touch it.

Chapter Eight

Kyan awoke in the dim dawn of the next day, more energetic than she had felt for some time. Glancing over at Rupert, she noted he was still asleep and thought to wake him before dismissing the idea shortly afterward. She could do without him talking at her, spewing sentimentalities like the night before. Did he think she cared?

Maybe he just needed someone to talk to...

Kyan felt utterly disgusted with herself. Since when had she grown so utterly reasonable? For a moment, teeth on edge, she thought of waking Rupert again, if only for a good argument.

"Cripes, what is wrong?" Kyan spat furiously, staring out at the bushes to the left of them. They would have to make their way through those if they expected to—

A movement from the direction of the bushes caught her eye, and she went still. Had there been--?

Yes! There it was again! A glint of something...something valuable? It had made a pretty sound too, a tinkle, sort of like a bell. A silver bell? Kyan crept in the direction of the bushes, licking her lips unconsciously, watching...

There it was again! More to the right this time, Kyan caught a look at the object, and was pleased to notice she was right. Whoever had the silver bell was moving fast along the bushes. Kyan sped up, poised to strike. When she judged she was sufficiently ahead of the tinkling, she stopped and stepped through the bushes.

Kyan found herself face to face with a young gray squirrel, female, only a child. She was staring at the magically appearing stranger with wide eyes, a stick grasped in one paw. From the stick dangled a piece of corded meadow grass, and from this cord hung not one, but two, tiny silver bells.

Fingering the pouch around her waist, Kyan licked her lips. The squirrel child looked at her uncertainly.

"Hello, there," Kyan spoke in what she hoped was a soothing voice, breaking the silence. "What's yer name?"

The little gray frowned. "Granpa tells me not to talk to strangers. He says there's too much trouble in Beechwood right now."

"This is Beechwood?" Kyan feigned interest. "Do yew live here then?"

The squirrel backed up a few steps. "I'm sorry, I can't talk to you anymore. I promised Granpa. He says..he says be careful for strangers and red thieves."

Red thieves? Stupid, insulting Southern slang. She had forgotten about that. After all, she had only been in the South once before, and then not as far down as Beechwood. It had been when she was younger, not as wise. Her stupid younger cousin kept thinking he saw quartz in the river, but it was just fish, and then he drowned. The rest of the family had fun fighting over his possessions. There were only two casualties.

Kyan drifted back to reality, the dreamy smile slipping off of her face in time to notice the young gray trying to edge past her, bells jangling beautifully. The young one's home must be beyond, she realized. Desperately, she reached out and grabbed her arm.

"Look here, I just want to trade-

The young squirrel jerked away, frightened now, and ran past. Kyan grabbed at the stick she carried as she passed, and caught hold of one of the small, silver bells.

The two engaged for a moment, in a small tug-of-war, before Kyan bared her teeth and the young gray dropped the stick and started to scream ear-piercingly loud.

Rupert awoke to the sound of a scream somewhere off to his left, and was on his feet quickly. He felt well-rested, a miracle in itself, but already he could sense a splotch of pressure on this day as he drew closer to the end of his quest. He could feel it. He could also feel that something had gone wrong.

Coming fully awake with a jolt, he realized Kyan was no longer asleep, and was in fact nowhere to be found.

"Kyan?" he called, warily. The air was silent now, the shrill edge of the scream fading out. Without a moment to lose, Rupert headed in its direction.

Cutting to the source of the noise proved to be more frustrating than he had bargained for. The grass and shrub was thicker than he had surmised, and Rupert found himself growing increasingly lost the deeper he plowed through it all. There had to be a path somewhere, perhaps he had entered wrong…?

He came to a dead halt. The sound of voices drifted to him from somewhere slightly to his right. Slowly, as silent as he could, Rupert crept toward them. One of the voices belonged to someone very young The other was hard, authoritative, and unforgiving.

"…I'm very proud of you, Kira. You know just what to do by now, very proud. But I can't help but think this doesn't bode well for our home life. Now, I've heard rumors, but—

"You don't think they're true, Granpa? I hear things like war is coming in class, but how would anyone know…?"

"I don't know if its war persay, and you know better than to listen to those other children. It's trouble though, I'm betting. The appearance of red thieves this far out in the williwacks always bodes ill...some say they're working for those up north...That's the word at least. You wouldn't expect..."

The voices faded off again to the left of Rupert, and he realized that there must be a path somewhere close by. Pushing through the grasses closest to him, he soon came out into a spot of open air, and tumbled out onto the roadway, hitting his nose rather clumsily on a rock.

"Ow..." Rupert mumbled, rubbing the sore spot distractedly. He stared down the trail in front of him until he caught the sound of the voices once again, and was after them.

Awhile down the trail, the young gray squirrel called Kira stopped.

"Granpa...I think someone's following us," she said softly, tilting an ear back down the trail. "Do you think—

"Hush, Kira," the older squirrel said sternly. "If it's another one, we'll know what to do, right?"

"Yes, Granpa."

Rupert, from his hidden position on the side of the path, surveyed the two squirrels with a cursory glance. They were both grays, one aged, and one merely a child. The young one held a stick from which dangled two silver bells, which were now clasped in her paw to keep from jangling. But why carry bells around if you were set on keeping quiet? Unless the bells in question had recently been the source of some trouble...

"No..." Rupert groaned softly.
Of course.

What had become of Kyan? The two squirrels in front of him didn't look like killers, but if the younger one had been in danger…There was only one way to find out. Taking a deep breath, Rupert slid out from his covering to face the two others.

"Erm…Hello," he said to get their attention.

The older squirrel whirled around so quick that watching him made Rupert a bit dizzy. A fierce, grizzled expression held on his weathered face. Upon seeing Rupert it softened only a little as he held the other's gaze, sizing him up. Finally, he spoke.

"Who are you, squirrel?"

No points taken for honesty, Rupert decided. "I'm Rupert."

"Rupert, eh?" The old squirrel still looked suspicious. No reason for him not to, really. Rupert's sudden materialization on the trail behind him was not a good start to any type of trust. "You look like you're wanting something, Rupert. I'm no fool. State your cause and be done with it."

Rupert stared at the older squirrel. No fool, indeed.

"Well," he began, feeling more hopeless than ever. "I'm looking for a chickaree. She…erm…stole something from me, and I'm looking to get it back. I heard someone screaming over here, and thought she might've crossed your path."

It was the first genuine lie Rupert had ever told, and he was apprehensive that the older squirrel would see right through him.

But the other only stared at him for a while longer before speaking, weighing each word as he did so.

"As it turns out, we did come across a red thief earlier today. She claimed to be called Farrow the Fierce, terror of the Southlands. I don't think she had anything else on her, but there was a pouch around her waist. Perhaps what you're looking for is there."

"Do you know where she is now?" Rupert asked.

Pause. Then, from where she was nearly forgotten below them both, the little Kira spoke.

"Granpa, I like him," she said. "I don't think he's going to hurt us. Can't we just tell him where the red thief is? He looks sad."

Sad? This last came to Rupert as a surprise. Did he look sad? Maybe desperate was a better word. The little squirrel was looking up at him, and he smiled down at her warmly.

'Granpa' let out a worn, resigned sigh of acquiescence.

"Yes, all right. I don't see why not after all. We've stuck her in the thorn bushes back a ways. She's tied up there. It generally takes a while for any red thief…or anyone, for that matter—to get out of a fix like that. But I can see you're in a hurry."

The old gray's face softened, and he put a paw on Rupert's shoulder. Speaking in a hushed voice so Kira wouldn't hear, he whispered. "Just be careful. Things aren't how they used to be down here. I hope you find what you're looking for."

Breaking away quickly, the elder saluted Rupert, and turned his granddaughter around, starting down the path home again.

"Thank you!" Rupert called after them.

Kyan struggled experimentally against her bonds. She was stuck fast, and she knew it. The thorns from the large bush she was tied to poked into her, unforgiving, whenever she attempted to execute a move.

"C'mon, c'mon," she murmured, shifting one way and then the other. Nothing seemed to work. And even though Kyan told herself she was in control, she was truthfully starting to panic. If the gray had waken, he might already be gone, and then what hope would she have of following him?

"Then I could jist live in the Southlands, like, and call myself a Beechwood squirrel. Huh. That wouldn't be much of a tale. I wouldn't have any shiny stuff, neither. The Emp'rer's the key to the treasure…"

She paused, frowning doubtfully, then flinched at a sound nearby. Tensing herself, Kyan prepared to put up a fight. If it was that old gray and his stupid little baggage, she would teach them a lesson. She would—

The grass parted. It was a gray, but not the two who had captured her.

"*Rupert?*"

"*Farrow the Fierce?*"

"Scares you too, does it?"

"You'd be hard pressed to scare me looking like that." Rupert set to loosening her bonds. "Do you *have* to terrorize children for small bits of finery?"

"Yes. And that wasn't a child. It was a screaming likkle terror with fur stuck to it."

"Come off it, you red thief."

Kyan glared broodingly, stepping away from the thorn brush at last.

"Well, we'll have to double back now," Rupert began. "We can't take this path anywhere, if we run into those two again, they'll know I freed you. The old one'll probably have my blood."

Kyan, who was starting down the road already, spun on the spot.

"Huh? Double back? So this is completely outta yer way, is that what yer saying?"

"Not terribly so, but yes. We're heading southwest." Somewhere, Rupert realized that he had told Kyan the direction he meant to go at last, but he didn't pay it much mind. Kyan didn't seem to have registered that last statement in any case.

"Wha…? Don't tell me yew actually...actually…y'know, came back here to…*just* to…"

"Save you?" Rupert looked perplexed.

"Yeah. That." Kyan looked rather like she had swallowed something painful and was waiting to explode.

"Yes. Now we have to go, quickly."

Kyan spent the next couple uneventful hours of their travel casting resentful looks at Rupert's back, thoughts clattering about in her skull.

That was an unexpected turn of events. HAS to make it hard for me, doesn't he? Has to pull out the stupid honor code of his and come to save me. I could've escaped myself. On the other hand, it's sort of attractive…attractive? Stupid is more like it, isn't that what I've always thought? I don't have to do anything about it, wasn't MY decision to save me.

All the while she thought, Kyan fingered the contents of the pouch around her waist.

But still…no one's…saved me…before. Maybe I should give him something. Not something big. Something small. Almost like I don't care. Because I don't, you know. I care about rubies. Rubies are nice. But with all this honor, he'll be dead soon, saving someone, so I might as well. Then I could take it back once he's gone. Gone saving someone again, stupidly I might add.

Stupidly saving someone.

Saving me?

Kyan's paw closed about the gold coin in her pocket, and she rubbed it.

Now don't look at it, or you'll change your mind. How to do this? I could chuck it at him, but then he might dismiss it as a pinecone. Maybe I could leave it somewhere with a note for when he wakes up again. From, Mysterious Generous and Thankful Coin-Giver. I could lay it off on the south. Honky tonk customs and all that.

Rupert turned around unexpectedly.

"We'd better find a place to settle down, it looks like open-

"Here!" Kyan nearly screamed, throwing something hard so fast he could barely register the movement. It landed on the ground in front of him, and Rupert studied it dubiously. A gold coin glinted at him from the mud.

Kyan was standing, her head turned away, squinting as if the dull light from the coin was enough to blind her.

Rupert stared in puzzlement, trying to hide a smile.

"Kyan…what?"

"Thankyoupickitup," Kyan said so fast he could barely understand her.

Finally Rupert understood. Taking the coin in his paw, he sat in shock. He had never known a chickaree to—

Kyan glanced over at him, drew in her breath in a sharp gasp, and quickly looked away again.

Rupert quickly pocketed the gift, understanding. He stared at her.

"This must be *killing* you," he said , a trace of awe in his voice.

Kyan dropped her paws to her sides again, seeing the coin was gone, and breathed out slowly.

"Not really."

"Thank you, Kyan," Rupert told her, smiling. He looked like he might have said more, except at that moment, something blew into his face, catching him on the cheek.

Surprised, Rupert jumped back and ripped the thing from his face. It was only a harmless ladybug shell. But as Rupert stared at it, suddenly he was hit with a sort of terror that could not be created from nothing.

"Zirreo," he whispered.

Kyan just stared at him, not comprehending.

"Zirreo is in trouble," he said, letting the shell fall to his feet.

Something in Kyan's brain clicked. Zirreo. The white squirrel the Emperor was talking about.

"How…?"

"I don't know. He sent this to me though. It's a warning," Rupert breathed.

"Warning of what?"

Rupert didn't answer.

"We can't rest tonight."

Chapter Nine

As it turned out, Rupert and Kyan could not go any farther that night. Somewhere along their way it started to thunderstorm, and they pressed on until they could hardly see through the rain, taking to the trees as soon as they could. When the storm showed no signs of abating, they were forced to stop. The wind and wet was too much for them, and surely they would catch a chill if they kept at it.

The desperate quiet that had lingered about Rupert since he had received the message from Zirreo seemed to snap and fall around him in pieces then, and Kyan, watching him, got the sense of something utterly sad, something indecent for her to see, and turned away.

They found a clearing, a dry patch on a wide branch of a generous beech tree, and huddled close to the trunk for warmth, watching the rain chase the shadows and pour all around them with a frightening intensity. Soon, the unnamed fear which had found a place inside both squirrels began to unfold, and they talked to keep it away, to fight off the loneliness of the night.

"Kyan," Rupert began, after a time. "I haven't told you nearly enough about anything, have I?"

"No," Kyan said, but without her usual bluntness. She was staring off into the wall of rain beyond them, looking, for the first time Rupert had seen, like her mind was occupied.

"Okay then," he said, casting a lingering glance over her. She looked back for a second to show she was listening. "Well. You know how I said, there was a way to get back at the blacks? Well, there is, but it's actually...the black squirrels aren't naturally immortal. They aren't Astrippa's chosen."

Kyan snorted.

"You don't believe in Astrippa?"

"Can I touch Astrippa? Is Astrippa *shiny*?" Kyan smirked. "Then I don't have use for her, real or not."

Rupert frowned, feeling almost sad for reasons he couldn't put his paw on.

"Fair enough. Anyhow, this...immortality thing for the black squirrels can't go on. They've become corrupted as leaders over the past decades. There's an object which, whenever held directly by one of a certain race, has the power to turn that race immortal—

"The chesknut..." Kyan breathed.

"What?"

"Nothing. Go ahead."

Rupert stared at her, hard, and then continued. "There is a golden chestnut that is enchanted somehow. It got misplaced...don't ask me how it got this far. I like to think it's enchantment, but really it doesn't matter. What matters is that I have to find it and to take immortality from the blacks so that we can all have a fair rule again."

Kyan sat still, blinking intermitted with the pitter-patter of the rain.

"Yer going to rule, are yew?"

Rupert flushed. "It's possible. I wish I could say I'd make a good leader, but I'm scared, I think."

There was a pregnant pause in which the two just listened to the rainfall and took comfort in the dryness in the face of what lay before them.

"You know," Rupert said. "Before my mother died, she told me that...that even though there's all different types in this world, we're more united than you'd think. She said our souls are only a dewdrop away."

He stopped, and Kyan couldn't tell whether he was embarrassed, or just finished with putting himself out in the open.

"I guess I just got lonely on this quest, being the only one who knows, so I had to tell it to somebody. Even if you're not really with me. Hopefully, you will be with me. Hopefully, you'll see in the end, too. I didn't understand either at first, but I think I'm beginning to."

This time, Kyan was so taken aback that she was literally rendered speechless.

Could he know what she was going to do? What she had planned to do?

No.

If he did, she figured, he would be angry. But there was no anger in Rupert's face as he waited for the storm to end. Just a patience that she, in all her impatience couldn't understand, and that same quiet determination from before.

It was then that she realized she had intruded on something quite private, and now she felt she couldn't back out. She needed something shiny to stare at, but around them it was dull. Except for Rupert. His silver necklace flashed in the corner of her eye. Like a beacon that would inevitably lead to trouble, she tried to ignore it.

The rain stopped in the morning hours. Neither squirrel could remember sleeping, or much of the night before. Everything was covered in a dim haze, and to Rupert nothing mattered but what lay ahead. He could feel that the falls were close now, even if he couldn't see them yet. But on the edge of his determination, there was a prickle of fear.

Too late, it whispered. An image of Zirreo floated to the top of his mind, and he pushed it down, quickly, jerkily.

Rupert traveled very quick that day, his feet eating up the bark in front of him almost before he could register the sight of it. Kyan lagged behind, her mind a turmoil.

She finally knew the meaning of what she was after, but now everything else didn't seem clear at all.

Just get the chestnut, kill the gray, come back, get your reward.

There was a knife in her belt. She had almost forgotten.

Yes. Kyan could do this. She was the mistress of deceit.

Well. Maybe don't kill the gray. As long as he stays out of the way.

Mind only half decided, Kyan continued on. But they did not speak, and the effects of the night before slowly faded as they separated.

Rupert traveled with authority, a type of strength he maintained for the sake of not falling apart as the feelings of despair moved in on him. He shot through a maze of branches, picking the strongest and winding around it only to fly on air a second later. Closer, closer. He no longer paid attention to direction, and he found it wasn't necessary. Intuition, bare, animal instinct, was enough now. Closer, and trying not to think the one thought padlocked in his brain, threatening to claw its way out.

…Zirreo?

Venul lay back in his chambers, breathing peacefully. He was content for the first time in a long time, feeling as if things were finally going his way. The old white squirrel had been given the chance to speak the whole day long, and had done nothing. He would give it a few more hours, and then it would be time.

Time for the kill. There wasn't anything personal in it, he told himself, but he had to admit that ending the legacy of mystical white squirrels was quite an accomplishment. He'd be remembered for that if nothing else.

It was about time. For Venul knew that hardly anyone believed in magic, just like hardly anyone believed in Astrippa.

The era of the black squirrel wouldn't be over. It was just beginning.

It was dusk when Rupert reached the falls. He felt a jerking in his chest, and stopped short.

It was the grandest sight he had ever seen. If he had felt he had the time, he would have sat in awe for much longer. The water roared with a life of its own, frightening and exhilarating at the same time, the great rocky wall of the falls rising up through the trees that surrounded it profusely. For a time, Rupert wasn't able to tear his eyes away from the sight.

Under the falls.

Rupert, from his position in the tree, was unable to see any opening between the water and the rocks. The noise from the falls was overpowering, and he found it hard to hear himself think.

Looking behind him, he realized Kyan hadn't caught up to him. Just as well, he didn't want to take any chances. Climbing down from his tree, he tried to keep from flinching back at the enormous power of the falls, tried not to think of how the water could crush him in an instant. The spray bit at Rupert's face, thrown up from the rocks below, but he kept going closer. He had found a passageway up and behind the falls, a narrow one where the rock grew flat and worn. It had been in plain sight, but he hadn't noticed it for what it was, the water casting illusions over the rocks so that it appeared there was not an inch between them.

Rupert was already starting up the passage he had found, apprehensively, looking ahead with each step. And then he was in, behind the water, on a ledge that curved around the sheer mountain of rock. It was an odd thing, but not unpleasant really, now that he was here. He could imagine the river up above him, feeding the falls which poured down in front of him in an almost transparent sheet in which light and color played and reflected themselves on the wall behind him.

Rupert kept going, keeping to the slowly curving path for what seemed to him a long time, and worry began to dance at the corners of his mind. Was the waterfall really this big or was his mind playing tricks on him? What if the chestnut wasn't here at all?

But then, just ahead, he saw it. A dark shape, round, off to one side of the passageway. He might have missed it entirely had not he seen a tiny glimmer of gold through a split in the leather casing it was wrapped in.

So this is it, Rupert thought. He let out a long sigh, though whether it was from relief or anticipation he couldn't tell. He had started toward the chestnut when the blur of orange came out of nowhere, brushing up against him, almost knocking him off balance. Steadying himself, he looked up to see the chestnut cradled in the paws of another, and a sense of dread went stabbing through him, making his insides crawl with cold.

"Kyan?"

The doors to Zirreo's cell creaked open on their hinges, and two chickarees came in to take him away.

"We're going for a likkle walk, aren't we?"

"Shh, lets just get 'im outta here, Verk."

Zirreo glanced up without a word, and allowed himself to be dragged from his cell. For a second, he let his mind flash to Rupert, hoping, then he closed himself off again.

The guards brought him to Venul's chambers and knocked briskly on the doors. Zirreo shifted, and one of the chickarees hit him in the side, causing the other guard to hit the first. Their tussle came abruptly to a halt when Venul's voice sounded from the other side.

"Enter."

His time had come.

"Kyan, give me the chestnut," Rupert said, his voice low, trying to keep the panic inside him from rising to the surface.

But Kyan was off, running off the edge of the ledge, curving upward with a thrust of her lithe body and clinging to the mountainous rock from which the water poured, the chestnut dangling from her mouth.

Rupert gave chase, his insides squirming now, filled with rage for himself. Of course. Kyan, one of Venul's squirrels, sent after him for this express purpose. He wanted to scream. He might have actually screamed, but the water was too loud, pounding in his ears like his blood, so that he couldn't hear a thing save for the constant pounding.

Climbing on Kyan's tail, he followed her up the rocks, keeping her darting red body in his line of sight at all times. Once he almost caught her, catching hold of her leg violently, knocking her askew. But she surged upwards with a burst of strength, freeing herself from her larger pursuer, and was climbing to the very top of the slope, stopping now, next to the river.

Rupert's heart was beating unevenly in his ears now as he heaved himself over the edge, trying not to look down at where the water shattered against the rocks below. He would mix blood with that water if he had to.

"Kyan…" he said, his voice raised in warning. "Think about what you're doing."

Kyan moved, and he started toward her quickly. But already something in him was screaming *Too late, too late.*

Kyan grinned at him, ripped open the casing of the chestnut so that half of it emerged, glittering crazily, having almost the same effect as the water pouring below them.

Rupert froze on the spot.

Venul and Zirreo faced each other across the room.

"So," Venul began, talking slowly, forcing a smile. "Are you ready to leave this world?"

"I am, Venul," Zirreo said calmly. "Can you say the same for yourself?"

"Don't try to scare me, old one; your threats will be void soon enough."

Zirreo didn't answer, but closed his eyes as though to gain some inner peace, and only opened them when he was jerked to one side by the chickaree guards, who forced him to a stone block in the middle of the floor, tying him down.

Venul came around, letting his face drift into Zirreo's line of vision from where he lay strapped to the block. He motioned to a guard who handed him a large, crudely fashioned hatchet.

"You know, old one," he said, stroking the hatchet blade lightly with one paw. "You always hear about those leaders who have other creatures do their dirty work for them. You may be interested to know that I am not one of them. I want you to know that your presence offends me…personally."

Kyan stared down at the chestnut as though fascinated, held by it in some way.

"Kyan…please…" Rupert said, shaken and feeling ill. Somehow he got the sense that she couldn't, or wouldn't, hear him. Rupert crept closer, and Kyan moved farther away, looking up at him for the briefest moment. Her eyes were unreadable.

Almost lackadaisically, before Rupert could do anything, before he could move one inch closer, she had turned the paw holding the casing upside down over the edge of where the river came crashing down.

When Rupert realized what she was doing, it was too late.

Venul had the guards leave the room; he didn't want anyone but himself to witness this.

Raising the hatchet over Zirreo, lining it up with his neck, Venul waited for the flash of fear to come to the old squirrel's face. It never came.

He had grown impatient.

With that single, purposeful, lightning-quick motion from Kyan, the chestnut glittered with a sense of finality, almost lingered in the air a second before plummeting hard and fast, freed from its casing, falling, mingling with the water from which it could have been made, shattering alongside it as it hit the rocks below.

Venul brought down the hatchet.

In that instant, it seemed to Rupert as if the world had darkened, as if everyone everywhere must know something of great importance had happened and then there was a moment of silence in which everything stopped. Perhaps even time stopped, and the gap between dimensions shuddered.

Then the sky brightened, and the magic was sapped from the sky of dusk. Rupert was facing Kyan, who looked as if she had felt it too.

The silence lengthened.

"It's over," he breathed, finally.

She caught his eye, and nodded.

The center of Firwood, where the gray compound stood, was moving along at its normal pace, when Venul burst from his chambers, running white-faced into Callisto and another black squirrel, both of whom looked at him as though he had lost a few acorns.

"A—ahh— Venul stuttered, growing paler under his dark fur by the second.

"What is it?" the anonymous black squirrel asked. Callisto just stared on in astonishment. They were gathering a whole lot of onlookers.

"Ah…" Venul choked, and collapsed at their feet. Callisto bent down, and upon touching him, gave a strangled scream.

"Argh! He's dead!"

"Dead? Here, you," started in the other, elder squirrel. "He's n-not d-

Suddenly he wheeled backwards as if a dizzy spell had taken him, and started breathing heavily. Callisto, utterly frightened now, ran away in case what they had was catching.

He didn't stop running once he reached the edge of the camp boundaries.

Chapter Ten

Atop the raging falls, time had gone back to its normal pace. Rupert was standing, in a day that could have been any other, and all he could feel was a curious sort of calm, mingled with something like sadness.

Rupert looked at Kyan across from him. She didn't meet his gaze like she had in that world-changing moment, but turned to stare to one side absently.

"Why?" he asked her, a dull sort of anger trying to be born in him.

"Oh, you wanted to be king then?"

He should feel angry, angry with Kyan because she had betrayed him. He should feel furious, but the emotion couldn't seem to come.

"No, and that's beside the point! I was instructed to take the chestnut and use it for good, and now that you've destroyed it, who knows what got screwed up! Don't you understand?!"

"No," Kyan spat. "I don't, and I never will. Yew grays, and yew blacks are all the same. Yew pretend yew've got honor, but yer really jist looking for power, power someone else has and yew think yew can do it better."

"Where are you from, Kyan?" Rupert's voice was dangerous. "Were you sent after me? Did you work for him all along?"

Kyan ignored his tone.

"Swearing on yer immortality doesn't mean nothing. Alright, I'll answer yer question. Yes. And until a while ago, I planned to go ahead and bring the chestnut back to him. But then, swearing on yer immortality doesn't mean nothing. Like I said. And first it's him, then it's yew. And I don't want—

Kyan stopped, winded, breathing hard. She looked as if she was frightened by some sudden realization.

"What don't you want, Kyan?" Rupert said, softer. But Kyan wouldn't answer. A smile crept across Rupert's face.

"You don't want me to be like him? You don't want me to be immortal, do you?"

"Hmph."

"But…why?"

"Now yer jist coming up with stuff. I didn't say anything like that. Now maybe yew should go back to yer grays, and teach 'em not to be as stupidly honorable as yew."

"…Kyan?"

"Go build a city!"

"Fine, I won't prod. As to building a city, I'm not sure I'd be such a good leader anymore. I've been thinking on everything and on what—

"You lead me fine. Now go."

"But aren't you coming with me?"

"I'm staying here."

"On the waterfall?"

"No, yew lump! In Beechwood! I'm thinking of starting a new title."

"A…?"

"Don't ask me to explain."

"Fine. But wouldn't you…you helped me, you know. I probably wouldn't have made it without you. Isn't there something I can do, since I might not see you again…?"

Kyan shrugged, looked away, then turned back to Rupert quickly, her eyes bright. She walked over and whispered something in his ear. Rupert laughed. Kyan looked offended.

"Okay, deal."

They sat in silence for a while, before Rupert said, "I'd better be getting back. If things turn out like I've been warned, it'll be chaos back there. And it's a long journey, if I remember correctly."

He turned away, and Kyan, who looked like she had been struggling with something up until now, shouted out behind him.

"Rupert!"

"Yes?"

"I kind of—sort of—well—

"What is it?"

"Go build a city."

"I like you too, Kyan."

"That's NOT what—oh—then we're even."

"Yes, we are."

And Rupert continued in a northeasterly direction, retracing the steps of moments before, only turning back when he couldn't see the falls anymore.

"Hmm..." he muttered to himself, feeling the lack of company already. "It's a new beginning, isn't it?"

A faint breeze went tumbling from the northeast, ruffling his fur. Rupert smiled.

"Well, I'm ready," the young gray announced.

When Rupert got back to Firwood a week later, things looked as he remembered, but the air felt different. Everywhere there were feelings of uncertainty thick on the air, squirrels wondering how to go about patching up their lives and building new ones in light of what had happened. For a lot of the grays, this would be the first time they would ever live free, and they found themselves frightened of the prospects.

Rupert was told that the black squirrels had all but abandoned the area, leaving quickly for fear of some sort of plague. It wasn't only the black squirrels, either. Many of the grays had barricaded themselves in their shabby houses for fear that the sickness might spread on to them. The only good news seemed to be that the Emperor was dead, and most didn't even know what to do with that.

"I feel there's lots to explain," Rupert said, when talking to a wide-eyed mother gray about where he had been. "If there was some way to—to rally everyone…"

And then a thought occurred to him.

"Zirreo! That's it, but why hasn't he explained it all? Zirreo ought to be here somewhere, I've got to tell him…"

"What, the white squirrel, you mean?" an old, wrinkled gray asked, casting a suspicious eye over Rupert.

Rupert nodded. "Yes, where is he?"

"There's no 'where' about it, I'm afraid. He's dead."

Rupert's insides jolted.

"Yes, the Emperor killed him with his own paws before dying himself. There's been rumor that the white put a curse on him before he died, and that's why this is happening."

The old one gestured around at the barren land around them as if to prove her point. The mother squirrel he had been talking to earlier had gone off to rally the others, feeling maybe desperate enough that she felt Rupert could save them.

Rupert alone.

Without Zirreo.

Rupert attempted to move his mouth, to tell the old squirrel that it wasn't true, that they were in no danger, but he couldn't. Zirreo had been all he had left. All the family he had to come back to was gone.

All the optimism of earlier had gone as well, draining out of him until he felt weak, and then tears were threatening at his eyes.

Rupert looked up, and in the blur in front of him was a crowd of timid, scared, weathered or beaten faces. All staring at him. All expecting him to put things right, to pick up all the odds and ends and sew them together. To tell them something they wanted to hear, for once. They didn't understand that without Zirreo, these things weren't possible. Rupert was just another like them, had been exactly like them. A brief trip into freedom and into how things should be hadn't changed a thing.

But the eyes were upon him, and murmurs now swept through the crowd, as they waited for him to speak.

And then he was speaking, speaking of the chestnut and how things really were, and what they had to fear and what they didn't. He told them there was hope, and that this was a perfect opportunity to start anew, to build their houses up in trees and not underground, to hold a proper ceremony for all their lost loved ones. He spoke, his voice rising and falling, and at some point through all the words, he started to believe himself.

When he had finally finished, his voice died out, and a hush fell over the crowd. It didn't seem as if the words of before had even come out of his own mouth, but now they were clapping, hesitantly at first, and then chittering and bruxing their approval. And Rupert was up in the air before he knew what was happening, passing over the heads of so many different squirrels, so many furry bodies that he grew disoriented. Feeling that his heart was finally content, and clutching the silver acorn around his neck, willing his father to see him and to be proud, and willing the same for Zirreo, Rupert allowed himself to pass out.

It had been a long journey, after all.

Epilogue

Far down south in Beechwood, a ways from the great falls, near the edge of the water, there was a great forest of redwoods. The enormous trees towered over the world, beautiful, and seeming isolated, as if they hailed from some other time entirely. A mist hung in the air, warm and balmy. The occasional croak of a hidden frog or scurrying of a mouse or chipmunk broke the silence every now and then, before properly fading back in respect of the sanctity of these trees.

From atop one of said trees, Kyan sighed.

It was so peaceful here, so lovely, so… shiny. A while ago she had not liked it too well out here. But that was before Rupert came. Rupert and at least five others. Carrying pouches. Pouches full of…

"So…much…" Kyan croaked, staring into the hollow she now called home. Overflowing with rubies, diamonds, rings, coins, silver and gold, there was hardly any room for anything else. Let alone *anyone* else.

Except me, Kyan thought. A satin bed with a crown hanging overhead marked the place she would spend much of her happy days here.

Rupert had kept his promise well.

At first, it had taken awhile, and Kyan had feared he had forgotten. But then, just when she had decided to go after him, to terrorize a couple of grays and demand her payment, he had come.

He had been sleeker, more mature, in charge of a colony of grays learning to thrive under the rule of someone as

Honorable

as him. And then he had gone back to his colony, the others who accompanied him looking a bit confused over why they were making a trip practically across Arborand to give a dead Emperor's gold to a chickaree who grabbed it like they had only come to wave it in her face.

That was all well and good, Kyan thought as she sat atop one of the uppermost limbs of her redwood, looking out over the water far ahead. She had what she wanted.

Perhaps she had been sad to see Rupert go. A little bit. She could permit that. Perhaps she could admit she found him attractive, sort of like a shiny thing. Except not like that.

But it was all right here, even without his particular kind of shine. Squirrels like Rupert lived to make words like honor and justice more than just words. Kyan could never live in the way he did, and he knew that probably, and had gone back to his colony to live in his particular way, and then to marry a lovely gray squirrel who had eyes on him awhile, and to have children and to make life stop long enough to notice he was *living* it.

For perhaps, Kyan thought, it was squirrels like Rupert that made things happen.

BOOK II: *The Silver Compass*

Prologue

She heard them before she saw them, low ominous murmurs, deep voices in the hall outside the doorway. They were talking to her parents; she couldn't hear what they were saying. When the knock had come at the door, her father had taken a look out the window and told her to hide under her bed. She had been about to argue, but something in the way he said it warned her not to.

The voices were rising now, getting agitated, and Mae curled herself into as small a ball as possible, her little heart thumping in her chest a thousand beats per minute. And then she couldn't hear anything. The voices had receded, and it seemed they were gone. It seemed her parents were gone, too. Mae wanted to crawl out from under the bed; she wanted to see if everything was all right. But some instinct warned her not to, and she remained frozen in place.

A floorboard creaked next to the door.

Her breath caught in her throat.

"Mother, father, where are you?" she thought. For already she knew that this was neither of them.

Then there were shadows in the room, three of them. They had filtered in as if by magic, and the room had been permeated with cold from the outdoors.

The shadows which Mae knew to be squirrels, other squirrels like herself, were searching the room. Their vision swept along the walls and finally down to the floor. One of them crouched and peered under the bed where she lay still, petrified. She was sure he had seen her.

But the squirrel straightened up again, leaving Mae to her petrified silence, and they had gone, drifting from the room just as they had come in.

Mae lay under the bed for as long as she thought necessary, painfully afraid that when she came out, they would be in the other room, lying in wait for her.

But when she finally did crawl out, they were nowhere to be found, although she searched the shadows at the edges of the room quite thoroughly. Her parents were also gone.

Mae climbed down the tree where her house was situated, a hard packed mess of sticks and grass that seemed to glint in the moonlight behind her as she looked back. It no longer looked safe or welcoming to her. It had been marked by those others, those shadows, and she had to get away.

Far away from here, the squirrel child thought, and ran.

It was only later that the tears which had been threatening to come, came. And by then, she didn't recognize her surroundings at all.

She had wandered around, lost, scared and crying, knowing she had not been old enough to go off alone, and sure she would die for it, when she felt a paw on her shoulder.

"What's the matter, honey?"

All she could do was whimper, and try to keep from fainting.

"Here, come with us," the voice had said. She tried to find its face, but she was far too tired, and passed out before she could hear much more of what the voice was saying.

Chapter One

"C'mon then!" Mae yelled in mock derision, speeding up as she spiraled down one tree and leapt to the next, feeling her claws catch on the solid wood. She was up, and wasted no time in going round and round, faster up this time, trying to ignore the ache beginning in her legs.

Flor was catching up. Yet again. It was infuriating, she thought with a laugh that was only half sincere.

In the instant after the thought had crossed her mind, Mae's tail was snagged from behind, and turning, she faced the smug other, who was holding it up like a trophy.

"Okay, fine, you've won again," she sighed, attempting rather unsuccessfully to hide her wounded pride. "Don't smile at me like that, I'm *never* going to win the Treetops racing and you *know* it. I know it. If it weren't for you—but I'm always second."

The young gray squirrel threw her tail of sleek black fur to the side with an offhand shrug.

"Oh calm down, Mae. We've plenty of time before this year's. Besides, if it really means so much to you, I'll *let* you win."

There was a moment of silence. Then Mae lunged at Flor unexpectedly, and they were off again.

Up, around, in the air all at once, it *did* mean something to Mae, more than she would ever have admitted to her best friend, that she beat him just once. She had felt, from an early age that she *must* be good at something, and had discovered that something was speed. The annual Treetops Racing event was something she practiced for, early, before Flor or any of the others in the

Firwood community woke up, something she looked forward to every year.

With a burst of excitement, Mae realized she was catching up with Flor; she could see him clearly now, there was only a bit to go—

"Stop for a minute. Stop, stop, STOP!"

The flustered, irritable voice broke through Mae's ecstasy, and a second later, she bumped into Flor's immobile backside. Shaking her head groggily and looking around, she saw why Flor had been stopped. Or rather, whom he had been stopped by, the reason not yet apparent.

Mrs. Fennel was possibly the fattest and the bitterest squirrel in the community. Mae wasn't quite sure whether these two things went hand in hand, but she hadn't been foolish enough to ask, as Mrs. Fennel already nurtured a special dislike for her in particular.

Other than the fact that she was a black squirrel, Mae could see no reason for this dislike. But color was the only reason the older squirrel needed, and in this day and time, Mae supposed she could see where she was coming from. Just a scant number of years ago, the black squirrels had taken over the grays of Firwood with the help of immortality gained from an object known only as the golden chestnut. They had acted as vicious dictators, repressing the grays horribly. Finally, saving grace had come in the form of Flor's father Rupert, the squirrel who now ruled their community. Mae liked Rupert a lot, almost like her own father. He had been one of the few squirrels in the community to trust Mae, and the one who had found her when she was orphaned, alone and lost. He had taken her in, and she had soon become close friends with Flor, who was only a season younger than Mae. As a result of this, Mae was the sort of leader between the two, the one who instigated the sometimes mischievous tricks the two would pull off together. She supposed this didn't help some of the older squirrel's prejudices much, but at such a young age, she found it hard to be overly bothered by this. Firwood was all she had known, all she could remember knowing. It was her home just as much as theirs.

Mrs. Fennel stared at Mae with a beady, wrathful eye before snapping at them both.

"How is it that you two always escape hearing news of any serious event, eh?" She was breathing as if it had been she and not them, who had just run a long way.

"Serious event?" Flor said.

"Yes, that's what I said, isn't it?" Without waiting for either of them to respond, she pressed on impatiently.

"The whole community is having a meeting, in the main tree, *now*. I've been asked if I could please round up those who are always off somewhere *else*," she said, giving Mae another disapproving glance. Mae ignored this.

"Meeting for what?" she asked immediately.

Mrs. Fennel gave her a long look before saying, "It appears there have been some uneasy happenings in the area of late."

Mae's heart beat faster. She hadn't expected anything like this.

"You mean danger?" she asked. "Like what?"

"Cripes!" Mrs. Fennel swore, apparently repulsed by Mae's inquisitive nature. "It's not my place to tell. You'll just have to wait and see."

And with that, she turned around, beckoning for them to come after.

Exchanging glances, Mae and Flor followed her to the large main tree, a massive thing which towered over the rest of the community. It was where some squirrels made their home, and also where most events were held. Formerly the place the dark Emperor Venul had ruled from, the massive tree had undergone quite a few changes of decoration, and was always brightly lit, glowing firefly lamps hanging from the wide, arching ceiling every few feet. The smell of acorn pancakes and other such delicacies could be caught drifting through the hall from the direction of the kitchens, down a narrow flight of stairs from where they had entered. Mae rubbed her stomach. She had forgotten her lack of breakfast before now. Several times, she attempted to speak to Flor, but Mrs. Fennel was walking so fast that they were forced to take small bounds to keep up with her. The halls were strangely empty, giving her a sense of how important this meeting must be.

Mae had only had occasion to be in the meeting room once or twice, but it seemed she still managed to forget how large it actually was. With an arching, domed solid wood ceiling, oddly shaped by two intersecting branches above which served as towers, the meeting room appeared spacious and daunting. Wooden shelves carved from the sides of the chambers stuck out, hulking and shadowy, at even intervals, spiraling up the sides of the room. These were used for seats, and by the time Mae and Flor arrived, all of them were taken up by whispering, chattering squirrels, looking menacingly shadowy, surrounding them from above. Mrs. Fennel moved off to one of the lower shelves. Someone had clearly saved her a seat. Mae and Flor took places along the wall.

"I wonder what- Mae began, but Flor pointed, and she saw a solemn young gray squirrel mount the wood podium in the center of the room.

"Attention, please!" he called, in an unnaturally shrill voice. "I said, attention!"

Gradually, the murmuring died down, and the shrill young squirrel continued.

"Rupert would like to speak!"

A hush fell over the room, and the young squirrel left the podium, looking rather cocky. Another, older squirrel appeared, a silver acorn dangling from around his neck, his expression placid. When he reached the top of the podium, he looked around at them all, almost as if surprised that so many of them had come.

"I suppose you're wondering what this is all about," Rupert began. "I'm sorry it's so early in the morning, and we couldn't break for pancakes first, but—" he broke off, and this time his face was tinged with worry. "This, I feel, is more important. You've all heard the rumors of the Dark Wanderer, have you not?"

Shock spread across the room in a wave, and squirrels throughout turned their heads to glance at each other, skeptical, frightened, or confused.

"It appears," Rupert continued, as if unaware of the commotion his words had caused. "That it might be more than rumor."

"How do you know?" squealed a female voice from somewhere above.

"There's been a sighting on the border of Oakwood."

"Oakwood! I knew we hadn't seen the end of the black squirrels!" said a pompous old squirrel with dusty fur.

"What does he want here?" gasped someone in fright.

A squirrel wife collapsed in a faint, almost hitting the podium as she fell from her spot on the floor.

Rupert allowed himself to look sympathetic, not bothering to hide his concern.

"I can't possibly tell you whether this was a genuine sighting or not, but it is clear in any case that we must take extra measures of precaution. Parents, keep your children close. If anyone sees anything suspicious, report it immediately. The purpose of this meeting is just to warn you, to let you know. Going on what we have heard of this Dark Wanderer, he—if it is a he—does not have any respect for life."

Rupert looked around at them all, his face hard with resolve.

"I've told you all that is in my capacity to tell, and now you may go. First, however, someone ought to pick up this one," he said with a small smile, pointing at the fainted squirrel wife. A couple of others nearby complied, and Rupert drew back from the podium. As Mae watched him walk to the side, she thought she saw his face revert to a troubled expression, before it was covered in shadow.

The others were moving now, heading out of the meeting hall, abuzz with conversation about what they had just been told. From somewhere off behind she and Flor, Mae heard Mrs. Fennel loudly telling some of her lady friends how she thought she'd seen something dark in the trees only the day before.

Mae, like practically everyone else, had heard the tales of the Dark Wanderer. Mostly, she had thought them to be fictitious, until now that was; there was something in Rupert's apparent belief that made her suddenly unsure. Flor had always taken the tack that they were at least partly real; where had the stories come from after all? After this, Mae had to reluctantly agree with him in her mind. She had heard of the Dark Wanderer as a shadowy, crooked old squirrel who visited homes, inquiring about others' beliefs in Astrippa, the goddess of the squirrels. If they were not parallel to his own, or if they refused to conform, rumor had it that the Wanderer cast dark magic upon his unfortunate victim. No one knew what kind of squirrel the Wanderer was, though most in the gray community of Firwood pictured him black as night, unavoidable runoff from past experience.

"Do you believe all of it?" Flor asked Mae as they were leaving the hall.

Mae paused before answering.

"All that we've been told just now, yes," she said.

"I don't believe about the magic," he told her. "Whoever heard of a black squirrel doing magic? Supposedly, only white squirrels could ever have that power, and they're all gone, since…"

"Since the death of Zirreo," Mae agreed. "I know."

Zirreo had been the last of the white squirrels, and had set Rupert on his quest for the golden chestnut, before he was killed by the Emperor Venul.

They walked in silence for a bit longer, the sounds of the others pushing around them filling up the space where their words might have gone. Mae didn't feel so hungry anymore.

They had reached the outside air once again, and were about to exit the main tree, when a touch on Mae's shoulder sent her spinning around. Rupert was standing behind them both.

"Could I request a word with you two?" he asked, with that small, friendly yet serious smile he had.

"Yes, of course," Mae said, startled. A looming feeling of apprehension filled her, but she couldn't divine its cause. As they followed Rupert back the way they had come, Flor seemed to notice Mae's uneasiness.

"Father," he said quickly. "Does this have anything to do with the Dark Wanderer?"

"In a moment, Flor," Rupert said quietly. They had reached a door to the side of the hall, and Rupert led them in, closing the door firmly behind them all. It was a small storage room, the only place they were likely to get privacy now that the tree was overrun with excited squirrels.

Mae turned around uncomfortably in the small space, and looked to Rupert questioningly. He smiled slightly.

"Now, you two don't kill me for this, but I would feel a lot more comfortable if you did not stray away from other, elder squirrels. I know you like your adventures, and games, but it's dangerous."

"So you believe, then?" Mae asked. She didn't need to explain what she was referring to.

"Yes," Rupert said simply. "I believe that this Dark Wanderer is real. Very real," he added. "I care a lot for you. Your mother does too."

Mae cast her eyes to the ground. She could not help it. Much of the time it seemed as if Rupert's wife had to stretch herself thin to accept her, though she didn't know why. Rupert saw her look, and gave a half-smile.

"Both of you," he said firmly. "Just...remember."

Mae felt touched for a reason beyond her complete comprehension. Rupert wasn't her father, didn't have to be her father, especially in a time like this where being a black squirrel made you seem one with the enemy, the Dark Wanderers, the nightmarish shadows on the edges of minds, undefined threats that didn't necessarily exist. It was then that she realized Rupert was different from everyone else in the gray community. He was unchanging, immutable, but there was something he *knew*, something she wished she could know. In that moment, she wished very much that she could be his daughter.

"That's all I wanted to say," Rupert said after a time, opening the door for them. The buzz of the hall filled Mae's ears again, and Flor walked out in front of her. She felt a paw on her shoulder as she turned to follow, and Rupert said, in a voice that only she could hear, "Watch out for him, okay?"

Mae looked at Rupert, and knew, startlingly in that second, that he knew they would wander anyway, knew they would not stick to his advice.

"Okay." She nodded as she said it, her voice alone being too soft to discern. When she stepped out into the corridor, Flor was standing waiting for her on the far side of the hall. He gestured to her impatiently. She glanced back, but Rupert had gone, and she followed Flor out into the sunlight, pushed along by the crowd that eased about her.

Chapter Two

The days passed with no event since the meeting at the main tree, and most of the grays in the community at Firwood began to feel as if they were in no danger once more. There were tentative whispers that maybe the Dark Wanderer was only a tale after all, or that he had decided to pass their community by entirely. There came a point, inevitably, where the threat faded, and everyone went back to their normal ways of life.

Then came the day of the sighting. Whether by coincidence, or by some dryly humorous twist of fate, Mae and Flor were the only ones present when it happened. And by yet another twist of fate's irksome paw, they were nowhere out of the way when it happened.

Dusk was settling in on the community, and most of the others were already at home, though there were a few grays still out and about, laughing with each other, talking. Nothing was out of the ordinary, except for the speedy approach of that year's Treetops Racing tournament eating at Mae's mind. In the blink of a couple seconds, her worries on that subject became meaningless as Flor took a sharp breath of air.

"What is it?" Mae asked, not thoroughly concerned, her mind floating to other topics even as she spoke.

"*Look!*" Flor gasped, pointing discreetly over at a stand of trees to their left. Mae couldn't see anything, save for an old gray couple walking together between the trees. She was about to turn back to Flor, a grin on her lips, when she saw it. A slash of black against the green-brown of the forest, further back from the old couple, flickering in and out of her vision, once, twice. Her grin fading, she stared a while longer but could not make out any more movement.

"Something's back there," Flor said unsteadily.

Mae took a step toward the forest grove, squinting in the dying light. There, another flicker of black, deep as night. Whoever it was, they appeared to be merely skirting the community. Waiting to attack? Mae's heart was pumping fast, filled with curiosity.

"We should go back," she heard Flor say as if from a distance. "Everyone's heading home, we should as well. We've got to tell my dad. C'mon. Mae?

But Mae was entranced by what she was seeing.

"There's more than one of them, I think," she whispered slowly. "Flor, what d'you think they're doing?"

"For bark's sake, how am I supposed to know? We've got to tell everyone!"

Mae shook her head, dazed. She felt oddly drugged. What was wrong with her? What Flor was suggesting was the smart thing to do, the right thing, and she knew it. Yet…she felt an unexplainable, strong pull to the woods in front of her, to follow the movements, to find out what she needed to know…

It was ridiculous, of course. There was nothing she needed to know, after all. What could she possibly gain from following an elusive shadow into a forest, endangering her best friend…

But…

"You're right, Flor. Look, go tell the others what we saw."

"What about you?"

"I—I'll be along shortly."

Flor stared at her.

"You're going after it, aren't you?"

"I didn't say anything of the sort!"

"It doesn't matter, Mae. I know you. You might as well have come out and said it. But the fact of the matter is, you're crazy. I won't allow you."

Mae smirked. "Stop me."

A brief silence followed before Flor blurted out, "I'm coming too, then."

Mae's smirk fell away.

"No, look Flor, you can't!"

"Stop me."

The two stared at each other evenly for a few seconds, and both smiled tentatively. A noise echoed across the forest, the sound of a branch snapping. Mae turned, and headed in the direction of the disturbance, hoping against hope that Flor wasn't following her and knowing he was.

They crept across the leaf-strewn ground of the forest, taking to the trees almost immediately. Going in the direction they had seen the shadows moving in, they could not find anything for a long time. Mae had just begun to think that they had lost whomever it had been, when a faint voice sounded from behind some nearby brush. Heart pounding again, she looked over at Flor. He nodded, indicating that he had heard it too.

Mae leapt over to where a conveniently placed fir tree allowed her to peer down behind the brush from which the voice had emanated. Her breath caught in her throat. Flor landed beside her and stiffened, his body going completely rigid.

Down below, was the most grotesquely frightening squirrel Mae had ever laid eyes on. He was large, in the prime of life, but his fur was mussed as if he hadn't bothered to groom himself…or as if his mind had not been in the state to care. But it was the squirrel's face that made Mae truly frightened. Though the rest of the stranger's fur was pitch black, there was a wide, bright white streak of fur across his face. Mae had never seen a half-breed before, had never known they existed—though looking upon this one made her think it was a knowledge she could have done without. Next to this squirrel, there was another, much smaller than the first. He was small and burnt red in color, and carried a sort of sack across his back, which he would reach up and stroke occasionally as if he constantly needed to be reassured that whatever was inside was still there. The two were stopped behind the shrub, arguing fervently.

"Idger, I told you to keep your voice down," hissed the large squirrel angrily.

"Yessir, sorry sir," the other squirrel muttered, not sounding sorry in the least. "When do I get my payment fer the last raid?"

"When I feel like giving it to you!" the other growled. "She's not happy at all, not with you, Idger. She doesn't care about you."

"Please sir, will yew *stop* talking like that," the chickaree called Idger groaned. "All the time, it's 'she' this, and 'she' that. 'She' doesn't even exist—

The half-breed's paw shot out and tightened around the chickaree's neck. His voice was raised dramatically, violently crazed.

"She doesn't CARE about you!" he screamed. From her place on the fir tree, Mae could see Idger trembling. He didn't speak. She was sure his life must be over.

But then suddenly, the bigger squirrel suddenly loosened up, letting go of the red squirrel in an almost sedated manner, dropping his paws to his sides.

"Idger, we need something to eat. It is a long way to Ashwood."

Mae turned to Flor, mouthed "Ashwood" to him. Flor gave Mae a horrified glance, which reflected her own thoughts back at her. This squirrel was obviously unhinged in some way, and seeing as he and his companion seemed only to be passing through Firwood, their best bet would be to go quickly and silently back to the colony. Mae wasn't even sure why she had gone out here in the first place. She felt terribly cold, damp, and chilled to the core.

The black squirrel shifted on the ground below, just a shadow with life breathed into it, and a slash of white. She thought she shouldn't be afraid. They should just turn and go.

Mae touched Flor, tugging on his forepaw. He didn't hesitate, and the two started to leap to the next tree, back the way they had come.

It might have worked, Mae later thought, if it hadn't been for their timing. Just as she started off the branch, Flor beside her, a voice erupted from below.

"I think we have some guests, Idger. Can you find our guests? She knows where our guests are, but do you?"

The awful madness thick within the voice of the large squirrel made Mae's heart do a strange thumping tango in her small chest, and she found, too late, that she had lost her concentration and was falling, her jump coming up short. She hit the ground in a flurry of crisp golden-brown leaves, and leapt to her feet immediately, praying that Flor had made his escape. Feeling disoriented, Mae hobbled toward the nearest tree, but a voice called out behind her again.

"I wouldn't go anywhere if I were you." This time, the chickaree had spotted her, and he came scurrying over delightedly, rubbing his paws together as if he had discovered a big treat.

Mae tried again to make a dash for freedom, but the big half-breed was behind her now, grinning insanely. Clenching a paw on her shoulder, he began to speak conversationally to her.

"Hello, honey. What's your name?"

Mae didn't say anything, keeping persistently silent, refusing to meet the eye of the other.

"Shy, are we? Why don't you ask your gray friend to come down, honey? Maybe he can tell me."

Mae flinched. Looking up overhead, she could see Flor peering down at her. She saw his face change expression as he realized he had been spotted.

Following Mae's gaze, the big black squirrel grinned his terrible grin up at Flor.

"I'd come down if I were you, gray," he murmured, his voice taking on an almost dreamy quality. Mae got the sense that his voice was as ever-shifting as his moods, and knew she had never felt so scared in her life. If it weren't for her stupid curiosity, they would be safe in the Firwood community now, and these squirrels would be passing them by, well on their way to Ashwood.

Flor was coming down from the tree. She could hear his claws scratching on the wood, slowly. She could picture him, tentatively moving, gauging the situation. She wished he would just run away. But Flor, in his sense of honor, would never run. He never did. Except to effortlessly beat her, she thought, thinking of the races that no longer mattered.

Flor had reached the ground. He stood there, nervously, body tensed.

"You're not going to hurt her, are you?" she heard him ask.

"Oh, I should," came the low grate of the big squirrel's voice. "But I won't. You were spying on me. I know it, so you can just admit it. She knows it."

Mae cleared her throat nervously. They were dealing with a loose cannon here.

"Look…can't you just…let us be on our way, then? We can't possibly have anything you want."

"Or…" the big squirrel breathed, taking his paw from her shoulder. "You could."

Mae attempted to move, but found that she had been bound by a thin, fibrous rope, made from some sort of vine. She looked over at Flor, who was now being held still by the chickaree, who was at work rendering him helpless in much the same way.

"You may know me," the big squirrel said, "As the Dark Wanderer. But you can call me Callisto. You're with me now."

Chapter Three

And so Mae and Flor traveled with Callisto and Idger, finding no way to get out of the helpless situation. Mae found it hard to look at Flor, ridden with guilt. She had gotten them into this. She had to get them out.

On the first sign of dawn that night, Callisto stopped short and had them camp in the split of an elm tree. Mae was unpleasantly surprised, but didn't dare say anything.

"We sleep during the day, honey," Callisto said, as if reading her thoughts. "And wander at night. Dark Wanderer. Haha." His laugh was strangled and joyless. Mae feared for their lives that day.

As soon as they were settled in, Callisto snapped at Idger.

"Go get us some food, will you? Quick, now. And take him," He gestured to Flor as if he were an interesting foraging implement of no real consequence. Idger opened his mouth, looking like he would argue, but Callisto gave him an ugly look.

"Don't talk about payment. I'll give you payment when I feel like it, won't I? She likes that method, don't you know..." his voice trailed off, and so did Idger, dragging Flor behind him. Flor glanced back at Mae, his words unspoken but present all the same. He was afraid for her, alone in the presence of this mad beast of a squirrel. Well, so was she.

There followed a moment of silence after Flor's leaving, in which Mae looked anywhere but at the larger squirrel, hoping to avoid any confrontations. After a moment, she glanced him out of the corner of her eye, shifting into full view and her heart sank; a confrontation seemed inevitable.

"Do you have a name, honey?" he asked, in perfect harmony with her dread. His voice was low and grating and made her stiffen with nerves.

Mae thought fast.

"Juniper," she decided. She had always liked that name.

Callisto looked in thought for a moment, then said. "The truth, this time."

Mae breathed in fast. "M-Mae," she could not keep the unintentional stutter out of her voice.

How had he done that?

"Mae," Callisto repeated, as if judging the value of the name. The way he said it made her view her own name in a worse light than she ever had. "I like that name."

"Oh. Thank you." Mae became determined not to show any fear in the face of the enemy. Maybe if she were nice enough, Callisto would let she and Flor go. It had been a mistake to lie about her name, she realized. That sort of thing made others think you had something to hide.

"Hmm." Callisto did not ask about Flor. Instead, he moved up one side of the split in the elm tree and took a seat, eyes bright with thought.

"Come sit by me, Mae," he told her. Mae hesitated, then sat a good bit to the left of him, haunches tensed. Callisto was quiet for a good bit more.

"What sort of activities do you enjoy, Mae?"

Mae was taken aback by the suddenness and apparent spontaneity of the question.

"Well…I like to run about in the trees. Racing. I don't know what else, I've never really thought about it."

"Do you pray to Astrippa?"

The question hit her like cold water, triggering something in her memory and she sat for a moment like a fish out of water, gasping.

"It's only a question."

"Yes. Of course I do," Mae responded truthfully. Her heart was pounding heavily by now, but Callisto didn't say anything more. The big black squirrel assumed his thoughtful pose once more, and hearing a noise, Mae turned to find that Idger was back, dragging a disgruntled Flor along. Flor looked concerned, but his face relaxed a good deal once he saw that Mae was not in any apparent danger, other than the obvious.

Idger had found several berries and acorns, along with some cold, fresh stream water, which Flor carried in the open halves of a chestnut's shell. After they had eaten and rested, they set out again under cover of darkness once more.

This pattern continued relentlessly. Every time they stopped to eat, or to sleep, Callisto would send Idger off to forage, Flor tied to his side, forced to help, and Mae would be left alone with the dark squirrel in an uncomfortable silence in which he would stare at her and grin, or talk to her. This was what bothered Mae most. Callisto was indeed often generally cruel to Flor, almost as if he were of no consequence. But he seemed strangely interested in Mae, always keeping the same tone with her, asking her bemusing questions every time they were alone. And only when they were alone. Sometimes, she got the feeling that he would send the others off just to engage her in this sort of helpless cycle, one from which she dearly wished for the opportunity to escape from, and to take Flor with her.

But it seemed that no opportunity for this ever presented itself, at least not in a fashion that would not get them killed. Callisto traveled in a purposeful, straight march toward the setting sun every afternoon, sleeping during the day, secretive in the night hours. Mae did not know what he wanted with her or Flor. She could not imagine what importance they would be to someone like the fabled Dark Wanderer. There seemed to be a pattern to the way the large half-breed traveled, and often Mae wondered where they were going. But as it turned out, she could never get a satisfactory answer to this question either, though she had only dared to bring it up once. Callisto had just given her a sly smile and said something to the extent of "all in time." Mae didn't intend to wait for time to spell things out for them. She and Flor were leaving as soon as the opportunity arose, even if they had to make that opportunity for themselves.

One evening, Mae and Flor found a rare chance to talk, and shielded themselves behind the leaves of a bramble bush as a sound barrier.

As soon as they were a safe distance from their captors, Flor cut to the chase. "Mae, what is it that Callisto is doing with you? Why does he always have me leave to forage? Is he hurting you in some way?"

Flor had been concerned a long time about this, Mae could tell by the way the worry shone out of his eyes now.

Mae answered truthfully. "I don't know, really. He just has me sit with him, mostly. Then he asks questions, but they all seem fairly harmless. Like what I like to do, what I like to eat, what's my middle name, you know."

"You don't have a middle name."

"It was just an example. And anyhow, Flor, that's not the most pressing matter on our paws. We need a plan."

"Sorry. Yes, of course." Mae could tell her friend wanted to pursue the matter further, but he desisted. "Did you have an idea, then?"

"No, I was hoping you might," Mae admitted.

"I could try to escape from Idger while we're foraging, and then double back and rescue you."

Mae only needed a second to think on this.

"No way! That would be putting you in too much danger. Look, I don't know what Callisto's about, but you don't want to mess with him. I know that much."

"Well, then what do you propose we do?"

"I don't know," she said, after a time. "It's just...I got us into this mess, and if we're getting out of it in a risky fashion, which is inevitable, *I* should be the one taking the risks."

A snapping of twigs sounded and Idger sidled through into their clearing. Both squirrels stopped talking and turned to the newcomer.

"Well, c'mon then," Idger said loudly, gesturing at Flor. His eyes were narrowed suspiciously, and he looked shiftily about as if expecting enemies to be camped close nearby. "C'mon. Gray one, yer coming with me. Now."

Idger looked in a temper, and Mae thought she knew what it was about. For the last few days, the chickaree had been asking Callisto about 'payment', and so far Callisto had ignored him. Mae was a little puzzled as to what kind of payment the big squirrel possibly had for the chickaree, but it was none of her concern whether the little savage got paid or not.

"Oh, and likkle blackie?" Idger's irritating voice caught Mae in her tracks.

"What?"

Idger narrowed his eyes at being spoken to in such an impudent manner.

"Yer supposed to go see Callisto. I would be quick about it, he doesn't like waiting much."

Resigned to her habitual visit to Callisto, Mae found the squirrel in question sitting in the center of their camp, which consisted of some damp leaves beneath a sheltering brush. He was staring at the ground, mouthing something, some sort of rhythmic mantra under his breath. At the sight of Mae, a smile which only pretended to be friendly crossed his face.

"Ah—I told Idger to come get you. She wants you near. So do I, you know. You interest me, Mae."

Never had Mae gotten so much information from the ominous squirrel at once.

"Callisto," she said politely, in a moment of unrivaled bravery. "What are you keeping us around for? It's not that it bothers me too much, but we don't seem to be of any use to you. Aren't we just hampering you down?"

Waiting on tenterhooks, Mae held her breath, but all that Callisto said was "No. Of course not. Everyone has their use, Mae, surely you must know that. You and I especially, we should know, and she of course. But you and I, we have fine lineage. Only we can really decipher what is right in this world."

Mae stiffened.

"If you mean that the black squirrels are superior, I don't believe you. Gray squirrels like Flor, they're just as important."

"Flor, is that the gray's name?" Callisto asked. "I had gathered as much." He did not respond to any of

Mae's indignant exclamations, and Mae began to feel the strains of anger rising in her breast.

"What *do* you want of me?" she demanded again, but Callisto was now concentrating on the inside of his paw, his eyes turned to hard stones of effort. Mae was surprised to notice he was muttering again, softly, just as he had been when she had first come across him. She thought to cut across him, to demand an answer, or to take her chances and dart off to find Flor and leave, when her thoughts subsided on the eve of a warmth. Not a warmth, a glow, really, coming from Callisto's paw. His recitations had turned to a low hum, and flecks of gold dancing in a soft light were radiating out a small distance from his paw. His head was still bowed, his eyes still determinedly fixed on the growing light.

Mae began to feel frightened. It was not just from the light that this feeling entered her; she felt indeed as if there were another being, not quite palpable, in the tent of brush, one that she could not see, flitting on the edges, concentrated in the small glow she could not tear her eyes away from.

Then, as suddenly as he had begun muttering, Callisto stopped. The light that had filled the space between where the two squirrels stood slowly faded and they were left to the dull, brightness of the sun as it began its descent once more. The night was almost completely upon them again.

Still, Mae's eyes were fixed on Callisto's paw, which was curled around something, as if holding air. Instinctively, though it made no sense, Mae knew that it was not just air that the big mutant black held. She could not control herself.

"What is it?" she asked, a tremor in her voice.

Callisto looked sideways at her, not answering for a moment. Then he smiled wryly at her and opened his paw. A good sized sheaf of what looked like gold glimmered up at her.

"Payment," he said, in answer to her question.

Mae collapsed, trembling, to the ground. She was sure she had just seen magic, and nothing less. Magic, which until now, was just a whispered fairy tale, something of old, just like the white squirrels. Here, in this bright and loud and clear world, such a thing shouldn't think to rear its head, to prod the chest of nonbelievers. But what she had just seen, surely…

Callisto had them continue their trek as soon as Idger and Flor had returned. Flor traveled in the darkness next to Mae, sensing something had come over her. Several times, he would reach out to hold her paw in his own, to catch her when she tripped, which happened often. He could read it in her movements; something was wrong.

What?

Mae squeezed his paw as he helped her up yet again. Idger was getting impatient with them lagging behind.

We have to get out of here, Flor.

Chapter Four

It was still dark, toward the wee hours of the day, when they came to the nest situated high up in the crook of a birch tree. Mae fully expected they would pass it by; it was indistinct, not any different from any other home. But just as she turned her eyes from it, taking a step forward, Callisto stopped on the spot. He engaged himself in an odd sort of act, standing on his hind legs, swaying towards the spot where the small home lay nestled in the branches of its guarding tree. Mae looked over at Idger, who was showing no surprise at this sort of behavior from his master. Mae was then seized with a type of horrible fear, afraid that once again she would see something unexplainable take place.

But as soon as she had had these thoughts, Callisto stopped swaying, and grinned his ghastly, mad grin.

"Here," he said to Idger, who perhaps on receiving his payment at last, had no objection to the statement. The chickaree started forward, and Mae and Flor were held back from following. Flor gave Mae a questioning glance, and Mae shrugged back subtly. Together they watched as Idger leap deftly to the tree in question and began to scale its height. He stopped when he reached the brightly lit home, appeared to compose himself, and then knocked. The thatched door opened a crack, though Mae found it hard to see whoever was inside. Idger appeared to be talking to the owner of the home. As he spoke, the door inched toward closing, then snapped all of the way open on a sharp word. A head poked out, and looked around, past Idger, deep into the night. A sneer formed on Idger's features, and he stretched out a paw to where the rest of them lay just out of sight. They could hear the nasal tone of his voice rising and falling, and the door opened still more until they could fully distinguish the figure of another squirrel, full-grown. Mae could not tell what to what race he or she belonged, but they were certainly not a chickaree, judging from their size compared to the one on their doorstep. Mae guessed a gray.

Callisto put a paw on her, and she jumped.

"Closer," he murmured. The three of them edged around until they had gotten quite close to the house now, and were able to hear what it was the two squirrels at the door were saying.

Mae had been right. The squirrel standing in the door was indeed a gray. A gray who was looking very nervous, grinding his teeth together and staring out into the black. Idger was still speaking.

"—an honorable effort. If yew decide to join."

The gray looked uncertain of something.

"You say there is another with you?"

Idger smiled crookedly.

"Oh, yes. But tonight, he will only join us once you have made your choice."

"And what is his purpose?"

Idger looked about to make a snide answer when Callisto stepped out from the shadows. The gray squirrel in the doorway gasped. Mae couldn't see why he had taken until now to come out into the open, but she now saw what a grand effect it had on the body in the doorway.

"The Dark Wanderer..." he breathed.

"Ah..." Callisto said. "But why do you seem so afraid?"

"You...you will kill me," the gray said faintly.

"Do you not believe in Astrippa?"

"…Yes."

"Then why must you die? The Dark Wanderer is not here. But he will come, if you do not let Astrippa into your life. If you do not join with her forces. My messenger has told you what will happen, has he not?"

"…Yes. It's just…difficult to…"

"Believe? Yes, I know. I am not so horrible as you would think," Callisto said, his voice oddly gentle. For some reason, it sounded even more frightful this way. Mae shivered, willing the gray squirrel to close the door.

"I am reasonable. The Dark Wanderer exists, but I can save you from him, if you join the forces of good. You need not do anything until the time arises. In the meantime, I can protect you."

Callisto motioned to Idger, who took from his pack a rolled piece of birch bark and a stick of charcoal. He handed these things to the gray squirrel in the doorway, who hesitated for only a second before writing down his name. Smiling, Callisto rolled up the birch bark again and handed it back to Idger. The gray squirrel in the doorway looked nervous still, but Callisto turned to him.

"You will be protected. A small price to pay, don't you think? And you're doing it for *her*."

He then turned, and left the house, Idger trailing behind. When they had reached Mae and Flor, Idger said, "Sir, that isn't how we normally do it, I thought." He sounded a bit disgruntled.

"Do you have a complaint to make, Idger?" Callisto asked. He completely ignored the two young squirrels with him, offering no explanation for his actions. Idger opened his mouth, but Callisto cut across him.

"I deserve to have more of a part! Vengeance for the unfaithful ones is not enough for me, I need to tell them face to face. Last night I was thinking. Do you want to know what I was thinking, Idger?"

"No, sir," Idger said, deeply unhappy now.

"I was thinking how she cares for me, and how she doesn't care about others as much. Others like you. I was thinking that maybe I should be the one to tell them about my mission. They would listen to me, they would see the truth better, I think. There would be less casualties, more followers. More *support*," he said this in a unnaturally loud voice, and Idger involuntarily moved back.

"Okay, sir," he said, casting his unhappy glance at the ground.

Callisto looked amused.

"What's the matter, Idger, do you think I have no need of you anymore? Well, if we are speaking of *need*, I suppose I don't. But...I foresee that there may be a time you will come in use, so I will not dispel you yet."

Idger heaved a sigh of relief.

"Thank yew."

"Sir."

"Sir. Of cirse."

They set off again, and Mae and Flor were again forced to follow with no idea of what they were headed toward, or why they were being forced to come along. Though keeping the last interaction they had seen in mind, Mae was sure it could be for no happy reason.

She was lost in thought again when Callisto pulled back to walk beside her. She flinched away instinctively, but all he did was whisper in her ear.

"I trust you saw all of that, Mae." And then he was back in front of them again.

Flor turned to Mae.

"What was that?" he mouthed.

Mae didn't have an answer.

The next dawn they camped, Flor whispered to Mae, "I don't care what the chances are, if a day from now we haven't found a plan of escape, I'm getting free of Idger while foraging, and coming to get you."

Mae was going to argue, but she knew she couldn't dissuade him. There was a hard firmness in his eye that reminded her for a brief moment of his father when in the middle of a brief for-your-own-good lecture.

"Okay," she agreed, reluctantly. And resolutely, she set about thinking of some other way to go about what must come. She didn't have long to think however, for Callisto called her name in a singsong voice, and she was once again forced to sit beside him. Once again she asked him why he kept her, not with much expectation of an answer.

"Because you are central to a noble cause, Mae," he told her.

Mae started. She hadn't expected him to reveal this much, but still she could make no sense of it.

"What cause, sir?" she asked. Again, she did not expect an answer, and again her expectations proved wrong.

"Her cause," Callisto said, softer this time.

A thought occurred to Mae, lingering only a moment in her mind before she voiced it.

"Sir…When you talk of *her*, do you mean…do you mean Astrippa?"

Callisto turned his face to her, half bathed in shadow, and smiled grimly.

Mae finally told Flor everything late that day, for she still found it hard to sleep at this time, and Idger, who usually remained awake, poking them with a stick and cackling, had fallen into a stupor which was humorous to gaze upon. Callisto never slept where they could see him. Often Mae wondered if he *did* sleep, and so she glanced around nervously before imparting her findings to her friend.

Once she had finished, Flor stared at the ground for an indeterminate amount of time. When he looked up, it was with the eyes of someone who has finally made a decision.

"We should leave now."

"Now?! But Flor, we don't know where Callisto is, he could be..." She stopped as the small snap of a twig sounded outside their sheltering bush. Mae stared through the foliage, trying to see in the fading light.

"Could be out there," Flor finished, his voice a deadly hush. "But we have to risk it. We *have* to, Mae. Dark is coming, and we don't have much time before he," (he indicated Idger) "starts to stir. We just have to trust to Astrippa, and make a getaway while we still have a chance. Who knows what will come of us if we wait another night? And Mae, I think it's clear that this Callisto wants something from you, and knowing the little we know about him, it can't be anything good. We both saw how he intimidated that gray two nights ago...now I don't know what he's playing at, but we don't want our name on that list of his, and I don't want you, Mae, to be his 'central cause'. Let him find another, we're done with this."

"He did magic," said Mae, suddenly. Flor's words had moved her, and she wanted to tell him all she knew. The incident of the payment appearing had left her mind until this moment, but now the memory came rushing back to her, keenly. "I'm almost sure of it."

Flor's eyes widened.

"Magic? But—

"I know. No one but the white squirrels. Legend, in other words. We have to leave, you're right about that, Flor. But it's dusk now. Are you sure it's the right time?"

"It'll have to be." He smiled wryly. "Mae, you can't make all of the decisions, all of the time. If we *run* fast—

Mae caught the allusion, and elbowed him in the side roughly.

"Very funny. Alright then, let's go."

With Mae in front, both squirrels crept to where they could peer out from the brush. Mae thought she saw a billion shadows flit around at the corner of her eye, but she knew they were only imaginings borne of fear. Still, a bad feeling remained, fluttering in her chest.

"Clear?" came Flor's voice behind her, shattering her fearful imaginings.

Mae gave a barely discernible nod and looked back at him.

"We should go diagonally to the right," she said. "There's a stand of trees not far from here, and if we can get to them, we should be able to start back the way we came under sufficient cover. I just hope we don't get lost. I'm only vaguely sure of the direction we should head for home."

Flor shrugged. "I'm pretty good with direction. I'll lead, if you don't mind. Which will, coincidentally, work out perfectly."

Mae glared at him. "Will you *stop* with that? Someday, Flor, I'm going to beat you, and then we'll see who's making the jokes."

Flor laughed easily.

The pain was in the first few steps, in revealing themselves to whatever lay ahead of them, just beyond their sight. Once they had come out into the open, relocated the stand of trees, and started running for them, everything fell into place. Mae pumped her legs hard, chasing Flor toward the clump of black, which was getting closer and closer, more definable as the dusky clump of trees it was.

Mae was actually beginning to think that they would make it, when suddenly she felt something pull her tail roughly from behind, jerking her to a near stop. Tearing her eyes from Flor's fast-retreating back, she saw Idger latched onto her tail. Kicking out frantically with her hind legs, she knocked the smaller squirrel from her and put on a new burst of speed. She was getting tired, and she chanced, in her fatigue, to look about for the first time. The shock of horror she got was so strong that she had to keep herself from falling over. She was not, in fact, running alone. Next to her, far off to one side, Callisto ran too, a wild smile pulling at his mouth. The ugly half-breed looked at her, a burning in his eyes, and she sucked in the air around her rapidly, trying with every fiber of her being to keep going.

Why, why did we think this a good idea? How could we have been so deluded to think it would work?!

The trees rose suddenly up in front of her. Flor, who was already in the act of climbing one, turned back and saw her predicament. Ignoring her cries not to turn back, he did exactly that.

"Flor," she groaned, "Keep going!" Callisto was closing in on her from one side. Idger had stopped the chase, apparently distracted by some sparkly rock or other. Flor was almost at the base of the tree when Mae saw his eyes widen, staring at a point behind her. Even

Callisto appeared deterred for a moment, surprised. But before Mae could turn to find out what it was they saw, she felt herself grabbed from behind. She struggled frantically, kicking out at what felt like more than one captor. For one delirious moment, she regained her grasp on freedom, but it was short-lived, as the next moment she felt the impact of something hard as rock collide with her head, and plummeted into the realm of unconsciousness.

Chapter Five

It took Mae a while to realize she had regained her senses, for dark continued to surround her. Then she realized that it was not complete dark, that there were small lights bobbing in her line of vision. It seemed as if she were lying down. Strange... Breathing in, she shifted her body, and found nothing hurt. Was this some sort of dream? It all seemed oddly surreal. She was lying on some sort of soft, hammock-like material, which she could feel bobbing and swaying as if she were being carried. Mae looked around for Flor, but didn't see him.

"You're safe," a voice whispered in her ear.

Mae started. A face had popped up nearby, over the edge of whatever she was being carried in. It was a face of a sort she had never seen before, with a small round face, and equally round ears to match large, round black eyes, which glittered not unpleasantly. Once again, Mae had cause to wonder if she were dreaming.

"Who--?" she began to ask groggily, but the head had ducked down again at the sound of her voice as if its owner were skittish. Mae wanted badly to move, to attempt to crane around to get a better look at these strange creatures, but she didn't quite dare to, for at the smallest movement the hammock swayed alarmingly. A sudden spell of dizziness came over her, and she leaned back, face turned into the hammock, wishing she were again unconscious.

Once Mae had calmed her senses, she found that she could see a ways around herself, by way of the bobbing lights, which she now recognized as intense firefly lanterns being held on a level lower than she. Attempting to relax, she thought back to the last thing she could remember, running from Callisto and his crazed smile, being snatched away and knocked out when she resisted. Were these strange creatures of which she had only seen a bit really trying to help her? Where were they taking her, and where was Flor?

Her last question was answered almost immediately after she thought it to herself.

"Mae? Mae, are you okay?" Flor poked up next to her.

"Flor!" she said, startled. "Thank goodness! I thought maybe—but where are we anyway?"

"Would it sound awful if I said I weren't sure?"

Mae looked incredulous.

"Haven't you been with me for a while? These creatures, what are they? They're all around you, Flor, you've got to know!" But the feeling of unreality was creeping back to her, fast approaching, and it made her feel a little sick.

"They're not going to hurt us, I'm sure of that," Flor reassured her. "I just can't make heads or tails of them aside from that. I've tried talking to them, but they seem to be fully concentrated on toting you somewhere safe."

"What are they like?" Mae asked, intrigued.

"They're smaller than us by a good deal. There's about four of them carrying you. They've got large eyes, and they don't seem to talk much, though I get the feeling that shouldn't be taken for lack of intelligence…deep thinkers, perhaps." He shrugged. "But Mae, wait until you see how they get around. It's amazing, but odd. Frightful odd. I don't know what to make of it."

"What, haven't they got feet?" Mae asked in a hush, conscious that the mysterious creatures in question might overhear her talking about them.

Flor snorted. "Of course they've got feet. But the way they jump. They've got—well, I can't do it justice. But Mae," he leaned down and whispered the last bit close to her ear in tones of excitement and wonder. "I think they can fly."

Mae jerked her head up.

"No."

Flor didn't seem to have heard her.

"It's amazing. Amazing. The way they hold you between them when they go between trees, it's so startling...If only someone like us could move like that."

Seeing that he was completely serious, Mae laid off the subject. A moment later, Flor's head snapped back, and he caught up to where Mae's hammock was still being promptly carried off, slower now.

"We're here, I think," he whispered.

As if in answer to his remark, the air about them suddenly got cooler. Mae was now being carried into a hole, or a tunnel or nest, or whatever sort of home these creatures kept. She wondered if they were a colony of sorts, similar to the Firwood colony she and Flor called home.

Mae could hear the dripping of water coming from somewhere close by, but all she could see when she moved from side to side were dark, smooth wooden walls. A tree, then. The creatures lived in trees. Mae only had a second or two to think about this, for the little creatures had come where they wanted, and set her down at last.

She found herself staring around at several of the strangest creatures she had encountered in all her existence. They were squirrels, thankfully, for this was the only bond of familiarity Mae could feel she had with them. They were small, furry staring creatures with eyes like lamplights and thinly furred tails. Mostly brown in color save for the downy white of their undersides, the creatures possessed a strange crinkling, a flap of downy skin between their hind and forelegs. Mae's mind went to Flor's words of earlier

I think they can fly…

"Good night to you," came a small, hushed voice, soothing in its approach on their ears. The foremost of the gathered squirrels had spoken. Mae caught the sound of the drip-dripping water again, behind the walls, and addressed her apparent savior.

"Thank you. You can't possibly know the extent of what you've done for me. If that black squirrel…"

"The Dark Wanderer," interrupted the little flying squirrel, in his soft murmur of a voice. The others behind him remained silent, only a few turning to each other and murmuring in the same beautiful tones. Mae was entranced by these creatures; every aspect of them was like some sort of pleasantly drug-induced dream.

"Tell me, who are you?" Flor's voice sounded from behind her, and she turned to see that it was he who had been supporting her for some time.

Mae expected an answer from the squirrel who had spoken before; she had assumed him the leader. But another spoke up, from behind the first, her voice almost musical.

"Most call us Night Whisperers. We don't personally have a name for ourselves. We have decided we don't have much of a use for one. You are welcome to use whatever name you like."

Flor breathed out behind Mae, long and low, and she could feel the small night creatures having the same effect on him as on herself. What sort of creatures were they, with their calming, almost soporific effect?

"How is it that we've never heard of you before?" she asked suddenly.

Yet another squirrel spoke this time, and the others patiently moved aside a bit and gave him the floor.

"I suppose it is because we are a bit reclusive. And we prefer the night to day. You are daytime squirrels, we assume. Now if you will allow us, we will bring you to your quarters. Follow Lunesta, she's set everything up earlier."

Mae and Flor complied, following the same female with the musical voice who had spoken earlier. They were off, down the hollowed out innards of branches, dimly lit by floating firefly lamps. The atmosphere this created was extraordinarily relaxing, and Mae found herself longing to sleep.

Lunesta lead them into a small room with water running down one wall. Mae registered this with shock and was on the verge of warning Lunesta of it when the flying squirrel explained.

"That is a liquid wall. We have them in several of the rooms. We have created a network that recycles any rain water we get in the top cavity of this tree. We spent the work on it because it makes a lovely sound when we turn in for the day. See how you like it tonight."

The water trickled along the wall, sounding like a slow moving stream. Mae's eyelids were heavy. Flor, who seemed to be holding up better after their exertion, asked the question that would have come to her own mind eventually.

"How" he asked. "Do you know about the Dark Wanderer? Have you had…run-ins with him?"

Lunesta looked caught for a moment, before answering. "Well…yes and no. The Dark Wanderer is common knowledge. Because we are isolated from the rest of the world in a way, it would be hard for him to find us. His night travels are pretense; he does not really belong to the night, and so poses no threat to us. I suppose it's daytime squirrels like you who need the protection."

She started to move to the door.

"Wait!" Mae said, coming awake a little.

Lunesta turned, her normally calm demeanor slightly apprehensive.

"Do you know what his plans are?"

"You should sleep for now." She said it gently, and before Mae could argue, she was gone.

"Now what do you suppose *that* was about?" Mae heard Flor say, but she was already floating into the realm of sleep. She felt him try to pull her back, but his attempts grew weak quickly, and soon they were both lying half-asleep in the darkness, listening to the trickle of the liquid wall over the smooth, dark wood, and in that moment they felt a stirring of a feeling of being blessed, and both knew what they shared without communicating it.

"Tomorrow," Mae whispered.

"Mmm," Flor replied.

But they never got to sleep the night out, for midway between dreams, a sound, a stirring in the black of unconsciousness woke Mae from her slumber and forced her into the world at hand, as dreamlike as that world might have been. Flor was still lying nearby on the downy bed the like of which they had both been provided with.

For a while, Mae could not see why she had awoke. Nothing seemed amiss and she could not hear a thing. She lay still for a moment, watching the strange reflection of the water on the opposite wall, listening to it, calming herself, for her heart had leapt in that brief moment. Finally she attempted to go back to sleep, but her own body, in fierce revolt borne of uneasiness, would not allow her. She tiredly opened her eyes once more, and then she understood.

Someone else was in the room with them.

Chapter Six

It was under the cover of darkness that Idger followed his master through tangled forests and across dark expanses of land. His ribs burned from the exertion of moving so quickly, and his master showed no signs of slowing down. If it weren't for the payment, Idger swore, he would turn around and leave at this moment, just let himself fall behind. It would be easy enough to do. But even here, even at a distance, Idger feared his master. He resented it, in the way all materialists resent the bonds they choose. Patting the sack containing his payment, Idger thought of its lovely shine and ran on, fervently wishing the two stupid little squirrels they had lost had already died somewhere, or never existed to begin with. He should've been paid double for looking after them. But they were important to his master, or at least the black one was, and now his master was angry at losing them. Idger let out a hiss of frustration, which died in his throat when he realized his master had stopped.

Callisto stood, staring up at a colossal, deformed ash tree. Idger felt a stirring of recognition within himself, and had to restrain from appearing curious. They had been here before. A long time back, a wintry day…but Idger couldn't remember much of it. He was a young chickaree then, and his attention span had been even shorter than it was now.

With a start, Idger noticed his master scaling the tree now, clearly wasting no time. He followed at a distance, cautious of rebuke should he find out he wasn't wanted here. But Callisto didn't seem to care. His movements were too purposeful, and his face was like stone.

The big half-breed stopped short at a place where a thick branch came out from the trunk, cast a glance at the one window in view, high up in the curve the tree made before plummeting back to earth crazily, and knocked.

There was no apparent door in the spot he had knocked, and afterwards a silence rang loud through the night.

There, he's crazy, Idger thought with a relieved sneer. *Not as if I didn't know it, but he gets crazier every year.*

But a part of the trunk swung inwards after a moment, and the head of a young chipmunk peeped out nervously, took in the sight of Callisto, and nearly shut the door again. He stopped himself just in time.

"W-what can I do for you, good sirs?"

"Get your master out here to talk to me. Now."

The chipmunk scattered, and the hidden door swung shut again.

Long minutes dragged by in which neither of the waiting squirrels said a word to one another, and then the door opened again slowly to reveal a wizened old fox squirrel, once large in size, now withered with something that was not quite age. He looked, in fact, like someone who has gained a lot of age in a short time, age brought on by stress. Now, as he looked into the face of Callisto, his body shuddered and his face clouded over.

"But why do you look so miserable, Pernil?" Callisto said quietly. "You knew our meeting again was inevitable. The sooner this is done, the better for us, the better for *her*. Hand it over, then."

Pernil sighed, almost collapsing as he did so.

"Now, Pernil, you are normally a strong leader, this is not becoming in you," Callisto murmured, then let out a cackle of laughter as if he had just said something wildly funny.

"Callisto, Callisto," Pernil gasped in a wheezy voice, barely above a whisper, as if he were hoping by speaking softly enough Callisto wouldn't hear or care about what he was saying. "It—I don't know, I am not responsible, I do not know how…"

Callisto looked suddenly dark.

"But—but Callisto…it's…gone."

"Gone?" Callisto hissed, his paw reaching out and grabbing onto the other, who flinched in response. Closing his eyes, Pernil mumbled something that could've been a prayer, going limp in Callisto's grasp.

"Spare our colony," he said, his voice loud and uncoordinated.

"Spare your colony, eh?" Callisto said. He looked angrier than Idger had ever seen him, ever. The chickaree turned and ran to the base of the tree to wait for his master; he did not feel he needed to watch things further. Overhead he heard Callisto, wild in anger, and then a wail of anguish from Pernil. There was silence, and then the sound of something hitting the ground nearby. Idger moved to the side in the rustling leaves, and in the glint of the dim light from the one window up above, he saw a glittering eye to his left, staring up at him from the ground sightlessly. The head of Pernil rolled over a bit as Idger ventured closer, disturbing the ground nearby. Something wet and slick spilled out of it to meet eh leaves below.

Idger, who had had nothing to eat for longer than he would have liked, promptly threw up. He almost ran away that night, but his master was on the hunt for something, and Idger did not want to be on the list of the hunted.

Chapter Seven

Mae sat still in the darkness of the room, hoping that the sound of the water from the liquid wall would mask her breathing. But she knew thinking like this was useless, that the other presence already knew they were there. And so she waited, afraid to wake Flor, straining to see what she already felt there in the room around her.

A sound, someone coming closer, and then something touched her side. She froze, almost forgetting to breathe. Then, from the dark right next to her, "Don't be afraid of me. Instead be afraid of what I have come to impart."

This made no sense to Mae, and she still could not see whomever it was who had hold of her. Satisfied that they would not hurt her for the moment, Mae noticed Flor come awake.

"Hello?" he asked turning his head wildly. "I hear things, Mae…"

But the thing in the darkness between them had also grabbed hold of him, and now they were both in the hands of someone they could not see.

"Who are you?" Mae demanded.

The shadowy something released them, and slipped toward the door, past the liquid wall, which illuminated a ghost of a shadow for a second, not long enough for Mae to make heads or tails of their visitor.

"Come with me," the thing whispered to them, the voice coming from the door this time.

Flor looked over at Mae, and she could sense what might have been a grin on his face.

"How is this amusing?" she asked him sharply, unable to control herself.

"Mae, I think it's one of them," Flor said. And as they stepped out into the lit hallway, she realized he was right. Their intruder turned out to be one of the flying squirrels who had shown hospitality to them. This squirrel, however, was stranger looking than any of the others by far. She was older, her voice less like a dream, and she wore a dark, gauzy material over her body, an odd sort of shawl which caused her to appear phantomlike and shapeless. Her large black eyes stared out from under the material, not blinking, and as she turned up a passageway, the two friends followed her in puzzlement.

The veiled squirrel took them up a curving passageway and into a small door to the side. The wood of the door was rough and splintery, as if it had been made in a hurry, and the walls of the room gave off the same feeling.

The room was also terribly small and stuffy, warmer than Mae was comfortable with. A high table stood in the middle of the place, and some mysterious boxes were strewn around the edges of it. On the table stood what looked like a large, pulsating drop of dew.

"Uhm.." Flor murmured, sounding almost comical in his incredulity, but perhaps out of caution neither he nor Mae asked what the thing was.

The little flying squirrel stood across from them, and tore off her veil. The effect was horrifying, until they realized they were seeing her face through the strange water drop. The distorted face smiled at them, and Mae wanted to look around the drop of water, if only to assure herself that the squirrel behind it was not deformed in any such way, but at that moment the small stranger spoke again.

"Do not move, you are perfect where you are."

Mae knew she should probably feel more alarmed. The strange squirrel could be positioning them so that she could use the odd bubble-contraption to harm them. But somehow, she doubted it. In fact, she doubted very much that this squirrel, secretive as she seemed, would do them any harm. There had been, and still was, a feeling of inexplicable safety about this place, and it had not dissipated upon the discovery of this newcomer.

"If you don't mind my asking— Mae began, but the stranger put a paw to her mouth to signify that she should be silent.

"You were in trouble with the Dark Wanderer," she whispered. "Do you know why that was?"

"How—well, no," Flor admitted.

There was a moment of silence in which the strange squirrel's eyes went shut, and when she opened them again, they rested on Mae.

"He wanted you," she said. It was not a question. Mae was starting to get a vague idea of what kind of squirrel this was, but she almost didn't want to indulge the thought…after all, seers weren't supposed to exist among squirrels, were they?

"You wonder who I am, perhaps?" the small flyer inquired in a tone of politeness from across the suspended dew drop. Her face contorted and twisted weirdly through the water as she talked. Not waiting for an answer, she went on. "My name is Kiroba. I am sorry for startling you and your friend, but you must understand, though *I* am welcome here, my talents are not. So I must take you here in private. I—had noticed something about you, Mae, when you entered our dwelling place. You didn't see me, I imagine, I am rather good at hiding myself when I do not want to be seen. There was an aura of purpose about you, but one of uncertainty as well. It seems to me that you are important in some way, but also that you do not know the purpose which I sensed." She paused. "I have brought you here, Mae, to see if I cannot divine this purpose, as well as that of your friend. Flor," she added, looking now more curiously at Flor. "It seems not a coincidence at all that you both were found by the Dark Wanderer, and you both may be the ones…well, never mind about that. All I have is theory. You look at me as if you are impressed, and I'm thankful for that to some extent, but you must know that I am not as powerful as you think me. All I can do is hope to help."

Mae didn't know what to say.

"Thank you," Flor said, moving slightly beside her. "I feel honored that you would want to help us. All we really want, though, is to get home."

"Don't thank me," Kiroba said swiftly. "I assure you, it is as much for my sake as it is for yours that I do this. As for going home, I fear you may not get that wish. Your lives seem tangled in something which my mind can barely broach. You are both needed."

Flor voiced his opinion quickly, and Mae looked over, surprised by his vehemence.

"But we need to go home! It's the only place we're safe, and my father thinks we're both dead now probably. I nearly thought Mae had had it back there, and I don't want to risk that again."

But Kiroba didn't seem to have heard him, or if she did she gave no sign of recognizing his voice. Her large, round eyes, normally bright and black, had glazed over, looking milky, and protruded farther from her head. It was both frightening and comical.

"Er…" Mae said, feeling she should go ahead and try to break the silence. Nothing happened. There was nothing they could do but wait for Kiroba to come out of whatever she was in. The silence felt powerful and thick, and the odd drop of dew shone faintly in answer to the stare Kiroba was putting on it. It was several long minutes before anyone stirred. When Kiroba finally let a breath out, in a low, ragged "ahh", both Mae and Flor jumped in alarm at the sound.

"Ahh," Kiroba sighed again, walking around her crystal ball of sorts, and retrieving her veil from the ground as she did so. Draping it over her eyes again, she faced them.

They both waited for her to speak, but she kept silent, looking almost sad and strangely excited at once. Finally, she broke the silence.

"There can be no going home, Flor."

Mae looked at Flor and knew he was angry, but helplessly angry, and knew also that everything was as Kiroba said.

"What must we do, then?" she asked, and was surprised by the calm in her own voice. She knew Flor didn't want her to accept, but like he had said himself, Mae had always been the one to lead.

Kiroba, satisfied perhaps that they had not argued further, said "I do not know everything, and I cannot pretend to. But it seems necessary that your path must cross that of the Dark Wanderer once again."

Flor sucked in a breath and put a paw on Mae's shoulder unconsciously, protectively. She was glad for his nearness. When she asked the next logical question, the 'why', her voice seemed farther away.

"Your fate—which I can only see partially, and then only when the stars are out--requires it," she said simply. "There is an object, the value of which I know not, which is of importance to the enemy. I cannot see the Dark Wanderer's purpose, as indeed it seems shaded over by some other kind of mystical spell, far more powerful than any I could ever weave."

Kiroba paused, and an air of unease settled over the room. Mae could sense the seer was deeply troubled, as if she were keeping much of her thoughts to herself, and they were not pleasant ones.

"But this object…" Kiroba finally spoke up again, giving a start like she had forgotten they were standing there, "you are to stop the dark one before he can get to it. Fate has regrettably not been able to tell me what this object is, as that appears to be cleverly hidden from me as well." Again, her face assumed a troubled expression. "But it will surely be disastrous in the paws of the dark one. The Dark Wanderer knows this, and will go to considerable lengths to retrieve it."

Mae thought she could see what was coming, and was filled with foreboding.

"You want us to get this object before Callisto does?"

"You—how do you know? Is that his name, then?"

Mae blinked.

"What? Does no one know?"

"No one knows the name of the Dark Wanderer, no. He does not give it out to anyone. Well, he may give it to his victims, but they're all dead. There's no way of knowing."

She stared at Mae, entranced for a moment, then a small tremor went through her body and she shook her head slightly. Then Flor spoke, calmer now.

"Everyone is in danger, aren't they? This Callisto, he's trying to take over, isn't he? Could it be that this is no different from the black squirrels' attempt several years ago?"

Kiroba looked at him, thoughtfully. "I would acknowledge that theory, and I consider it highly possible. But the black squirrels then had immortality, something they believed to be a gift from Astrippa herself. What does this one have?"

Mae moved, opened her mouth and closed it.

Magic. He has magic, doesn't he? But she didn't say it. Something stopped her, and she sat mute, hoping Kiroba hadn't seen. But the flying squirrel's eyes had disappeared up into her head under her veil, and she no longer seemed to notice their presence. After several moments of this, Mae and Flor gave each other uncomfortable looks. Should they leave? Was something wrong? Finally Mae motioned to the door, and Flor hesitated for a second before following her to it. The still, mystical air was beginning to tingle, to bite at her skin, and she wanted out. They were in the act of leaving when Kiroba's voice came suddenly, unbidden to them from across the room. Mae turned back to see her standing in the same place as before, breathing fast. Her voice was strange and leaden.

"South. It is south you must go. Southwest. You must do it for us all. You must stop his plans from being carried out."

They waited, but Kiroba said nothing more. Flor stepped outside, and Mae went to follow, but again the mystic squirrel spoke.

"Neither of you will see home again."

Mae stepped outside and closed the door. No protest came from the other side. Kiroba must still be in her haze of premonition, or oblivion, or whatever it was that kept seers so isolated from the rest of the breathing world. In this moment, standing outside the splintered door in the dark hallway, looking at Flor with the silent question *what has she said?* in his eyes, Mae felt she understood the fear others felt when they pushed the ones like this up here and locked them away. The prejudice.

Only natural.

She was instantly repulsed and ashamed by the thought.

Looking at Flor again, staring at him; he was asking if she wanted to go back.

"Yes," said Mae. Yes, she did.

Why am I so angry?

She and Flor took a while to find the bedroom again, and when they had at last, the two of them collapsed on their simple beds and attempted to talk about what had happened through the haze of tiredness coming back to them.

"I reckon she's right," Flor said. "We've seen the way Callisto pressured that squirrel into signing his parchment, or list, or whatever it was. I really can't make heads or tails of it, Mae, but we can't do nothing. Whatever he's doing, it's nothing good."

"You really think we ought to try and stop them, then?"

"Yes, I do. Don't you?"

"Yes. We will go after them. And then..."

We will *see home again.*

Mae pushed the sentiment out into the night with her mind, letting it hang there, poignant and solid. It was a promise. Feeling considerably and surprisingly better, she settled down to sleep once more, this time blissfully uninterrupted.

Chapter Eight

The next day-or night, rather--, Mae and Flor left the flying squirrel community. The little creatures seemed worried for them, making sure they were equipped with enough food to last for a week at least. They warbled their goodbyes in their lovely voices, giving Mae an aching feeling of nostalgia, though nothing had passed which should make her feel this way. They crowded out over one thick branch, singing their goodbyes at the two young squirrels, who left quickly if not eagerly under cover of darkness. They did not see Kiroba among those seeing them off, though Mae supposed she had no reason to believe the seer wasn't watching, sprung from her isolated prison.

The night air was cold, and made her shivering natural. At first, they walked in relative silence before Flor spoke.

"You know, Mae…we never really asked them where we were. A bit stupid of us, don't you think?"

"It doesn't matter," Mae said. She felt like her mind were full of fuzz, but she looked around at the trees all the same, and admitted to herself that Flor had a point. "We have to go southwest, Flor, so it's not pressing that we know exactly where we are."

"I think we're in Maplewood," Flor said excitedly. "Maplewood is supposed to be magic. My dad told me something about it being connected to strange creatures in the night and—

"Wait—you *knew* about the flying squirrels?"

"Oh, no, not really," Flor said, sounding instead as if he were confessing to knowing a good deal. "It's just—I used to hear stories. Their fear of magic…well, it's said they had a run-in with a white squirrel, and that's how things got how they are."

"What kind of bunk is that?" Mae snorted.

"Well," Flor said defensively. "You asked. And they're only stories. The flying squirrels seemed rather old-fashioned, didn't they? They're not cowards, after all they saved us, but they keep out of things that don't concern them. It seems like they're in a sphere of their own with a desire to keep it that way. The fact that they're night creatures helps, I suppose."

"What are you trying to prove?" Mae laughed. "That your story is true? That an encounter with a white squirrel changed this colony's life forever? Okay, maybe. But I'm doubting it. How many colonies of flying squirrels *are* there anyway? And Madame Kiroba said—"

"Kiroba's different from the rest of them though, isn't she? They don't seem to interact with her at all. As weird as they all are, I think she's the only one with any sort of magic. Or at least, the only one who shows it. You had to have noticed how quickly they got rid of us."

Mae had to admit that he had a point. As they walked on into the night, rain started to mist softly from the sky, falling and beading on leaves and making the skin of the trees more treacherous to walk on. They didn't converse much after that, Flor naturally more silent and thoughtful, Mae reverting to a fierce brooding session over what she had to consent to be imagined wrongs.

"What's magic anyway?" Mae asked, when the coming of day was approaching in the air, making the worries of the night seem somewhat preposterous as day always had a habit of doing. "I mean, just how much of it exists?"

Flor gave her a pained expression. "And I'm supposed to know this how?"

She continued to stare at him and he sighed.

"Okay…well, the way I hear it, there are three types of magic. Or are supposed to be. Really, before we got sucked into this, I didn't think it existed."

"Three types?" Mae prompted.

"Yes. Magic of the seer, magic of illusion, and pure magic."

"Explain, please."

"Well. Magic of the seer is the ability to see into the future to some extent or other, to make predictions, or in some cases, to read the mind of another."

"Like Kiroba."

"Yes. Magic of illusion is probably the most dangerous type of magic because in some ways it's not magic at all. It's the ability to create something that is not there, but which appears real to all the senses of others, whether it be material, or…an urge in someone else."

"What?"

"Well, if the magic's really strong, it's said that the one who possesses it can make others do things they wouldn't normally do…manipulate them."

Mae felt a shiver go down her spine, but ignored it.

"And? Pure magic, what's that about?"

"Hmm…that's the one that sort of escapes definition in many cases. It's supposed to be the strongest, because pure magic has no bounds. I guess those who have it can…do everything the other types involve, but also…bend time, move things with the mind, or even disappear."

Mae was aghast.

"Is that real?"

"How do I know?" Flor said mischievously. "It could be illusion."

Mae growled and swiped at him, but he scampered around the other side of the branch they were standing on, leaving her peering down at him.

"Flor…" she said, but let an accidental laugh out all the same.

They chased each other around, keeping southerly as well as they could in the midst of their games, until Mae found herself slipping wildly on one particularly wet maple tree.

"Argh!" she cried, still in some fit of hysteria, and attempted to grab Flor by the tail as she went over the edge of the branch. Flor turned around, laughing, and then a surprised look came over his face as they both fell to the ground.

Letting go of her friend, Mae twisted her body in the air, preparing to land on her feet, and landed…

Right in someone else's footprints.

At first she blinked, startled, down at the tracks stretching away in front of her and underneath, before her bafflement wore away and she cried for Flor to come see.

"What's that?" Then, "Oh! Do you think it's them, Mae?"

They stared at each other in the dawn light, their minds running along the same track. Mae moved her foot, picking it up from the muddy ground. Whoever's footprints she had landed in had bigger feet than she.

"Mae! Look!" Flor cried out, from where he had walked a ways away from the scene she was surveying. Mae came over, and what she saw left no doubt in their minds.

Next to the set of largish tracks, some smaller, struggling footprints skipped along.

"It's them, all right. Thank Astrippa," muttered Flor. Mae felt dazed. They might have missed the signs altogether if she had not chanced to fall at the moment she did.

"Thank Astrippa, indeed. It looks like we're headed in the right direction. In any case, now we have something to follow."

"Not now, Mae," Flor groaned, looking at Mae's expectant face. "Aren't you tired in the least?"

"Grown used to being nocturnal, have you?"

"Haven't you?"

Mae made a noncommittal sound, but grinned all the same.

"Okay, sleep. The tracks have got to be fresh, don't they? They have to have been made when it was raining."

"Good point," Flor said, yawning. "I guess then, that you will not object to me dozing off on you."

The two found a low clearing amidst the confused branches of a stunted tree, and were soon asleep. Mae stayed awake a bit longer than Flor, excitement coursing through her at the thought that they were almost caught up with the enemy. It took a while for her to realize that she had let go of her bitterness over what the seer had said. Predictions could go rot, because Mae was winning this. She was doing it for Firwood, she was doing it for Rupert, and she was doing it for Flor. Her sense of adventure had come rushing back fully, and in the comfort of that familiar thing, she could at last rest.

Chapter Nine

Idger was in a temper by the time he and Callisto crossed the border into Beechwood. He had never been made to travel this far in a few measly days, and his lust for more payment was mounting. Still, he was a spineless creature, and could not bring himself to face up to his master at all, especially when said master was in a worse temper than he.

Callisto plowed on for a day or two, deep in thought. Only when he could see the Redwood Forest on the horizon did he stop for more than a couple of hours. They had recruited only two since the night at the fox squirrel community, but he had less interest in recruiting now.

"What use is it, without the compass?" the black squirrel grumbled wrathfully. "None, that's the answer. The compass is the key."

"The compass, yew say?" Idger spoke up for the first time in days. His sullen brooding pushed aside, he realized his curiosity. His master had never mentioned this before, not to my memory. "Is that what we're after, then?"

Callisto turned to him, and for one fiery instant Idger thought his time had come to an end. Then the big half-breed lapsed into some sort of reverie, staring dazedly off into the distance, where the tops of the enormous redwoods could be seen fading into the gray sky.

"Of course it's what we're looking for," he murmured, voice subdued. "That's what she said. The compass and then her plan."

Idger was disappointed. When Callisto had asked for this 'something' from the stupid old fox squirrel, he had assumed it was some sort of priceless treasure, silver, gold, or rubies. But a *compass*? What did a compass have to do with anything?

"It doesn't matter," Callisto muttered, still seemingly lost in his own mind, or world, or wherever squirrels like him went to live the nightmares they dreamed. "It doesn't matter because she doesn't care about *you*. I promised to build her an army and I will."

Suddenly his face contorted, twisting into something thoroughly horrifying. In that instant, Idger thought he could see right through the eyes and into the burning, hell-like mind beyond. "There will be," he rasped, "no peace for the non-believer."

Idger, who was used to his master's rants, had never seen anything like this before. It seemed to him, in his own, dull coward's fear, that the dark one was talking directly to *him*. He felt a warm, burning trickle down his leg and moaned deep in his throat.

"Idger," Callisto laughed, suddenly easy. "Idger, Idger, you fool."

But Idger had made his decision. Fool indeed. Fool for thinking that this was worth a few meager slabs of gold brick. He could get treasure somewhere else, perhaps. Better treasure, away from this mad vestige of a devil.

Idger, yew fool. Yer movin' out.

It took a while for Callisto to finally fall to rest the next morning. He muttered himself to sleep, then muttered as he slept, sometimes in fast-paced monologues, sometimes as if he were conversing with someone else. When Idger could be sure his master was actually asleep, and not just pretending as he sometimes feared, he began to make his way down the tree they were camped in, and paused at the base. Where should he go? Back the way they had come was perhaps the best option, but the wall of redwoods rocketing up in front of him held his attention in a hypnotic way. The trees seemed magical, and indeed, once he had submersed himself in them, he found the air was rich with an oddly perfumed mist. The croaks of some sort of frog sounded off to all sides, intermittent and slow, and every once in a while, something seemed to move in the mist, shadows darting across his vision. At first the chickaree was frightened by these apparent mirages, but grew eventually calm under their influence, and forgot his thoughts on turning back. Here was better than there anyhow, and Idger began to feel drowsy.

The trunks of the trees he passed through were so large around that it seemed they were many trees wrapped into one, and from where he now stood among them all, he could not see the tops of them.

"Interesting," he mused, and his voice was cut short, muffled by the wet mist.

Climb them. He'll have no chance of finding you then, what with all this mist. You'll be able to see better too. Climb them.

The thought came unbidden, and made Idger's heart race with a kind of heady exhilaration borne of nervous fear.

"I could climb them," he said to himself, and tightening the straps of his sack to avoid losing any of his precious gold, Idger did just that.

The climb was steeper than he had imagined, and the chickaree found himself taking a breather on a branch once, in order to keep his stamina up in spite of the heavy pack on his back. When he reached the top, bitter thoughts of escape subsided from his mind, and he gaped openly. The view was spectacular. Water! Spreading out from the shore of Beechwood as far as the eye could see. And, almost hidden from view lay what looked to be more land on the horizon. Unexplored, perhaps? The possibilities seemed endless, but when he looked again it was gone. Idger leapt to the next tree, nearly missing his mark and falling. He was fatigued entirely.

"It's his fault, of cirse," muttered Idger. "If I hadn't stayed so long wif him…well, now I'll make sure he can't find me." Casting his mind back to Callisto's latest outburst, the red squirrel shivered. "He's crazy. Crazy. And he keeps getting crazier every day. I don't want to put myself in wif his lot, and cripes, I wouldn't have, but—

His paw leapt consciously to the pouch on his back, feeling the hard treasures within. "Then I wouldn't have my beauties, now would I?"

Moving along down a thick branch, something caught Idger's eye. At first he blew it off to illusion at work once more, then noticed it again. A rich sparkle, a lustrous shine. Eyes wide and greedy, the chickaree crept back down the branch, identifying a hole in the trunk of the tree from which the shine was emanating.

"Mmm…" he moaned, mouth slackening to hang half-open. "What *is* it?"

Approaching quickly and rather mindlessly, Idger had to make a conscious effort to stop himself just parading into the hole. What if someone else were lying in wait? Scaling the trunk, he peered into the hole from a side angle, hoping against hope that no life was evident.

No one was there, but even this lucky fact could not make it through to the mind of the stunned chickaree, for what he now saw before him was the most beautiful sight he had ever seen in his life. There were rubies, and emeralds, a few silver gauntlets, gold chains and mystic discs from days long past, even a crown hanging from a high place on the wall, which gave him some pause. Could this place belong to a king, the king of the redwoods, perhaps? Imagining what kind of fearsome creature would have rule over all this, Idger was momentarily put off. Momentarily. Soon enough, the pleasure of all this wealth was too much for him. King or no, they would have to deal with losing some of this. There was plenty to spare, after all.

Idger made one last thorough sweep of the dazzling room to confirm the lack of occupation, and noticed something he had missed the first time around. Sitting off in one corner, propped up by a couple of coins, a small silver disk glinted, reflecting back the light thrown off from the other treasures. A compass.

The compass?

Could it be, just possibly, that this was what Callisto had been looking for?

If I could get it back, the master would be so pleased.

But how did it *get* here?

I would be rewarded, perhaps more than I can imagine once he gathers this army he keeps jabbering about.

Idger needed no second thought. Stealing into the hollow, he rubbed his eyes to keep them from watering at the prospects. Really, this was just too much! Excess was always good, he liked it that way. As his aunt Tufter had said, "Excess is bliss." It had probably been the second time he had ever agreed with anything that old bag had said.

A wise squirrel would have cast a look out the hole once again before taking what he could carry. As it happened, Idger was not a wise squirrel. And so, when the voice from the mouth of the hollow sounded, Idger's arms and pack were full to bursting with finery, and there was no quick plan of escape apparent to his dazed mind.

"What d'yew think yer doing?"

Idger whirled about, the gauntlet he was inspecting clattering from his paws. Another chickaree stood framed in the doorway, one he recognized from somewhere…Perhaps serving with Venul? This last thought was a trigger, and recognition dawned. It was not pleasant.

"Officer Kyan?"

The female chickaree snorted distastefully.

"That e'nt me. The name's…eh hem…*Trevvor the Terrible*, and—

She darted forward and bit his ear, hard, knocking everything from his startled paws.

"And yer going to *die*."

Chapter Ten

This last was said dramatically, but Idger didn't doubt she was serious. Judging from the amount of blood coming from his ear, she had already made a good start. But Idger was beginning to form a plan.

"Wait--!" he said, his eyes glinting craftily. She dodged at him again, and he swung his pack at her. It missed and hit the wall, making a delicate shattering sound as it hit the floor. The crown wobbled precariously from its position on the wall.

"I'm in now, that's yer fault. Apparently yew don't guard this place well enough."

Kyan bristled and scowled but didn't say anything. Evidently she had decided to wait for him to say his piece. Idger didn't know how long he would have, so he wasted no time in cutting to the chase, painfully aware that he was the one with his back to a wall.

"Yew know I won't leave unless I can get something out of this, or die trying. I say we barter."

"Barter?" Kyan looked incredulous. "Go find yer own hollow. Yew sound like my whiny cousin."

"I might *be* yer whiny cousin." (It was true. Chickarees were not very selective about breeding) "but I only want ..." He pretended to deliberate. "That gauntlet, that crown, and that compass." He added this last in a light tone, trying to make it seem insignificant in the face of his blighting awareness that it may well be worth more than the others.

"No deal," Kyan said, sneering. "What do yew think I am, a fool?"

Idger strained not to answer this question. Avoiding argument was hard, but he needed to get a foot up here.

"Okay, jist the crown and the compass then."

"First off, yer not getting that crown, so firget it. If yew mention it one more time, I'm biting yer tail off and using it to line my bed."

Kyan was circling him, prepared to attack at any moment.

"Jist the compass, last offer," Idger said, though it pained him to do it. "I'll go in peace then."

Kyan turned to the compass and surveyed it keenly, as though she were truly seeing it for the first time.

"I'm very fond of this here," she grumped. "If yew want it, yer going to have to play for it."

"Fine," he snapped. "Gamble, then?"

This was getting ridiculous. Idger was tempted to just fight for the thing, but the uncertainty of winning couldn't be risked. He was starting to regret coming up into these monster trees, now. A coward's life behind a stronger, albeit squealing mad master suited him better. If he could get the compass to his master, he was sure his absence might be overlooked.

"No," Kyan said, and he could tell she was enjoying very much denying him an easy way to what he wanted most desperately. He remembered her more clearly now, from the days at the gray compound. He had only been a minor type of labor enforcer, below her in rank. Kyan was a slippery creature, and he remembered this if nothing else.

"We're going to play chessnuts. Whoever wins, gets to keep the compassy thing. Got it?"

"Do we really have to?" Idger asked prissily.

"Yes. I like the compassy thing a lot. It's one of my best. Valued stuff, this is." She tapped the compass as if to prove her point.

Idger had the distinct feeling that Kyan would have said this about any of the thirty-something items in her collection, but consented all the same.

Without further ado, Kyan stopped pacing like she wanted to kill Idger, and took out a badly scarred set of chessnuts, settling herself down at a small table stuffed in a corner. She waited, and while Idger seated himself, she sorted the pieces into two teams, making sure to give herself the shiniest of the nuts. Idger scowled at his team of young, green chestnuts while he waited for Kyan, who was taking her time setting her dark brown, lustrous ones in neat rows.

"There," she said with a sigh after what Idger would have estimated to be a good, round century. Then, quick as a flash, she made a possibly illegal move and knocked out two of Idger's team.

"Right then," Idger said tersely. He made a strategic move, biding his time. Kyan caught his game quickly and followed it.

A quarter of the way through, Idger was pleased to find himself winning by a hair. He leaned back, gave a fake yawn, and attempted lazy conversation.

"Lived here all your life, Trevvor?" he asked, sneering.

"Not at all," Kyan murmured, ignoring his jibe and concentrating on the board between them. So she still refused to recognize him. This irritated him a bit, but as his Aunt Tufter had said, "Keep your eyes on the gold." It was the only other advice of hers he'd ever agreed with, and Idger decided to do just that.

"How'd you come across such pretty likkle things?" He spoke the thought out loud. "Is there more in this area? It seems a magicky sort of place, eh?"

"Why don't yew go out in the magicky fog and look fer it," Kyan snickered derisively. Idger bit into one of the discarded chestnuts just to spite her. She spit on his side of the board.

The game went on in such a fashion until Kyan, in a move Idger had not seen coming, took his last piece from the board, and leant back gloatingly. Idger only took a moment to glare at her, before making up his mind in a flash. And so, in a manner Aunt Tufter would have been proud of, he moved to one side before darting forward to where the compass lay in the corner. Kyan met him there, and did what she had threatened to do from the first.

Callisto awoke sometime in the morning at the sense of mutiny and, his suspicions confirmed by the absence of Idger, went storming through the thick, wet mists of the redwoods in a mood to kill. But when the dark one almost tripped over the dead body of his servant on the forest floor, he found someone had already done his work for him.

The discovery elicited mixed emotions from him. On the one paw, Idger had never been much use. On the other, he would now have to waste time searching for his own food and minor needs. Unless…he could get the two young ones back. They had escaped so unfairly, helped along by those big-eyed denizens of the night. He had searched for them of course, but his efforts had been fruitless. It wasn't as if he cared about the gray one; that one could rot for all he cared. But the young black squirrel, if he weren't mistaken of course, could be of use to him, in the end…

It was then that Callisto noticed the glimmer of silver beneath the leaves nearby, slightly to the left of Idger's motionless body. Lurching forward eagerly,

Callisto's mind gave a start. The compass stared up at him, its small, intricately formed needle pointing dubiously north. The great black squirrel smiled, making the white streak on his face contort strangely. He was back on track already. He had what he wanted. Well, half of it, he conceded, but half was a start. Callisto bent down and picked up the compass, holding it close to him with a manic glint in his eye. Leaning back against the tree from whence the compass had fallen, the half-breed stared down at his prize. As he did so, the small needle within did something it had not done for a long, long time: it started to spin, faster and faster, then slower and slower, coming to a quivering halt at long last.

Callisto chuckled darkly. Luck had come after all. It was just late in the coming.

"Astrippa," he whispered, his voice hanging ominously in the fog. "You won't be sorry. Your army is coming."

Poised on the redwood above him, Kyan shuddered. She had been going to retrieve the compass, fallen in the clutches of that nuisance of a squirrel, but now she wisely decided to leave it. Better to lose a piece of finery than to infringe upon the aura around this one.

Chapter Eleven

Mae woke feeling strangely unnerved. Looking around, she quickly located Flor, lying nearby, still deep in sleep.

"Flor," she whispered. He didn't budge, though she could see his sides gently heaving up and down.

Just go back to sleep she told herself, but there was a tugging inside her that wouldn't allow it. Her unconscious had received a warning, a warning of *what* she had no idea, but she could not drift off quite yet.

The air was misty, as if it had rained on some nearby body of water and the steam from such a shower couldn't resist chasing across the land. It was after noon, and Mae realized that she should probably still be sleeping. She might have thought nothing of it, if not for the fact that this was not the first time she had had such a feeling. The same feeling of unease had been present when she had been jerked awake by some unseen force in the lodgings of the night whisperers. Mae cast around her field of vision for something to hold onto, and caught sight of the footprints they had seen last night. She stiffened, an idea shooting through her unpleasantly, and darted to Flor's side, shaking him awake.

"Flor! Flor!" she hissed.

"Whatisit?" he mumbled groggily, turning over in his spot on the ground and pulling a dried oak leaf toward him in some quest for warmth.

"Flor!" Mae said again insistently, jabbing him hard in the side.

"Ouch! What…? Mae, is everything all right?"

Mae glanced at him grimly. "I don't think so." She was still staring uneasily off into the gathering mist, and Flor came to stand beside her presently.

"Mae...? I don't...I don't see anything." But his voice held a note of uncertainty all the same.

The mist shifted, and wound itself around the two lone squirrels, and Mae wondered whether she should say what was on her mind. Would it sound fantastical, or crazy? No matter. This was Flor. She could talk to Flor, and Flor would listen. Flor would believe her.

Mae inclined her head so that she could speak into her friend's ear.

"I think he's here," she whispered, as steadily as she could.

Flor looked startled.

"You mean...?"

"Yeah." She couldn't bring herself to say the name, just in case it would call the one they spoke of out of hiding.

"Then how come he hasn't come for us? Do you think he knows we're here?"

"No," Mae said, surprised at her own certainty. "But I think he will if we don't find a place to hide. I think...I think he's looking for us, Flor."

....*I think he's looking for* me.

But Mae didn't say what she thought, and they both made way for the same tree, even though she wished they could split up, go separate directions. Callisto wanted *her*, and he had since the beginning. Flor would never accept it. She wouldn't if he had been the one.

So she let it go.

What seemed like an hour passed, as they stared down into the mist, and Flor turned toward Mae once, but didn't question her. She was starting to wonder as well, though. Was she wrong? Had her premonition been for nothing? Or had Callisto already passed them by and they hadn't noticed because of the mist?

Premonition? Is that really what it was?

But then there was movement below them, and Mae came out of her thoughts into the realm of terror at the realization that he was here, moving below them, a dark shadow. Had he found their trail somehow, or sensed where they were? Was he coming back for them? For her?

The dark shape of Callisto passed underneath them, obscure and all too real at once. The dark mutant was muttering something to himself, such as he had often done in Mae's memory, and leaning closer, she and Flor realized they were in hearing range of his words.

"I cannot do it now...No, I can't. I need...I need someone else. Who will be there to command them if *I* do it? I can't be responsible for everything, I don't have your power."

Silence. Mae imagined Callisto to be deliberating in this space of time.

"Yes, it will work with her. Why not? I have seen her, and I am telling you...of course, my perception is not as good as yours..." Callisto's voice sounded angry, now. Forcing his tone to a calmer one, he continued lightly.

"But I do know that there is something there. How else could she have escaped my notice, when I was *this* close...?" A note of exasperation was back, and Mae felt odd. Was he talking about *her*?

The unformed shape of a memory, slight and fleeting, passed across her mind, and was whisked away a second later. No, it was more likely that Callisto meant someone else entirely.

Flor nudged her in the side and gave her a look that said they should climb up the tree farther. Mae obliged, half-reluctantly. Once they had gotten far enough away so that they could no longer hear the half-breed's one-sided conversations, Flor spoke.

"Mae, he's completely unhinged!"

"But...I thought we knew that." Despite herself, she was still thinking about what she had heard earlier, and of the feeling it had evoked in her.

"Well, of course, but now we *know,* know. And it's not only that. You know who he thinks he's talking to? He thinks it's Astrippa. He's called himself the Dark Wanderer, and he thinks he has special contact with Astrippa, that he's on some sort of mad, morbid quest to do her bidding, to raise some army...remember the list he had, the way he had others put their names down by threatening their families and making them feel guilty about their faith? It could be the work of an all-out nutcracker, which he undoubtedly is, but...Mae, now I'm really seeing how dangerous this is. How we need to stop him, like Kiroba said. I don't know how we'll do it, but we've got to keep him from getting whatever it is he's after."

Mae, seeing Flor like this, so determined and yet so unsure, saw that he had something that she didn't, and she turned to him, feeling somehow that there should be words.

"I'm glad you're with me, Flor," she said. It took a lot not to add some joking comment such as came naturally to her in the silence that followed. Then Flor gave her a smile and voiced what they had both been thinking.

"How are we going to stop him, though?"

Mae didn't know. Hadn't known, couldn't know. They were young, both smaller than the big black squirrel, and there were signs that he had magic of some sort. Mae thought about the types of magic Flor had described, and concluded that any of them would be extremely dangerous to them if the enemy possessed it. Looking down to the base of their tree, she asked "Is he gone?"

"It'll be hard to tell unless we get closer."

And so Mae and Flor moved downwards, as quietly as possible. Mae felt conscious of every little scratch her claws made on the bark, and was relieved when they came back to their old perch and no sound met her ears.

"He's probably moved on," she said, glancing about. The sky was darkening, and Flor stifled a yawn.

"Shall we sleep up h-

But he was cut off when a voice, a sickeningly familiar voice sounded from the other side of the tree.

"How nice it is to see you again, Mae honey."

Mae felt her stomach jolt uncomfortably, and something dark and soft brushed against her cheek.

Flor slowly turned around next to her.

"How will you stop me, Mae?" Callisto was saying quietly, and with another sick jolt, she realized that he must have been listening to them for some time. "The answer is," the dark squirrel paused dramatically, "you *can't*, Mae. But you can help me."

Callisto walked out onto a branch parallel to them, and Mae strived not to turn her eyes from the obscene white marking, zigzagging like a scar across the side of his face. In doing so, she noticed that he was carrying something. Small and silver, it hung from a hook that looped about his paw, swinging back and forth, forward and back as he talked.

"Did you ever notice how much power I convey?" he asked. Back, forth, went the silver pendant. Mae strained to see what it was. Was *this* the object that would cause great destruction? It seemed unlikely, seeing as it was already in Callisto's grasp, and the Dark Wanderer had done nothing catastrophic yet...

"Did you ever think that you might have a chance at half my power? Would you risk it, Mae, if all it took were a small sacrifice, nothing really. Would you help the noble cause of Astrippa?"

The words he spoke rang oddly in Mae's ears, making a tinny sound, and still the object swung back and forth, back and forth. The effect was almost hypnotic.

"What are you talking about?" said Flor slowly, speaking for Mae in her silence.

"Ask Mae," Callisto said sharply, and the object stopped swinging. It was a compass, Mae saw now. Callisto took it in one paw and turned it toward Mae, his eyes glinting crazily. The small needle inside began turning, faster and faster, then started to slow, but Callisto jerked it to himself, glanced at it, and dropped it to swing on its hook once more before Mae could see where it would point.

"See," he said, "This, Mae, is our tool, our key to success."

"I...I don't understand what you mean!" Mae blurted, frustrated and afraid. Flor moved discreetly out of the corner of her eye, but her attention was overwhelmingly on the large half-breed squirrel, who sat talking as if there was something between them.

"You don't remember me, do you Mae?"

Mae shook her head, staring at the compass, then at Callisto, back and forth, back and forth. She was starting to feel dizzy.

"I am the Dark Wanderer. I visit those who are lucky enough to receive me. And I visited you once. Have you forgotten, Mae, that you met me? Of course, it was brief, but..."

And now Mae knew. The memory which had flashed through her mind when she had heard Callisto muttering came back, full force, and suddenly her life seemed fuller. Fuller and more horrifying.

"You... you killed my parents, didn't you?" Her voice was shaking. "That night, when someone came to us. It was so long ago, before I came to Firwood. I don't even remember where...they told me to hide, and I did it. I was so frightened...and then..." She looked up at Callisto coldly. "They never came back."

"Yes, yes," Callisto said, as if the memory were somehow regrettable to him. "That was back when I was going through Oakwood. You see, I was part of the *great*" he laced a vengeful dose of sarcasm into the word, "Venul's little reign of terror over the Firwood grays. When our immortality was taken away, it was clear that Venul was not doing what *She* instructed him to. Of course, I doubt She ever spoke to him. At first we thought some great disease was befalling the black squirrels, so we fled, back to Oakwood, that cursed, drawling land we are consistently relegated to. But I had a plan. Astrippa has, through her divinity, informed me of what needs to be done, to bring honor back to those who are *really* faithful to her. An army of believers must be built, and then, once we perform the necessary rituals, she will *come to us* and make her judgments as she will. This is the will of Astrippa."

His eyes shone maniacally as he spoke these words, and Mae backed up fully to the trunk of the tree. Anger was flooding through her veins, rage at this vile squirrel who had robbed her of her family before she even knew the nature of being robbed. And here he stood, talking about Astrippa and salvation, and things he didn't know a thing about.

"Your parents, regrettably, were not able to agree to Her will," Callisto continued. "So, naturally they served no further purpose. We then searched the house thoroughly."

"And I escaped," Mae said tensely. "I slipped right out from under your nose. You could get the parents, but not a little child."

"Yes," Callisto said, his voice strangely calm. "I always wondered about that. I had them look for you. I looked for you myself. I could sense your presence. But I could never *find* you. And that is how I know!" His eyes glinted, again revealing the burning insanity within.

"I don't know what you know. I don't know what you're talking about. You're crazy. You're just..."

Mae looked around, searching for the right word, and noticed that Flor was no longer at her side. Her chest seized in panic, while the rational part of her gabbled that he must have hidden, he would be safe now. She noticed that Callisto had moved down his branch so that they were almost right across from each other now, the distance between she and the mad squirrel diminishing.

"You seemed almost *invisible*, Mae," Callisto said, still caught in his feverish recollections. "And then, again you alluded us when we searched for you in the surrounding land. Three of my followers were lost or killed on the wild forested border. But not you. Not you. And, Mae," He leapt to her branch, and moved closer. "Not me, either."

Mae suddenly understood what he was getting at.

"You think I'm magic."

"Oh, come Mae, aren't we all?"

"But I don't understand! I'm *not* magic. And even if I were, what difference would it make? Why would you need *me*? You have magic of your own!"

"Ah, well, that's for me to know and you to find out," Callisto cackled madly, now very close to Mae. "Don't be afraid, Mae." And he suddenly thrust a paw out at her. Mae flinched, and ducked, but nothing happened. She looked up to find the small silver compass dangling in front of her.

"Take it," Callisto snarled.

Seeing that she didn't have much of a choice, being cornered in this way, Mae hesitantly took the compass from him, staring at it in bewilderment. A moment passed, then the needle lurched into motion, spinning faster and faster. Callisto was staring at it, breathing fast and hard. Mae was thoroughly confused and frightened, but a small part of her felt the slightest bit intrigued. This intrigue was the only thing which kept her from bolting when the opportune moment arrived, and then passed away irretrievably when Callisto lifted his head from staring at the needle. It was still spinning. The half-breed looked beyond angry.

"What…" he hissed, drawing in breath, and lunged, both for the compass and for Mae. Mae jerked away, but not soon enough. Callisto was clutching her shoulder tightly, squeezing. The look in his eyes was beyond maniacal.

"All for nothing then, is it? You…"

"Stop it!" Flor's voice came out of nowhere, and before Mae could blink again, he was present, on top of Callisto. Tail waving wildly and angrily, he bit the arm that held Mae, and she staggered away, rubbing her shoulder.

"Flor!"

But Callisto had turned away from her momentarily to engage himself with Flor. His fury was like something unholy, and Mae heard her friend yell, before freeing himself of the bigger squirrel and dashing away.

Callisto turned back to Mae, but before either of them could do another thing, Flor was between them again, determinedly blocking Mae from Callisto.

"Go, Mae, go! We've got to run!"

Mae hesitated, wanting to make sure that Flor would come after, and Flor's eyes met hers for that second. Then Callisto's paws shot out, and there was a sickening crunch. Flor's head lolled to the side, and he swayed for a moment, before falling limply from the branch, his neck snapped in two.

Callisto's face was a mask of rage, filled with demented fury. Turning to Mae, he was caught in the face full-force by something hard and unforgiving. His insides buzzing

Astrippa, dear Astrippa, I will avenge you. Forgive my mistake

The large black squirrel lost footing and consciousness almost at once, plummeting a considerable length after his last victim.

Panting hard, Mae held the compass to her chest with both paws and stared down to the base of the tree. It was too dark to see anything.

Her insides were strangely empty.

How curiously dark the world is. How curiously lonely. How long have I been here?

And then Mae ran.

Mae ran along the treetops, darting and weaving, jumping and bounding. Faster, ever faster.

I am now the fastest squirrel in Treetops Racing.

Biting her lip now, sprinting, scurrying. Going.

Run.

Yes.

I've got to run.

If she stopped, she would die. The compass would stop spinning.

There seemed no horizon, just space. There was no one in front of her.

The night passed. Morning came, and she did not stop for it. Night. And then morning. And then both. And then nothing at all.

Chapter Twelve

The world was changing. She knew it, and so did the rest of the squirrels around her, for they were the rest of the world. Something was going to happen, and it wasn't good. There must have been a thousand faces surrounding her own, blank, or with tracings of fear, all staring ahead. Ahead there was nothing. Nothing but a thick fog. And what was to come. She was not one of them. She felt separate somehow as though she had been excused from the tensest of emotions, freer. There was a tingling in her blood as she felt her heart beat in time to those around her, and she knew soon they would know something they might not want to know. Someone next to her grabbed her paw. The mist was thinning, parting...

Mae awoke with a jerk, feverishly rubbing her eyes. She felt heavy-headed, hot and lethargic. Sick. Crawling down to the small, trickling stream that ran through the middle of her grove of trees, Mae drank and dipped her paws into the water, rubbing it onto her face as a wakeup call.

She had been here for two or three days now, and there had been no sign of life anywhere. Since Flor's death, Mae had found it better that way and so she stayed. In truth, a comrade to mourn with might have made it easier for Mae, but all she had was the compass, which lay on the ground looking neutral, and with less shine than it had seemed to have at first. Whenever she picked it up to look at it, which was less and less each day, it would spin ceaselessly until she threw it away in impatience. It was a pointless vessel which contained no answers, at least to the questions she wanted to ask. And even her natural-born curiosity was dimming by the hour. Sometimes she felt as if she couldn't feel anything, and then she would turn to her anger at Callisto, the monster who had taken everything from her.

Sometimes even her anger was slow. Callisto might be dead, she would reason. And she wished she had killed him. After all, wouldn't he be after her, would he not have found her by now? But something still gave her the feeling that Callisto's madness almost gave him an unnatural sort of strength, that he couldn't be killed, that he was still out there, living on twisted fervor and dust alone.

And still sometimes she thought she didn't care either way.

This morning—for she had come back into consciousness on a morning and had kept the pattern— was different. It had been the first night she had had a dream that she could remember upon waking. There had been many restless nights, but few memories of what happened during these nights to make them so. This was the first such memory, and it unsettled her.

Mae didn't necessarily buy into the premonitory power of dreams, but there had been something about the quiet insistence upon her mind this one had had which shook her. And even though she was a bit uneasy, Mae half appreciated it. It was the first time in a long time that she had woke with an edge of purpose, a tinge of wonder to her thoughts.

After sitting by the stream, letting the quiet of the woods have its effect on her, Mae ventured over to the compass again and ran a finger over the surface. The needle quivered, but did not move.

Over the past couple of days, she had lain around thinking, trying to keep her mind off of Flor, and she had come to accept that as terribly as she wished it weren't true, Callisto might be right. She appeared to have some sort of magic, latent though it may be. It wasn't only the compass's reaction to her which had given her the hint. There was the strange feeling she had gotten when Callisto and Kiroba had been near, the forewarning she got subconsciously before they had made themselves known. And there was the fact that she had somehow outwitted the Dark Wanderer, slipped past the magic of others to find herself in the safe company of Rupert. Rupert, who had found her in the woods, wandering, lost and had taken her in. Rupert, who had acted almost like a father to her. Rupert, who *was* a father to Flor.

Mae imagined herself in front of Rupert and the council of the grays at Firwood, burning in the accusing glares of the onlookers and saying *"I am sorry. It was all my fault. I have caused your son to be killed."* She saw Rupert shake his head, ashamed and disappointed in her, heart broken by the death of his only son.

Holding back the acorn-sized lump that had manifested itself in her throat, Mae realized how selfish she truly was. She had led Flor into danger that could easily have been avoided in the first place on that evening, seemingly ages ago, when they had eavesdropped on Callisto and his servant in the woods. Idger. What had happened to him? She didn't know and found she didn't care, either. It was naught but a passing thought. What mattered was that her best friend was now dead as a result of her rash, unthinking, *selfish* actions.

I've always been this way, haven't I? Making decisions on the spur of the moment, bending others to suit my own whims…no wonder the others at the Firwood community didn't take to me very well. I had felt so victimized, like it was the color of my fur that they judged on, remembering history, and not who I really was. But who was I, really?

Mae knew the answer. And in the moment of being hard on herself, Mae had one resounding thought.

Flor always followed. Sometimes against his better judgment and he always gave me his opinion on what I would do anyway, no matter whether I liked it or not. But he would follow me. He wanted to get this done, he believed in the prophecy about the destruction the Dark Wanderer would bring, and he knew we must do something about it. This…thing…we were thrown into was less about him and more about me. And now he's gone, and it is only me. Me and my role to play. But…he always followed. He would have followed me to the end.

Mae got up, took the compass in both paws and stared hard and blazingly at the spinning needle, willing it to stop.

It stopped for Callisto. Why won't it stop for me?

Mae did not, in fact, know why she wanted the compass's needle to stop spinning, because she was not sure still what purpose it served. Compasses pointed north, and even if this were some enchanted compass, she didn't see what good it would do, knowing what she knew of things.

But *why* could Callisto work it? Why couldn't she?

Something shifted from behind her, and she dropped the compass to the ground in surprise. She had not heard a sound since she had come here, aside from the burbling of the brook. She really had no idea where she was, what part of Arborand, but she had come to suspect and then to simply assume that no one else lived here.

She had regained her composure when she heard it again, and this time the sound was unmistakably identifiable as someone running on dried leaves.

Mae turned all about, heart thumping fast. Her thoughts had immediately flown to one squirrel, and if it were who she feared it was, she was doomed.

Out of the corner of her eye she caught the motion again, and held it. Aware of the crunch her paws made as they hit the ground, she followed the noises of the other, blood pounding in her ears. The other had stopped momentarily now, along with the rustling sounds and Mae closed in behind them, flitting up the trunk of the nearest tree.

Gazing down, she blew out the long breath she had been holding in. It was only a chipmunk. Utterly relieved, an idea came to her. Hoping not to appear alarming, she clambered down from her place on the tree, and cleared her throat. The chipmunk's back stiffened, and it turned to face her. It was a male, middle aged, she would guess. At any rate older than she. He would certainly know, then.

"Excuse me?" Mae began awkwardly. "But could you tell me where this is?"

The chipmunk studied her warily. Was her color going to get her in trouble here, too? But in the end, he gave in, perhaps sensing her sincerity and slight desperation.

"You'd be in Maplewood, miss. Just south of Willow Lake. That's where the stream flows from. Pardon my intrusion, miss, but have you hit your head?"

"No, no, I'm all right."

Maplewood.

The chipmunk was studying her skeptically.

"All right, it's none of my business, miss. Good luck to you, whatever you're about."

Mae had grown unaccustomed to casual kindness, and even though its source was a mere chipmunk it made her feel warmer.

The chipmunk had turned and was continuing on his way. Mae watched as he came to a dead stump of a tree and climbed unsteadily up it, muttering to himself and not looking down.

He had to serve someone to live in a tree…chipmunks were ground dwellers if left to their own devices.

Why did it matter?

And it likely wouldn't have, but Mae felt the familiar, odd tugging sensation in her stomach and without knowing her purpose, she followed once more.

Upon reaching the dead tree, Mae scaled it expertly before realizing she couldn't just climb in the door, confirming whatever suspicions the chipmunk had had of her. She would need to find some other way

What in the name of Astrippa am I trying to DO??

…some other way in. Her stomach tingling, Mae felt a surge of luck as she noticed a small window farther up. It wasn't big enough to fit through, just a small hole in the bark, cut or gnawed, perhaps for ventilation purposes, but she climbed toward it anyway.

Peering inside, Mae was glad to find that the only occupant of the room she looked in upon was fast asleep. For a moment, her insides seized up in knots at the sight of him.

Lying right under the window was a young gray squirrel, and for a moment in which she could not seem to breathe, Mae thought that it had to be Flor. Flor wasn't dead after all, everything was alright, and here he was sound asleep…

But she knew it couldn't be, and just then the squirrel on the bed turned over in his sleep contentedly, revealing an alarmingly white strike of fur across one side of his stomach and his right paw and proved that it was not. All the same, Mae felt curiously disheartened. She would have turned from the window had not the sight of the sleeping squirrel's strange fur made her stare. She had only ever seen one half-breed in her life, and that was Callisto...

Something tugged at her stomach again

Intuition? Premonition?

and she took the compass from where it hung on her shoulder. Spinning, spinning, spinning in her paws, she drew a breath and lowered it through the window, dropping it to lean against the squirrel within.

It continued to spin. The squirrel twitched in his sleep, and his eyes opened for a moment. Mae could have sworn the squirrel had stared right at her, and she let go of the tree in shock, falling to the ground and catching herself neatly and without injury.

Staring back up at the tree, Mae cursed to herself under her breath. She hadn't seen any confirming sign of her suspicions. If only she weren't so jumpy...

But a movement came again at the entrance of the home, and Mae left at once, following the stream north. For better or for worse, she was on her way home.

Back at the hollow of the dead tree, the chipmunk stuck his head out, searching for the source of the sounds he had heard. When he couldn't find anything amiss, he retreated back inside, perplexed.

In the room above him, the compass's needle came to rest.

Epilogue

Mae traveled for three days, almost nonstop, constantly going over in her mind the scene she expected to be a part of when she reached home again. She had stopped by the place known as Willow Lake, and had engaged in idle conversation with a kind pair of gray squirrels for only as long as it took her to rest. Since then, she had been alone, and in being so, had plenty of time to speculate.

At first they would gather around her, thanking Astrippa that she was safe and wanting to know where she had got to. Someone would eventually cry "But where's Flor?" And then she would engage in the task of telling them what had happened, of leaving no part out, and of seeking their advice, if they would see fit to give it. Rupert would arrive on the scene, and...

She couldn't think any farther on the matter. She felt as if she had betrayed Rupert. He had known she would get into some sort of trouble, and that Flor would come along too. He had even seemed to accept it, and had told her to watch out for his son, trusting her. She had promised...and what a job she had done screwing it up.

Mae might have cried then. But the fact was that she had cried so often in the past days, cried without a purpose. And now she had a purpose and her mourning must be done. It had been a subconscious thing, and she did not realize the depth of it, but the old Mae had drifted away and left someone foreign and somehow stronger in her place. When she worried about returning, she did not worry about how she would be received, but how her arrival would affect the one figure closest to a father to her. Her life had molded into one of purpose, into which dreams and intuition took the place of adventurous whims, and into which she walked, not knowing whether she would ever return or if what waited for her was better than what she left behind.

The needle had spun…where would it land?

Day had drifted into night, and Mae was nearing the northern border of Maplewood. She would have made the journey across that night if she had not spotted a small light ahead, and headed toward the deviant light with a small, fluttering sense of wonder.

When she got there she found it was really nothing to see, just a firefly lamp hanging to a tree by its handle, spilling its mellow light into the immediate area.

But Mae did not turn around and go back to the path she had beaten. She recognized this light…

A procession of small creatures, carrying her lightly off among the twisting limbs of the trees, night air all around…lights bobbing in and out of her line of vision…

The flying squirrels. Night whisperers. She could not believe she had actually found this place again, but the area looked more and more familiar as she gazed upon it. Should she go on and leave them in peace? Or should she go back and pay a visit to those mystical creatures of the night with voices like music and the sound of water always nearby?

Something about the light, that one lone light unsettled her. Just sitting there, glowing steadily…

It was too easy. She had found this place far too easily. Who among the little flyers would be so foolish as to leave this light burning, exposing the secretive abode she remembered?

Mae crept forward, up towards the light, body tense, listening with all her might for any sound, any trace of something gone afoul.

Only dead silence met her ears. A slight gust of wind wended itself around her body and let go, leaving the vicinity as soon as it had come. Mae had reached the hidden entrance to the community's living quarters. No sound reached her. There was nothing for it. Blood pounding in her ears, she stepped inside.

The familiar room where she and Flor had been deposited when they had been saved by the little creatures met her eyes. Its smooth wooden walls brought a fond burst of familiarity to her chest, and she let go of her fear to have a look around. There was no one in the large room, or in the two she found adjoining it.

There was something else wrong here, but she couldn't put a finger on it until she had gone up two flights of stairs and down a hall, looking in doorways always with the same result. Aside from the apparent absence of anyone living here, the sound of trickling water was missing. Coming across the room in which she and Flor had stayed the night, her thoughts were confirmed with a glance inside. The liquid wall had dried up.

The place is completely deserted, Mae thought. It must have been for a good amount of time too, for the liquid walls to stop working their display of almost-magic. In fact, it seemed as if it had to have been this way at least since when she and Flor had...

A terrible thought seized her, and Mae gasped. Could it be that Callisto had been able to track them to the flying squirrels, and had just missed them? What then, had he done to the friendly little squirrels who had helped them so much?

198

Almost in a trance, Mae walked on, at last finding what she was looking for. Kiroba the seer's door, at the dark, shadowed end of the highest hall in the place, splintered and cracking. Shut.

There was something strange, something terrible about all of this. The halls…the halls were lit. But no one was here.

Mae reached out a shaking paw and touched the doorknob. For a while she kept her paw there, steadying her breath. Then she turned it.

Locked.

Mae's heart rate leapt, and she looked down at her paw slowly.

Locked. From the outside.

Heart still thumping like mad, Mae undid the lock with trembling paws. Then she turned the doorknob once again and opened the door.

At first Mae perceived that nothing was wrong. She saw the orb floating above its table, just as she had last seen it. Then her eyes fell to the floor, and she walked around the table to meet a sight that made her blood run cold.

Kiroba was here, but her life was no more. Stiff as a board, she lay sprawled on the floor, mouth gaping grotesquely. Her veil had been flung back in the throes of death to reveal her face, and Mae had to swallow a couple of times to keep from shouting out.

Her eyes were rolled back in their sockets so far that the eyeballs were pure white, interlaced with dead, purple veins. Mae flinched and looked away, her eyes falling to Kiroba's left paw, in which she held a small, pointed rock.

Mae looked around, anywhere but Kiroba's face. She didn't understand.

Then she saw the message, engraved sloppily but unmistakably, into the wall a couple of feet from the floor.

What she read there hammered its way into her, striking her with full force. Her mind could not seem to register what her eyes were seeing; Mae looked away down at the ground, breathed in and out for two long breaths. And still it sat, when next she looked, staring her in the face.

The White Squirrels Live

Mae couldn't look away. It had to be a trick of the light, something…What she was reading was impossible…

Something moved behind her. Mae turned. The shadow on the ground and the shadow on the wall outside of the door merged into one.

"Do not be afraid, Mae," the squirrel in the doorway said softly.

"I'm not," Mae lied, and just like that she wasn't. She stared into the pink eyes, willing herself to know, to understand….

"Zirreo."

The other smiled.

BOOK III: *The Coming*

Prologue

I watch the world, for it is still my ability to do so. After all, all rights have been taken away from me, and quite unfairly so. It is a rude gesture which I shall not forgive. My forgiveness does not come easily, and though I am sealed off for now, make no mistake. I watch, and I have no need for rest.

I can look, but I cannot touch. The right to touch the breathing world has been taken from me along with everything else; I cannot say that this does not anger me.

If they think that I cannot fight back, they are wrong. I will come one day, one day soon, and I will punish all the wrongdoers. There will only be punishment, and no rewards, for they have attempted to reap more than they have sown.

But never mind all that. What has been taken away can be taken back, and when I come again I will make sure that they are mine, to do my will which has been ignored. I will teach them to be shameful of me! Their pathetic world needs me, and so I come, though they are even now pushing away from the truth of it, ignorant, savage beasts.

And so it will be, and all that I have said will come to pass. I will take them, cup them in my paw.

Caress them.
Destroy them.

Chapter One

Dawn, while habitually a peaceful thing, was not so on the morning it came rolling over Firwood in the form of a thunderstorm. All of Arborand had darkened, but it was Firwood now that was paying for the wrath of the brooding clouds.

Squirrels all about the Firwood gray community were jolted out of slumber, peaceful or no. Voices rose in indignant protest, muffled by wooden walls and keenly heard (and objected to) by those who chose nests of grass. There had not been a storm like this since a time that perhaps only the very old could remember.

Rupert had never slept to begin with. The thunderstorm was just another minor slight atop all he had had to endure the past bleak month.

The leader of the grays lay stretched across his downy bed, body stiff with the intensity of thought. Nearby, his wife Ciele was also assuming a position of guarded misery. Minutes rolled by with the thunder, until eventually the latter put her paw to her forehead, touching it lightly, and closed her eyes.

"They're going to want to talk to you."

Rupert stirred from his position as though relieving a cramp, his eyes never leaving the ceiling. If anything, it was a signal given that he had heard what she had said. Ciele seemed to know. Staring intently at her paws, now spread in front of her, she spoke slowly, weighing her words.

"There is nothing you can tell them which you have not told them already."

He at last turned to look at her, sliding from the bed and standing.

"No, but I can tell them something, and anything right now that comes from me will be, momentarily, enough."

Ciele looked him in the face, and there was strength there in her own, and Rupert looked away. He had what he wanted. His children may have been robbed from him, taken as victims of the darkness enveloping this place, but his wife was in the dark with him, maybe more so, for who knew the pangs of a mother's loss? And so were the others.

It had been a week since their son Flor and their adopted daughter Mae had gone missing, swallowed up by the forest immediately around them. They had both dealt with it in different ways, Ciele keeping inside for an unnatural length of time, Rupert sending out search parties every day around the clock and waiting for their return. But he knew this wasn't fair. Even in a search party of seven or eight, something could befall those he sent out. With the rumors of the nearly fabled "Dark Wanderer" going around, of a squirrel black as night followed by his accomplices of death, he knew this all too well. And they knew it too. None—well, almost none—Rupert thought, with a sort of inward smile, of his followers had not figured this out. They only continued to risk themselves out of loyalty to him, and he could not let it go on. He hadn't slept much, and when he did, it was to the music of strange dreams, dreams of himself and some sort of army, dreams of Mae and a strange squirrel he didn't know—or was it Flor? The constant foggy quality of his dreams, and the habit he had of waking up to remember barely a thing— and then often not sleeping for the rest of the night— gave him very little to speculate on…if there was anything at all.

But more than this, Rupert felt something in his gut, a stirring to action that would not be ignored.

Looking out of the corner of his vision at Ciele, he wondered briefly if he should tell her, try to explain to her about what he was feeling, if anything just to get a fresh perspective. Rupert felt almost as if his dreams from earlier in life and the significant meaning each had had, had turned him to looking for an essence which in the overwhelming majority of instances simply did not exist. But reoccurring dreams had always meant something before, so why not now?

Rupert leaned against the wall and studied his feet, lean, gray and sharply clawed. He flexed his body, tightening the muscles, then fell back again. The difference was, he supposed, that Ciele had not been there when it first happened. They had met after the first ordeal, when Rupert had had to save Firwood and, he supposed, all of Arborand from the threat of the power-hungry black squirrels when immortality had them in its grasp. Rupert had come back home with no expectations for the devastated land before him, and none for the bright wink in the eye of one squirrel in the crowd he spoke to that afternoon, an afternoon when no one else had dared to be hopeful. The afternoon he became King.

That spark had kept Ciele going on something as intangible as it was mysterious for their whole time together. Rupert couldn't imagine anyone better to live out his life and set up nest with. But while Ciele raised their son, Floridem, well, she had always been a bit distant toward Mae. It had surprised Rupert at first, as Ciele had never been one to judge by something as petty as the color of another's fur, but when Rupert had come in one day from an excursion in the woods with the small, frightened black squirrel trailing shyly behind him, Ciele's eyes had seemed to cloud over for a bit. She had done her best of course, to treat the two of them with no discernment, but every time Flor and Mae would go out to play together, she would retreat back further into her quiet, intuitive nature, and Rupert found it hard to get anything out of her on the subject. Lately, since Mae and Flor had gone missing, Ciele had seemed despondent almost constantly, something that he knew should be expected, but he couldn't shake it all the same.

So Rupert had not told his wife about the dreams. Nor had he told his friends, or quite frankly, a single unit of the populace. He had considered it for days, always knowing that he was fooling himself, because he had already made up his mind not to tell anyone. Before, when he was young and having dreams, he would go to Zirreo. And sometimes his mind reflected to the idea, as if it were still possible. It seemed that since there was no Zirreo, there were no dreams, or dreams of consequence anyway.

Dreams were just dreams. But now, inexplicably, they had meaning again. Only this time there was no one to tell him what they meant. So Rupert had not acted on them.

Until now.

Rupert straightened. There had been a knock at the door, and the head of Dewlim, leader of the search party and a trusted friend besides, peered around the corner into the small living space. Seeing Rupert and Ciele, he grinned apologetically, then came in at Rupert's smile, shaking himself off vigorously.

"Shows no signs of clearing up," Dewlim muttered, gesturing vaguely to the outside, where the rain could be seen plummeting to the ground with a vengeance. "At *all*. And I should know because when—

"You didn't find them, did you?" Ciele said.

There was a pregnant pause. Dewlim shifted his weight, and looking down, shook his head.

"We've tried. We try every day. It's—

"It's okay," Rupert said firmly. "You're not going to do it anymore."

Ciele looked quickly over at him, a mild question in her eyes. Dewlim had dropped his sodden manner, and was looking indignant.

"Come again?"

"I'm not going to have you guys go out there again. It's putting you in danger, and frankly I don't think you'll find them."

"What?" Dewlim sputtered. Then, before Rupert could open his mouth again, "Oh, I know what you said all right, but have you completely lost it? You can't give up like that! If my Mika…well, that's not here nor there…but the point is, just this morning Trevor found what looked like some tracks or summat, and you can't pass that up, so how about just one more day, you might be—

"Dewlim."

"…Really, we don't mind. And those of us who do just don't know any better. Haven't got kids of their own. Rupert, I must say I never knew you to—

"Dewlim!"

"…Yes?"

"You are not sending out another search party tomorrow because *I* am going after them myself."

"Well, that's all well and good, but—come again?"

"Dewlim," Rupert said, masking a bit of a smile. "Go and get any and all of the searchers who would like to accompany me. Have them equip themselves with some type of arms, or protection, and traveling supplies.

The whole lot. Then bring them to me. We'll leave today."

Dewlim's mouth was still working rather stupidly. Ciele's eyes were wide from across the room, but she made no comment.

"Where...where are we going, then?" Dewlim finally managed.

The question caught Rupert unaware, for he had only feelings on this, and no certainty.

"Where I lead," he said quietly but firmly. "You're not afraid of that, are you Dewlim?"

The look of indignity was back. "Certainly not! You've never lead us wrong before. All right, I'll get them right away, but mind you I'm not bringing Trevor. Never thought the boy was very reliable. And now that we're out in the open about everything and all, I'd like to say that the tracks he found...well, I believe he was hallucinating. Too much water."

"I trust your judgment." Then, after a space of time, "But the more suited you can find, the better."

Dewlim raised his eyebrows.

"If you don't mind me asking—and say if you do!—just who will—

"Rule?" Ciele cut in, softly. "I will."

"Of course," There was relief in the other's face. "Then you're not coming?"

Ciele looked over at Rupert, but it was only a glance. She answered for herself.

"No, I will not. But I wish you the best of luck, from Astrippa herself."

There was a moment where no one spoke, and a mutual silence was cast out between them. Then Dewlim moved to the door, respectfully keeping his peace. Reaching it, he turned back to Rupert.

"If that's all?"

"Yes. You can go now," he said gently. Dewlim took his leave.

The heavy silence descended again, and Rupert honestly did not know what to expect. He kept his eyes trained on the wall slightly to the left of his wife, not sure of her feelings on his sudden announcement.

Ciele stirred, and said "I have no need to tell you, Rupert, that I don't know exactly what you have in mind," she smiled at him in a puzzled sort of way. "But whatever it is, I know that you're doing it because you believe it is the right thing. I'm with you. You know I am. I'll pray to Astrippa that you bring them back to us. Both of them." There was a pause, and in it, Rupert closed the space between them, clasping her paws in his, and nuzzled her neck. He gave her a reassuring smile, as reassuring as he could make it with his insides buzzing strangely. When they broke away, Ciele's face went blank. They were done, and there was nothing more to say. There was something fateful about all of this, something destined, and if Rupert had perhaps thought on it, he might have done things differently. But as it was, he took his leave, and waited upon his followers.

His army.

They would leave this afternoon.

Chapter Two

The storms that had been raging over Firwood ebbed into nonexistence as one moved east and south across Arborand to Maplewood. Just under the placid Willow Lake, the happy stream burbling past, a constant wide ray of sunshine kept all under its watch. Warmth had been the order of the day for the past couple weeks, and the air was set for contentment. Frogs and crickets were chirping sleepily and erratically, and the young gray squirrel lying on the sun-warmed rock by the stream seemed to add to the picture of enjoyment.

But the truth is often sadder than what it would appear, and pictures can be misleading. Theo proved both of these things nicely.

Theo, for that was the young gray's name, was not actually a full-fledged gray at all, though lying on his stomach with his front paws overlapping under his chin, he bore every semblance to one: but there was white on his bottom-most paw, and white on his stomach, and so Theo in fact carried around the unlucky title of 'half-breed'. Not that there was really anyone living relatively nearby who would sneer at this, but Theo wasn't *dumb*. He had heard whispers and caught the sideways glances of others when he and Perris had gone walking in the woods around here. Laughter died on lips, even. It was like he was cursed. Which he wasn't. Perris had mentioned it might have something to do with the Dark Wanderer, but that was just a silly chipmunk superstition. Most squirrels agreed that the Dark Wanderer, whoever he was, was a black squirrel, dark as night, and more night than squirrel anyway.

But all of that didn't matter, because Theo had other things on his mind apart from the Wanderer and his own minor abnormalities. Normally, when he had something troubling him, Theo would tell Perris about it, so to ease his mind with the unbiased (if somewhat sarcastic) replies he'd get out of his servant. ("There's something above my bed, Perris." "Probably a moth, sir." "I think it's scary." "Pardon my intrusion, sir, but it probably thinks the same of you. Perhaps you should try closing your eyes when you sleep, sir. It helps me.") Theo had come to Perris with all his boyhood problems, having no actual parents to speak of, but for some reason he could not discern, he found himself hesitant to speak of this particular problem.

If it IS a problem, he corrected himself.

Days ago, Theo had awaked to find a cool sensation on his fur, and had turned quickly, causing something hard and compact to fall to the floor. When he had cautiously peered over the edge of his bed, Theo had been utterly confused. A small silver compass lay on the ground, its intricate needle lying still on the neatly styled "N" for north. He hadn't, and still didn't, know what to make of it, and herein was the problem. Theo might have, upon receiving the compass (for someone must have put it there, he thought) asked Perris about it, if not for what had happened when he went to retrieve the thing from the ground.

Theo remembered it more clearly than he wanted to. The needle had started to move, and this was normal for compasses of course, but then it started moving very, very fast, around and around, so that Theo could almost hear the little needle whining in its constant journey, and he began to get dizzy and dropped the thing. Immediately, it stopped spinning, and not even when it hit the floor but *before* that, as soon as it left his paw.

With a beating heart, Theo had picked it up again. The needle started whirring around as soon as he made contact with the surface of the compass, and this time he forced himself to hold on longer, even when it seemed the needle might break with the pressure of spinning so fast. And fairly soon, it stopped. The madness of the constant circular motion ended, and Theo had peered at the surface of the compass. It was stopped dead between "S" and "W".

Theo didn't believe in magic, so naturally he was very afraid of the stuff. He had shaken the compass, he had walked around and around his room with it, but it had been annoyingly persistent about things.

"Compasses," Theo had whispered accusingly, teeth gritted. "Are supposed to face North. All the time. And NORTH," he said louder. "Cannot possibly always be south west from where I am standing. I have stood in every direction."

Perhaps the compass was broken. Maybe someone extremely rude had come into the habit of stuffing their used and trashed junk through his window onto his prone form at night. But that even *sounded* stupid. So Theo had walked around some more, and the compass had moved from time to time, but never the *right* way. Maplewood, where he lived, was in the southern part of Arborand. So logically, the compass should not have *ever* pointed between "S" and "W". But it had. So if the compass didn't point north, what *did* it point to?

Theo knew, lying on the rocks this summer's day, three days after he had received the thing, that he shouldn't care. But he just didn't understand. And Theo *hated* things he couldn't understand. He hated that he couldn't understand why he was a half-breed, he hated that he couldn't understand why that should mean anything, and he hated that he couldn't understand why Perris always woke up so early in the morning. He hated that he couldn't understand why his parents were gone. There were a lot of things Theo couldn't understand. So Theo hated a lot of things, but he could not ignore them.

Case in point, the compass sat in his oak drawer; he couldn't use under the pillow, because Perris made the bed every morning. He took it out every day and walked around with it. Every day the compass seemed to get heavier and heavier— though he supposed that was his imagination, which he rather wished he didn't possess— and every day he remained stumped as to what the thing was trying to tell him. Or how to make it not matter, which was what he was really trying to do, he supposed, being honest with himself for the first time in three days which had seemed like three months. Secrets were hard to hold.

And so, today, Theo told Perris. His chipmunk was in the kitchen, making lunch.

"*Stew?*"

"If there is something exotic you would rather have, you should probably tell me now, sir."

"Okay, stew."

"Wonderful, sir."

There was silence as Theo took in the fumes of the slowly bubbling soupy liquid, and thought of how exactly he would bring this up without sounding like a crazy animal. He had already decided not to mention the voices, for in the past day he could've sworn he heard someone talking to him through his brooding silences as well.

Perris was dicing walnuts.

"Eh-hem," Theo began. "Perris?"

"Yes, sir?"

"There's something weird I've got to tell you about."

"Just the one thing, sir?"

Theo ignored him. "I…have…is this hollow haunted?"

"I do beg your pardon, sir. Are you having nightmares again?"

"No, it's not that!" Theo didn't like to be reminded of the constant night terrors he had seemed to be suffer as a child. "No. It's just that. Okay." He was having a harder time than he thought he would just spitting it out. Theo knew that the fact of the compass was unreasonable, and he hated to appear unreasonable, but finally he made himself grind it out.

"I found a compass in my bed with me three sunrises ago." Perris made no comment, so he continued. "The…the thing about that is, it doesn't even point north. It keeps pointing me somewhere else. And it spins like crazy when I---hang on…"

Theo left to scale the passageway up the inside of the long hollow stump they lived in to his room, and a bit short of breath, took the compass from its drawer and went back down to where Perris was sprinkling mint leaves into the stew. Theo's stomach made a soft rumbling sound, and in spite of his trouble, he hoped they would be eating soon.

"There!" he said a bit too loudly perhaps, for Perris turned to look at him, taking in the compass, which had just finished its spinning to land somewhere between the "S" and the "W" again. "I was…thinking about telling you, but I don't know what to think of it myself, so I held off until— well I don't know, but it was in my drawer…"

"Pardon my intrusion, sir, but in that case, I would have found it tomorrow anyway."

"And—wait, why?"

"Pardon my intrusion sir, but haven't you ever wondered why your drawers don't have cobwebs inside of them?"

Theo felt a bit foolish at that. "Oh," he sighed. "Well, anyway. Here it is, not pointing north." He had some sort of crazed notion that if Perris looked at it, if *anyone* else looked at it, it would make the compass seem less of a mystery and more of a mundane type of artifact.

"Yes, sir, it is definitely a compass. And yes, sir, it is pointing the wrong way. You say you have no idea how this thing appeared next to you, sir?"

"No, none at all!" Then, just to cover all his bases. "Do you have any ideas?"

Perris stared at the compass, his eyes doing a sort of weird thing Theo was used to them doing when he was trying to remember something.

"Ahhh…"

"What?" Theo leaned forward.

"Now that is bizarre," Perris mumbled to himself and turned back to the stew in time to keep it from bubbling over.

"What?!" Theo pressed, more loudly still, leaning all the way over the counter and trying to look at Perris's face as the chipmunk cut into a mushroom with unnecessary gusto.

After a minute, Perris said, "I honestly don't know anything that would help you much, sir."

Theo opened his mouth, but Perris forestalled him. "What do you intend to do about the compass, sir?"

Theo hadn't thought he'd been thinking about anything of the sort, but all of a sudden the words came to his mouth as though someone else had put them there.

"Follow it."

Apparently, his voice had also sounded strange to Perris, who turned around so fast that the boiling water from the spoon he was holding almost hit Theo in the eye. Theo knew how it must sound. *He* was amazed at himself. Logical, reasonable Theo was thinking of following a broken compass to the ends of the earth. But if someone had really placed the compass there, it must be for a reason. And what were compasses for but to show the way?

Except, he thought rather crossly, *most compasses are also there so you don't get lost, and this one is bound to do the reverse to me.*

"Pardon the intrusion, sir—

"We have *got to* follow it."

Perris looked shocked at the desperation in his voice.

"…Yes, sir. Try not to lose sleep over it. I'll pack tomorrow."

"All right. Okay. Good."

Lunch was incredibly silent that day. Theo sat in his chair by the window, forged by courtesy of termites years ago, and Perris took his place standing up by the counter. Theo couldn't enjoy his stew as much as he would have liked, because he kept being angry at the compass, at whomever or whatever had put it there, and at the compulsion he could suddenly not resist to follow the damned thing. Perris would send glances over at Theo every once in a while, though he did not speak, which was the mark of a good chipmunk, but Theo could tell he was worried anyhow.

That night, Theo couldn't sleep. As he lay on his comfortable bed, trying to rest, he kept hearing noises which put him out of sorts. Natural little noises like branches creaking outside his window caused him to roll to the edge of his bed, shutting his eyes against the black and into a deeper black, as he waited to drift away.

Theo.

"Wuh." With a funny sound of shock, Theo rolled off the bed and onto the hard wood floor with an ungraceful bump. Blinking around at the dimly lit room, he couldn't find anyone else. But then, he knew no one would be there. The voice was back.

The voice had only been coming to Theo since a couple of days back, and then it had been so faint that he could imagine it was other things, or even that it didn't exist. But slowly, the voice had gotten stronger, and all that was saving him from having a breakdown over the whole situation was that the voice was always mercifully brief, and normally came when he was very tired.

He never spoke back to it, as if not speaking back would encourage the voice to leave him alone, or make it think he wasn't here. He knew this didn't make sense, but little made sense lately anyway. It was despairing.

Sitting on the floor to his room, Theo waited patiently for a couple of minutes, waiting for the voice to have its say or just plain leave him alone. He didn't hear anything.

Shuffling back to his feet, Theo fell back into bed, in a horizontal form of rebellion, and stayed there until sleep finally took him.

What was probably a quarter hour later, his eyes fluttered open and Theo was staring at the ceiling. He was not tired anymore, and in his stomach was a horrible tightening dread, such as he had never felt before.

Something bad was coming.

Sitting up fast, Theo got up with his heart jumping through his mouth at twice its normal pace, trying not to breathe too much, or think too much or to throw up.

Something bad was coming. They needed to leave NOW.

Steadying himself with his paws clutching the sides of the walls like death, he inched down to the lower part of the house, where Perris always slept. He almost tripped over the chipmunk, who was sleeping on the floor close to the door. Hysteric thoughts like *I never knew where Perris slept until now, isn't that funny? I guess I just never thought about it…how come I can't feel my head, do I have a fever?* came over Theo as he blundered over, feeling heavy and hot, and his stomach curled in and out in a truly disgusting manner.

"Perris! Perris! Per-

"Yes, sir, what is it?" Perris got up quickly and almost collided with Theo, who could not seem to move his body properly, could not seem to get out of the way.

"We have to go, now!"

Perris looked like he might say something for a second, but his face, shadowed by the darkness, stared at Theo's and he didn't say a thing, just turned around and walked to the door like he didn't know whether to be calm or frightened, but apparently he was trying to be calm since Theo was definitely frightened enough for them both. Theo vaguely thought something stupid like how he admired that, but then they were outside and they were halfway to the stream before Theo remembered that he had left the compass inside.

Saying something to Perris (or at least he thought he said something) he turned back and ran quicker than his up-until-now sedentary life had ever required of him, up to his room and to where he had left the compass, sitting on his chest of drawers, glinting in the light from the moon. Snatching it, he paused and his heart slowed for an instant, as a random compulsion to look out the window gripped him. The night was black and deep, cut across with a cloud of filmy white, and the moon seemed somehow full of malevolence with its barren stare.

Yes. Coming. Tonight.

Theo ran back the way he had come, and out to where Perris had waited for him.

They would follow the compass, and they would start tonight.

Chapter Three

It was in a flurry of leaves the next day that Theo gained his feet, torn from a brief yet heavy sleep. It was light out, and a fragmented fear left over from the night before moved across the region of his chest again.

"Perris!"

"Right here, sir."

Theo whipped his head around and found Perris sitting up rather dignified on an oak leaf spread out around him. The way he had answered, and the placid set of his face told Theo his servant had been awake long before he.

"Wha...why didn't you wake me up?" Theo lashed out, upset and still fearful, casting his eyes about the clearing they were in. *Where WERE they?* "I mean, something could've happened!"

"Pardon the intrusion, sir, but you were sleeping very heavily. And very loud too, sir."

Theo was about to answer this, then realized he didn't even recall falling asleep.

"When—when did I fall asleep?"

"We were walking, sir, or more like running, when you fell down. Luckily for us all, it was a good enough spot you fell in, so I fashioned up some blankets, and then you started snoring loudly, sir, so I figured if anything was after us it was probable that they would have found us already, sir."

Uh. Theo couldn't think of anything to say. "You should've wakened me," he said crossly, after a length of time, and rolled over on his stomach. "What's breakfast?"

Perris took some oat scones and jam out of an emergency pack that Theo didn't even know he'd brought in his panic the night before. *Probably he went in while I was back in getting the compass,* he thought, which made him even more mad, except he wasn't quite sure why.

At the thought of the compass, Theo turned around quick, letting out a breath of relief to find it behind him, tucked underneath his own oak leaf blanket. Spreading raspberry jam thickly across his scone, he took a large bite, and chewed. Theo ate extremely fast, then got up and walked around with the compass, trying to determine which way to go.

"Oh no," he moaned after a while. "This thing doesn't point north, but I don't even know if it's being consistent in wherever it's pointing."

"Stand and turn slowly in a circle, then, sir," Perris said from where he was cleaning up the breakfast mess. "It always helps."

Theo felt a bit dumb. He had forgotten something simple like that, which made him wonder what else he would be forgetting as time went on. Theo hated feeling dumb.

"Right, fine," he said, snappish, and placed himself firmly in one spot. As Theo turned, the compass's needle also did. Looking up at the position of the sun for aid, he figured after some time that the compass was continually pointing him in a south-western direction.

"Right," he said again, dropping the compass to let it dangle from its shortened chain, and turning to Perris. "We can trust that it's set on an actual direction, which is puzzling seeing as it works like an actual compass, except it always points south-west instead of north." He realized he was babbling, and shut up.

As he and Perris started off again in the direction the compass was pointing, Perris said "Pardon the intrusion, sir, but I've been wondering—what exactly was the cause of the minor stress you appeared to be feeling last night?"

"Well, I felt…it doesn't matter. It's…I just wasn't feeling very well at the time," he finished lamely.

"Pardon the intrusion sir, but I had no idea you reacted so adversely to indigestion."

Theo sighed. He decided that it might be good to tell someone else what had happened, but he did not really understand how to go about it without leaving Perris thinking he was crazy as a chickaree in a room of gold.

"I got this really horrible feeling, like there was some sort of…of *evil*, just plain evil out there, and it was looking for me, and on the right track too. I had the feeling if I didn't leave soon, it might come and eat me up, or the moon would swallow me whole, or something. The moon looked creepy last night," he added defensively, "But that's how I felt anyway. I swear I'm not crazy. Except…one more thing. I heard…*sometimes* I hear…"

"Yes, sir?" Perris prompted patiently.

"A voice. Not *voices*, or anything like that," Theo said, rushing through it, knowing that it really made no difference, it sounded the same. "I hear a voice every once in a while. Mostly it's very brief, just says my name or something and leaves it at that. But, damn, I'm not sure I should've told you that. You don't believe me."

Perris stared at him for a long moment, in which Theo became increasingly sure that the chipmunk didn't believe him, and possibly thought he was now serving a crazy squirrel. Then he just said, "Of course I do, sir."

"What?" Not even a comment with its usual sarcastic undertones?

"I believe you, sir. Your fear last night was far too real for me to doubt you, sir."

"You're not just saying that? Like, so I don't hit you or whatever?"

Perris made a soft snort sound. "Of course I'm just saying it, sir. Words are all I have got to give you in this case, but I mean them, so I believe we can start walking again, sir."

Theo looked up, surprised that he had stopped. "Oh," he said, and they continued, Theo feeling as if a large burden had been lifted from him ever so slightly. He watched Perris carrying both their provisions on his back slightly ahead of them, and felt words in his mouth, but for some reason they were terrifying to him, so he left it alone and when they had passed under the shadow of a tall elm tree, the time had passed.

Rupert squinted his eyes against the sun, looking for the right course to take. A train of about twenty grays spread out behind him, all ready with small, bearable weapons and provisions. They had been traveling nonstop at a good pace, for the last day and night, and had made some good headway. Some of the squirrels in his troop were still doubting of the soundness of Rupert's plans, which he understood perfectly, and could not blame them. But they all followed him out of a sound faith that Rupert was astounded by and admired, though it made him a bit nervous, a feeling that he had almost forgotten from his younger days; what if he didn't live up to their faith?

He had been having more premonitory dreams, all of which showed Mae in a place he recognized, a place with humid steam caught somewhere between the ground and the air, somewhere where the feel of the air was almost magical. There was someone with Mae, though they were not fully visible to him—was it Flor? Where was Flor?—and Mae kept turning around and speaking to him, a sad look on her face, trying to tell him something.

Wherever she was, he was needed. That much was clear.

And, of course, he was not supposed to come alone. That much was clear from the danger any lone traveler faced these days, but it was also made clear in his dreams. He had to have others with him, there was something he needed to accomplish, he needed to bring others to Mae, perhaps to protect her, or perhaps to protect something much, much larger. He didn't know. He had shared as little of this as possible with his troops, without feeling like he was being unfair to them. He told them the basics, that he thought he knew approximately where they were headed, that he had been there before, and that if he was wrong, he was sorry, but in truth Rupert was desperate now. He would have followed just about any signal to find his son and adopted daughter.

What is it about south-west? Rupert thought. *I keep being dragged back there, surely as if I'm magnetized. There must be* something *to it.* But aside from what he had undergone there years before, the region of Beechwood had always seemed so quaint…minus the redwood forest, the distant waters, and the constantly foggy air…No, however quaint the rest of it was, there was something about the southwestern end of that region which was intriguing at the very least.

Whenever they made a rest stop on the way to their destination, they would make a habit of asking the first squirrel they could find if they had seen anything resembling the two that had gone missing, or as Rupert had added once, if they had seen anyone at all in the area who did not seem to belong there. He wanted as much confirmation that they were on the right track as he could get, but so far no one seemed to have any information for them.

It was at noon one day when they got the first scent of something gone horribly wrong. They had stopped at a stand of trees in the south of Firwood, moving to get out of the sun. All around Rupert, squirrels were unsaddling themselves and taking advantage of the brief respite to get some food in their bellies. Rupert paced around the area they had set up in, the dry needles from the fir trees crunching under his feet. He scanned the area for any sign of habitation, and saw, peering through a tree so close to them that he didn't know how he had missed it, a small, firmly built nest, settled in the crook of two branches. The lights were on inside, he could see, but only dimly, like whoever was in there didn't want to be too conspicuous.

"Everyone's finishing up breakfasting, I told them we were leaving soon—what're you looking at?"

Dewlim had come up beside him and followed his gaze to the home above them.

"Oh…do you want to—

"Yes, Dewlim. I think we should take a look. See what they know."

Rupert would never rightly know whether he had actually known things would be different here than in the other places they had asked, or if the air of anticipation was just something he had made up upon looking back on it that night, but when they reached the nest, approaching the door, the lights went out inside.

Dewlim frowned at this, and cast a glance over at Rupert as if to ask if they should continue. Rupert nodded.

When he reached the door, he gave it a good sound knock, scaring the wits out of a nearby dragonfly. The thing took to the air quickly and glided off, just as the door edged open a crack.

Rupert was surprised. He hadn't thought the inhabitant of this nest would be very keen to talk to them, much less open the door the moment they came knocking. But after waiting a few seconds, Rupert realized that a crack was about all they were going to get out of whoever lived here until they stated their cause.

Dewlim was looking nervous, and kept snatching glances at the camp below them. Rupert gave him a look that told him he was welcome to go if he wanted, no hard feelings, but Dewlim planted himself firmly on the branch, shaking his head in a semi-comical manner. Rupert smiled to himself, and addressed the door.

"Hello?"

No response. Rupert thought of peering through the crack, but thought better of it, and continued.

"We are looking for two missing squirrels, one black, the other gray, both young, though I suspect they will have matured a bit by now. Have you seen anything unusual in the area, anyone who didn't belong?"

As he spoke these last couple of words, the door creaked open farther, and they got a look at the squirrel on the other side. Rupert caught the gasp in his throat, but a little squeak came from Dewlim, who looked away to the side, and back down again.

It was another gray, like them except not at all. He appeared about middle-aged, and there would not have been anything to gasp about had it not been for his eyes, glazed over, whitish and murky. It wasn't quite like cataracts, and in any case, that was something that befell much older creatures. The squirrel looked almost as if he were in some sort of trance, and as his pearly, dead gaze fell on Rupert and Dewlim, Rupert got the distinct impression that he was not actually seeing them at all. He might have excused himself right then, but the eyes of the other held him in place, and then the stranger spoke.

"Are you with—her?" The voice was muted, a low scraping sound. Dewlim jumped, and Rupert didn't blame him.

"Her?" he asked, trying to remember that he had about twenty others just below them to back him up. "I don't know, who is she?"

The other's eyes narrowed, at the same time retaining their far off, drugged look.

"Astrippa. The goddess of all squirrelkind. I…" and here a note of some dumb pride came in, "I am in her army."

"I believe in Astrippa, if that's what you mean," Rupert said slowly. "I didn't know she had an army."

"Oh yes," the other said, still looking as if he couldn't really see Rupert at all. "I will fight for her when she comes."

Rupert opened his mouth, but the strange squirrel overrode him.

"Arborand belongs to her." His face convulsed with something like a mix of sheer anger and pain. "Soon," he said, shutting the door on them both.

Climbing down from the tree, Dewlim scampered ahead of Rupert, throwing occasional looks behind them at the nest.

"What was that?" he sputtered when they finally reached the ground.

Rupert shrugged, deep in thought.

"I don't know," he said with complete honesty, "But it clearly means there's more out of place happening than we could venture a guess upon."

As Rupert got everyone together and trekked away, his thoughts kept coming back to the expression on the other squirrel's face, the look like he had somehow been under a trance, trapped in his own body which had somehow become not so much his own anymore. Like...

Well, like a *spell*. But magic wasn't supposed to exist anymore.

There was the chestnut...but that was years back, when...well, even then it had been inanimate, an *object* of magic. A spell suggested that there was someone somewhere who had some control of magic themselves, who knew how to bend it to their advantage. But...that kind of thing had died along with the white squirrels. It couldn't have been a spell. Perhaps the stranger had been half blind. Magic didn't need to enter into it. Besides, Rupert decided, if it *was* magic, the implications *that* concept held were enough to make one go dizzy.

But all the same, he was not so sure.

Chapter Four

Mae woke from the first peaceful sleep she had had in a long time, and looked around the room she was in. It was an upper chamber of the abode of the flying squirrels, night whisperers as they were more commonly called, and unlike the other scantly furnished rooms, this one was filled with all sorts of interesting odds and ends. A cabinet sat off to one side, one of the little doors in it open a little, hanging at a funny, suspended angle. There was a dusty window on the end of the room with the cabinet, tree branches growing right up and pressing against it as though insistent on breaking and entering. There were cards of some sort scattered around on the ground, a few old pieces of furniture, a couple of clocks with cryptic symbols instead of numbers, and even what looked like an old crystal ball, lying discarded on the floor. The tick-tick-tick of the couple of clocks still working sounded through the room, at odds with each other in keeping time. No other sounds could be heard, and for a moment Mae even thought of drifting to sleep again, when it hit her.

Though she had known why she was here, somehow she had managed to forget, as if she had been drugged, what she had found here in the home of the flying squirrels, the night whisperers who had helped she and Flor so much, been so kind to them. Had she been imagining it? The message on the wall in the room of the seer Kiroba, the wise flying squirrel's broken, dead body, and the other who had appeared...

Head snapping toward the door, Mae was surprised to find it open a crack. With little hesitation, she started forward and pushed it open upon reaching it.

He was standing right there, staring her in the face. Mae jumped back, she was so startled, and fell luckily enough onto the dusty mattress she had been lying on moments before.

"Guh…" was all she could manage. So that answered *that;* she hadn't been imagining it.

The old white squirrel came in and stood over her, looking somewhat amused, which made Mae kind of annoyed, though she didn't know whether you could be annoyed with a white squirrel and get away with it. Apparently, you could, because after some time, Zirreo just said "Good morning. I did wonder if you might wake up today."

What?

"*Today?* How long have I been asleep?"

"Oh, days now. You are feeling very refreshed, I imagine."

Mae had gotten over her shock sufficiently enough to give him a small nod.

"Good. You will need it."

Mae wasn't really sure she wanted to know why, though her unquenchable curiosity was already begging the question.

"You have a lot ahead of you, Mae," Zirreo said, she guessed in answer to her unasked question. He went over to sit on an overturned old chair and the points of the stumpy wooden chair legs sticking up around him on four sides made a strange picture indeed, like an awkward throne.

You're supposed to be dead.

But Mae didn't say it because it sounded stupid, and irrelevant, because clearly he was not. She was uncertain whether he could die to begin with. And so

Mae sat, for once not sputtering questions all over the place.

She could remember having gotten here, after…after Flor's death—she firmly made herself think it— and how this place was all abandoned, and the seer in the upstairs room was dead, and the door was locked from the outside. A shiver went through her, and then she thought about how Zirreo had come in, as if he had been standing outside for some time, and he hadn't seemed surprised at all to see her, even though they had never met. And he had told her that the message on the wall was true, "The white squirrels live", and he said that's all for now, and wasn't she tired, and then she remembered her body going all limp and weird on her, even though she hadn't felt tired before, and she could vaguely remember him carrying her somewhere, must've been here, and her dreams were like nothing she'd ever had before, just colors, colors dancing all around in the blackness, and a feeling of overwhelming peace as she watched them dance, and she must have been asleep for ages, though it felt like time didn't matter in that sleep. She wondered if she had been drugged, because it had felt that unnatural.

But even through her hazy waking state, one thing tugged at her repeatedly, needing to be spoken, a sharp, nagging fear that demanded an answer.

"Where *are* the flying squirrels?" Mae asked. She did not know what reaction to expect from Zirreo, but he remained perfectly calm.

"They have gone into hiding," he said. "I can't see that any direct harm will come to them any time soon. They are amazing creatures."

"Well, then…why was she…"

"Ah, the seer. Correct? Yes, Kiroba was unfairly treated by them, I admit. Despite their mystical nature and given name, night whisperers don't take to magic at all. Anyone with magic abilities is, I am afraid, not given much of a chance with them. Kiroba had been with them for some time, and she had given a prophecy shortly before you arrived. It appears that she was locked in her room while the others made a getaway. The seizure that came with the prophecy killed her. Sometimes that happens, if the force working through a seer is stronger than the seer herself. And no matter what else she looked, Kiroba was rather old. She has been here a long time. She deserved more respect."

Mae had had another question all ready, hanging on every word, but the last words spoken by Zirreo were spoken with a controlled but unmistakable anger.

"Did—but the flying squirrels always seemed so kind. They didn't seem the type to do something like that."

"No, but they've grown frightened of magic, perhaps beyond what is reasonable. They fail to understand that magic itself is a neutral force, but that it is the way the user chooses to twist it which makes the difference between good and evil. They were foolish, but they have their reasons. Still…reasons or no, Kiroba did not deserve that. She has served them well, even though they never gave her much incentive to be faithful."

"Did you know her, then?" Mae asked cautiously, not knowing whether it was a good idea to broach the subject.

Zirreo was silent a moment.

"I did not know Kiroba, no. But I have crossed paths with Edgewood before, and I know of its history."

He didn't say any more than that, and for a while after he didn't talk.

Mae guessed that Edgewood must be the name of this place; it seemed oddly appropriate. There were more questions pressing in on her, and she feared she couldn't contain herself.

"I'm sorry, but I don't really understand exactly why the night whisperers left. I mean, Kiroba'd been with them for a long time, right, so it couldn't have been the fact that she was going into a display of mystics that made them leave."

Zirreo smiled at her. "I am guessing it was the prophecy itself that made them leave."

"Which was?"

"Well, I can't be sure, but if you'll look at the message on the wall, I think that may have something to do with it."

"The white squirrels. Magic. Right. So they're scared the white squirrels are going to find them?"

Zirreo didn't say anything immediately. "It's hard to discern the exact way the minds of flyers work," he said. "But that is a distinct possibility."

"It's true, isn't it? I mean, about the white squirrels being back. You're back."

"Ah, well there's the difference. *I* was never truly gone."

Before Mae could say anything to that, Zirreo's face turned intent and serious. "Now, Mae, I have come to guide you in what is ahead of you. To guide you, and to warn you. There is something perilous going on, which I am sure you know, but you do not know enough."

No kidding Mae thought, in spite of herself. She was fit to burst with more questions, but she also badly wanted to hear what Zirreo had to say.

"I was foolish back when I was helping Rupert," he said, "I overlooked several things I should not have overlooked. Now things seem painfully obvious." She felt as if she could truly see pain in his pink eyes, though she couldn't think what it was about, and it disappeared quickly to be replaced with the usual calm. "The compass that you had with you," Zirreo said, suddenly becoming businesslike. "It's as good a place as any to start. You have been doing all that is in your power to keep it out of Callisto's paws, though you were never quite sure why. Am I correct?"

At the mention of Callisto, Mae had flinched, her own thoughts taking a painful turn, but she nodded.

"I was told if he got his paws on it something horrible would happen."

"Indeed, it would, and still can if we don't keep him from having it. Oh, he lives Mae," he said, correcting interpreting the look on her face. "Although I don't believe we would have been wrong to wish otherwise. Callisto is a terrible squirrel. And even then, I overlooked him. He worked for Venul, back when Venul ruled, that is. Venul was horrible enough, but inconsequential. If I had known then what Callisto was yet to start, I could have rid Arborand of him then. Now he is considerably more powerful."

"Callisto," said Mae suddenly. "Callisto has magic. I've seen him use it. When...when, you know, Flor and I, we were traveling with him— he was making us— and he used magic. He did this thing where he closed his eyes and started muttering, and gold appeared in his paw. He used it to pay his servant."

"Yes," Zirreo said. "Callisto has the magic of illusion. He can give things which do not exist a sort of half-existence."

"So the gold…it wasn't real?" Mae asked, unable to keep the doubt out of her voice.

"Yes. And no. The gold came from nothing, and so is not real. No one has the power to create something from nothing except Astrippa. But he was able to give it such an appearance of being real, that it looked real and felt real. Very useful, I imagine, for keeping chickarees in your service. They'd never know the difference, and as long as they could feel it, I doubt they'd care."

"So what exact danger does he pose to us?" Mae asked slowly, afraid she was missing something.

"I'm not quite there yet."

"Oh. Sorry."

"That is perfectly all right. Callisto is in the habit of hearing a certain voice in his head."

Mae's head jerked up. "Oh, I know! He was talking to himself all the time, and he was barking mad, it seemed. He kept asking me questions too, taking me to the side and asking me stuff, mostly about Astrippa."

Zirreo was nodding as if all of this made perfect sense. Again he was quiet, and this time Mae didn't break the stillness. She felt somehow that she shouldn't, that what Zirreo would say next, and how much he would reveal to her when he did speak, depended on it.

"I am going to tell you now, Mae," he said, placing one old white paw on the top of one of the upturned chair's legs as he continued to perch there, "What I know."

Mae waited in suspense, and noticed Zirreo's eyes dart for a moment to the corner of the room almost nervously, but all Mae saw when she looked there was the cabinet, one door still hanging weirdly.

After a moment of staring intently in the direction of the corner, Zirreo looked straight at Mae. The intensity, the steadiness of his pink eyes almost made her want to turn away, except that there was also a type of comfort there, so she stared back as best she could, and Zirreo began to talk.

"You may have fallen under the impression, traveling with Callisto as you were made to do, that he is possessed, or crazy. You are not wrong on either of these counts. I do not know how it first came about, but when Callisto was younger, he experimented with something he ought not to, and someone or something much stronger than he was able to get into his mind, to speak to him by way of some sort of link. This may have been possible simply because both parties involved were magic, or there may have been something more to it. Either way, Callisto grew rather demented over the years, as whatever was possessing him grew stronger, starting telling him things, giving him instructions. Callisto, who had once been so power-hungry, was no longer entirely his own."

"He said he was building an army," Mae said. "An army that he called Astrippa's."

"Yes," said Zirreo, "And that is disturbing."

"I'm glad I'm not the only one who thought so!" said Mae, and he gave her a small smile, which lightened her up a bit.

"Somehow, Callisto is using his magic of illusion to make others join him, to enlist them in this army, as you call it. I have my theories about this, and it appears he may well be using a gathering spell, which I again failed to believe he knew how to do. Clearly, he needs the compass in order to follow through with the instructions given to him. Perhaps he is being required to go where it leads."

"And where *does* it lead?" Mae asked, perplexed. There was so much new information to take in at once.

"That does not matter as much as it may seem. Our direct task at the moment is to keep Callisto from getting to the compass by whatever means possible."

A wave of horror came over Mae, a very extreme sense of fear.

"Z-Zirreo. I gave the compass to someone else!" she blurted. She couldn't even remember why she had done it, except that some intuition that told her to, and now she had put someone else's life in danger. What if Callisto had the compass now?

But Zirreo just looked at her in that calm, sedate way of his and said, "Yes. I know. Did you not trust your judgment?"

Mae looked at him incredulously. She didn't understand at all.

"Well, it seemed like intuition, premonition, or something of the like when I got the idea, but I'm reckless, Zirreo—I always have been. I was scared because the compass didn't work for me, it kept spinning and wouldn't stop. It worked for Callisto, and I don't know, something told me it would work for the squirrel in the hollow, the one I gave it to. But he was sleeping, Zirreo, and I just ran away like a thief, it was unfair! I just thought…I can't even explain it—I *felt*, deep in me, that it was the thing to do, except I don't know *why*! If all we're doing is trying to keep the compass away from Callisto, then I should've kept it, and not put any more lives into the balance. I'm…I'm…"

Always doing this, she wanted to say, and she felt tears threatening in her eyes, burning and stinging. *Always doing this. First with Flor. And then with this other squirrel, the one who reminded me of Flor. Flor, who is dead now, and not coming back.*

"I'm always making others suffer for my choices," Mae said, looking at the ground. She didn't want Zirreo to see her face, she already felt so transparent here, in front of him now, and she wished desperately to be back asleep on the dusty mattress in this abandoned bedroom with the colors twisting in the dark and the peace. Things were too real now. Too real and too painful.

Mae felt a paw under her chin, and she attempted to turn her head to the side, but it was persistent, and finally she looked up into Zirreo's face. It was kind, and without blame. She forced her tears back in her eyes.

"Mae," Zirreo said. "You have your own magic. Surely you have felt it. It is nothing terribly strong, but you are not being entirely fair to yourself. You ought to put more trust into your own intuition."

Mae just stood there, trying to make herself do what he asked.

"Okay," she said, not at all sure she could. Then, "What are we going to do?"

The sky was getting dull outside the window with the tree pressed against it, and Mae imagined anything, everything, could be happening out there right now. Things could be ending, squirrels could be living, hoping, dying, and she didn't want to go back to sleep anymore.

"I'm glad," Zirreo said, it seemed in answer to her last thought. "Because we must go find the squirrel who has the compass now, and we must help him."

Chapter Five

Mae and Zirreo traveled for a good two days. Zirreo never seemed to need any rest, and fairly quickly, Mae began to notice that she wasn't getting tired herself. When she mentioned this to Zirreo, he just smiled.

"Yes, you won't be getting very tired for a very long time."

And he was right. Scarily so.

Mae would have been hard pressed to deny it as one of the weirdest experiences she had ever had. They traveled all day once, Zirreo sometimes making conversation with her when he sensed her spirits were down, telling her about different kinds of plants they found when they scaled the trees to their base, and then they traveled all night as well, and Mae's body didn't give her a single sign of fatigue. When the sensation persisted into the middle of the next day, Mae couldn't hold herself back any longer, for Zirreo wasn't showing signs of being tired either, though she wasn't quite sure white squirrels ever did. She still had a very fantastical, mythical view of them, she imagined, but this was to be expected, as she had never actually knew they still existed, much less hung around a white squirrel herself until now.

So it was that she waited to ask the question that was bound to be asked. Zirreo had likely seen it coming.

"Why aren't I getting tired?" Mae asked, adept at bluntness as she was. "It feels supernatural."

But Zirreo just gave her a look that told her his mind was on other things, and said "You have more strength to keep going then you know, Mae."

Mae thought of herself running when Flor had died, running far away, and then she thought of handing the compass off to the sleeping squirrel who looked like

Flor *except for the white,* she remembered, and then she thought of the bending, floating colors that were somehow part of instead of *within* the blackness of sleep.

Maybe he's right, she thought, and not quite understanding what she meant by this, she was not bothered any longer, and they continued to travel. Mae knew where the stump was, the one she had left the compass at. She remembered it fairly well, and Zirreo, who walked directly alongside her, assured her that *he* was following *her,* which made her feel weird. She had assumed he knew through some psycho ritual or other where they were going. All at once there was a lot more pressure to keep going, not to fall behind, to keep destination in mind.

All the way down into the lower part of Maplewood from the Cherry Forest, Mae's mind was consumed with what Zirreo had told her. Callisto had powerful illusory magic, his army was controlled by something called a gathering spell, whatever that was, and the compass…Mae still didn't understand the compass. If Callisto were truly possessed by something else, could it be that even *he* did not know the true use of the compass? Then she thought of how the compass only worked for Callisto. What if he were to follow it, what would he find? And how would it impact the plan for an army, and everyone else in Arborand? She didn't really want to find out, but she truly wondered. The compass seemed so separate from everything else.

If I could hold it again, maybe I could figure it out.

She sped up, still walking tirelessly. They had to get to the other squirrel…before someone else did.

Mae smelled the smoke before she saw it rising through the air from her place atop the tree. And though it could have come from any tree in the area, she knew what had been burnt. She took off, searching for it down below, found what she was looking for, and dove in a panic, emotions and words racing through her mind. Hitting the ground, she dashed over to where the small, dead stump was smoking wetly. Dead wood didn't burn so well, which she thought must be some sort of miracle.

Dashing into the house, she already knew she would find nothing there.

Please please please.

Tearing through the entrance, past things knocked over in the kitchen, everything out of order, up to the top where the bedroom was, where she had seen him, where she finally stopped and stared from the gaping doorway.

The bed was knocked over, torn apart, the drawers in what looked like it had once been a nice oak dresser ripped out, some of them broken.

The place has been searched.

Mae heard a sound from down in the kitchen and flinched, but it was only Zirreo, and he came up behind her a moment later, keeping a distance back.

Mae kept staring at the room with its carnage, the bed pushed far away from the window where she had climbed up to look in so many nights ago now, it seemed. She didn't even know how long. Things were so disjointed all at once. She heard Zirreo move behind her, or breathe, and thought

You.

"You didn't tell me anything!" she said, her voice loud and uncontrolled.

Anger. She deserved it. He deserved it. It was time it went somewhere. And then everything she had hated, everything she had done wrong, everything she was afraid of, everything that had been beating against her insides, knotting them up for these year-long days finally won the war they had waged.

"You! Why are you here? Where the hell did you go? Did it ever cross your mind that we might have *needed* you? No? Why aren't you saying anything? Even when you talk you're not talking, you're not telling me everything! You...you said it would be *all right*, remember, and now look! I've killed someone else, is that *all right*?"

She darted over to one of the boards, snapped off completely from the oak dresser, picked it up and waved it at the white shadow in the doorway without seeing him.

"Is this *all right*? Should I trust in my *inner magic*? I don't have any rotting magic, *all right*? If I do, it's damn useless! I couldn't figure, couldn't see this coming! You're—you're always walking around like since you're a white squirrel none of this surprises you or something, like you're above it because you're a rotting *mystic*. Well bully for you. You've been gone a while, you've missed things...things that could've been changed if you'd have cared to be there, and we deserve to know everything! What *is* the compass anyway, why are we risking ourselves over it, what's Callisto going to do with it?"

She stopped, just breathing for a second, the tears choking her vision and smearing it. "You...missed a lot of time. Where were you? There were things that you— some things might not have happened, and now...this."

Mae turned around, and went right to Zirreo, intending to fight if she had to, but he just stepped aside and let her pass. She hardly looked at him, even now. She couldn't look at him. She needed to get outside, rid herself of the smoke choking her lungs, the stench of blame and hopelessness.

Reaching the outside, Mae leaned against the stump that had once been a home, and let the tears come. A light rain started to fall, like pricks of ice, of relief, through the smoke, mixing with her sorrow, and she could feel the day change around her. Still no one came out of the house, and she was glad for it.

A couple hours later, or that was how it felt to Mae, tears dried, staring at an earthworm wriggling its way out from the ground against the force of the damp soil, she felt his presence behind her. The small sprinkling of rain had left a coating of dew over everything, condensing into small beads stretched over everything. Mae continued to stare at the worm, not feeling fit to speak.

Zirreo's paw touched her shoulder, and she flinched, instantly rebuking herself for the movement.

"It's not your fault he died," Zirreo said. His voice was soft, as if he too knew a private sadness apart from Mae's own.

She turned away from the worm. In spite of herself, she felt a sense of relief. It was a lovely thing, and she wondered why she had not been able to convince herself before. Perhaps she had just needed to hear it from someone else.

The squirrel whose home she leaned against had escaped. She had known it, she supposed, all along. The compass had not been there, but neither had anyone's lifeless body. It counted for something. The place was torn apart and burned and she could feel the anger that must have gone into it. Callisto's rage, at coming here too late.

The sun winked in a closed-off manner through the trees around them. She was still angry, and they both knew it, but now there was hope, hope for this other squirrel, the one she had handed into the arms of danger.

The best she could do was attempt to guide him through it, to find him before the black nightmare chasing him caught up.

Had he known? Was that why he left?

She turned to Zirreo and nodded. Time could not be lost, and they did not have much of it to lose.

Evening was dying into night when Theo crossed the border into southern Ashwood, and it was getting near impossible for him to read the compass in the impending darkness. Normally, they would have reverted to looking at the stars, but tonight it made Theo's head hurt even to consider them, and he was beginning to feel annoyed with everything all over again.

"How do I—what—ergh!" Theo realized he had been holding the compass upside down and flipped it around hastily, looking back at Perris to make sure he hadn't seen. His eyes felt glazed over and his mind was sluggish.

"Pardon the intrusion, sir, but sleep might be useful in this case."

Theo stopped short and Perris just avoiding running into him in the dark. His mind was too tired to think up any sort of rebuke. Instead, he finally admitted to himself that he had missed almost two full nights of sleep so far, and that in fact it might be a good thing to turn in somewhere for the night.

"W—where?" he yawned. Then, looking around, he spotted a bunch of lights off to his right, shining at differing levels among the trees. "Perris, d'you think there might be a turn-in house up there somewhere?"

"It is not unlikely, sir."

"Good. Then." Theo started towards the lights, more shambling than walking, Perris bringing up the rear with their bags.

Soon it became apparent that they had walked into a town of small proportions. It was organized rather messily, as if squirrels had moved in at various times, making their dray on whatever wood someone hadn't already claimed, and in this way things had built up in a stagnated, unplanned fashion. The atmosphere was quiet, aside from the slamming of doors now and then, the squeal of a naughty child, or the laugh of a drunk through the too-thin walls. Occasionally, the random shadow of someone coming in to dinner would slash its way across the darkening sky, making branches rattle. Theo noted that the shadows he did see all seemed rather larger than any squirrel he could ever remember seeing, which made him feel nervous. Perhaps it was just because he was not used to seeing other squirrels.

Theo crossed in front of a bar, small and built rather precariously on a low-hanging branch just on the edge of the beaten path. A large squirrel the likes of which Theo had definitely never seen leaned up against the trunk of the tree, crooning something softly to himself and swaying lightly back and forth. An acorn cap full of Dew Frost was lilting dangerously to the side in his paw. Theo, looking about, figured he might get somewhere a lot faster if he were to ask whoever ran this place about the nearest turn-in house. He looked back at Perris who nodded, indicating he knew what he was up to.

Theo turned in to the entrance of the bar. The squirrel outside stuck out a paw real fast and he jumped, before realizing the drunk was only holding out the paw that held his acorn cap.

"Could you be a pal and get me some more Frosty Dew?" he asked, his tone drowsy and slurred.

"Er…okay, sure," Theo said, taking the cap from him. Perris followed him into the bar, giving the squirrel outside a look as he passed, though Theo was not sure if that was his own imagination, as tired as he was.

The inside of the bar was fairly empty, with only about five occupants, sitting around laughing at varying volumes, depending on how many Dew Frosts or Birch Beers they had consumed. Theo deposited the empty acorn cap on the bar and leaned over, looking for someone who looked fit to help him out. Behind the counter a chipmunk was taking orders from an especially fat tawny squirrel, who kept belching in the middle of his speech. All the squirrels appeared to be the same kind, a large, fierce-looking tawny-gold variety, with proud tufts of fur on their ears to add to their height, though Theo was already getting the impression that despite all this, they weren't much of a threat to anyone.

Perris took the compass from Theo and stuffed it in their pack before anyone could take much notice to it. He happened to be just in the nick of time, too. No sooner had the compass disappeared into the pack then the squirrel from outside came tottering in, stopped right next to Perris and asked him for a drink.

"You have the wrong side of the counter, sir," Perris said, looking vaguely disgusted. The large squirrel looked confused for a moment, seated himself on a bar stool, and promptly fell asleep. A group of three squirrels got up to leave, and Theo heard one of them talking about it getting late, even though the sun had only just gone down.

Seeing as how the few squirrels left in the bar seemed either too tipsy to tell left from right or fast asleep, in the case of the squirrel next to him, Theo leaned across the counter and snapped his fingers for the now unoccupied chipmunk, who came bustling over.

"What can I do for you, sir?"

Theo opened his mouth and yawned real loud by mistake.

"We'd like to see the owner of this place, and rather quick too, if you can," Perris said for him, as Theo's eyelids were starting to droop. Catching himself, he forced his eyes open, and stared ahead in a glazed manner at some particularly interesting bottles on a back shelf.

The chipmunk had gone off, and now came back through a door in the back of the bar that Theo hadn't noticed before. A pretty young female squirrel of the same type as the others came out behind her. Catching sight of Theo, the new squirrel looked surprised. He guessed they didn't have gray squirrels here every night, and on second guess, supposed it didn't help that he was half breed at that.

"How can I help you?" she asked, looking between he and Perris curiously but not impolitely.

"You're the owner?" said Theo in a voice that could be categorized as curious *and* impolite. Immediately he flushed, but she took no notice.

"My mother is, but she's out. What can I do for you?" she repeated.

"Yes, of course. We're traveling and we need to be directed to the nearest turn-in house." *Before I fall down snoring,* he thought, staring at the sleeping lout next to him with a twinge of envy.

"Oh," She looked pensive a moment, which couldn't be a good sign. Theo was about to get grumpy all over again when she said "Well, we normally don't have others coming here, if you know what I mean. It's very small here. Oh, here, your eyes are closing as I speak!"

She pushed across a mug of something warm. Theo took it up carefully and had a tentative sip. It burned something fierce going down.

"Oww…" he moaned, but his vision was already clearer. He got over the pain quickly, and went for more, until he felt the glassiness leave his eyes. Theo sat up straighter.

"What *is* that stuff?"

"Hot ginseng tea. About the only thing here 'sides water that won't make you tipsy. And don't worry about pay, it's on the house. Now," She leaned across the table to him, and Theo was overly conscious of how much bigger she was than him. He bet her fur was soft. "You want a place to stay. Like I said, there're no turn-in houses around here, we don't get anyone up here. I would tell you to walk up a ways— there's a larger town not too far north of here— but in times like this I wouldn't feel clean about it."

Theo thought he had a pretty good idea of what she meant. He nodded.

"So what would you suggest, then?" he asked, the epitome of politeness, trying to erase whatever first impression he was sure he had made. The chipmunk bartender was standing against a back wall, looking intently at Perris, who was avoiding eye contact and holding tightly to the pouch containing the compass.

"We have a couple of rooms upstairs. We've never leant them to others before, but then, we've never had the occasion to. It's family quarters, and like I said, we don't get others up here often. Especially not with the rumors going round. Not that I'm saying I've got any suspicions on you," she said quickly. "If I stare too much, it's only because I've never seen a gray…or a well, whatever you are," she finished, obviously thrown off by Theo's markings.

"No, no offense taken," he assured her. "We're pretty much even, actually, because I'd never seen a…a…well."

"Fox squirrel? My name's Brinna, by the way."

"Oh. Exactly. Theo." They shook paws.

"There're plenty of us here in Ashwood," Brinna said. "The north has got an amazing colony, we used to get a lot of, erm, literature from them but— she broke off, then spoke softer. "We're not supposed to talk about them anymore."

"Why not?"

"We're not on good terms at all. None of the rest of Ashwood really likes them either, though, so it's not just us. See, their leader had dealings with the Dark Wanderer." She whispered this last, and did a sort of shiver. "Most think the Dark Wanderer wouldn't have known about Ashwood if they hadn't conspired with him, could've passed us by. There are those who've said they've seen him, though I haven't myself, and Relph, who used to be so nice has gone all creepy, taking to the edges of town, hanging around getting thin. He came into the bar only once and scared everyone out. My Da thinks someone put a hocus on him, that it's the black mark of the Dark Wanderer. My Da even thinks *he's* seen him once, out for a walk."

"I haven't seen him," Theo said, and from the obstinate tone of his voice, it was apparent that a nerve had been struck somewhere. "I haven't seen anything."

Brinna looked surprised at his tone.

"Well, you must be tired. Here I am, chattering on. I've been known for it. I'll get Drayil to show you up to your rooms." She motioned to the chipmunk to her right, who immediately parted herself from the wall.

"If you'll come with me, sir," she addressed Theo, and he and Perris followed her up a set of stairs so far back that they could not have really been seen where they had been standing formerly. The stairs were lined with soft down and long yellow grass, and it was not a very long way up before they were met with a small bedroom, bare and simple with only a few possessions stacked neatly against the walls. The chipmunk Drayil opened an adjoining door, and led them into another room, but before Theo entered, something caught his eye. He looked back and noticed that someone was lying in one of the beds, but he couldn't see their face.

He wondered if Brinna had meant something else when she said her mother was out, and felt ashamed for snapping at her.

Upon entering the next room, Theo saw that it was even smaller, with its one bed pushed up against the wall. He nodded to Drayil to show that he was satisfied, and she hesitated before leaving, looking very nervous.

"What is it?" Theo said rather incredulously, before realizing she was looking at Perris.

"You could, erm…there are servant's quarters…"

"No thank you," Perris said in what Theo perceived as a rather coldly formal tone. Drayil turned a gratifying shade of pink and positively fled from the room. Theo looked around at Perris curiously, but he was busy stuffing their sack under the bed. Theo unconsciously thought of Brinna.

"This Dark Wanderer stuff has got me a tad miffed," he sighed, slumping down on the edge of the bed and throwing the extra blanket on the end to Perris.

"I was sensing something of the sort, sir," Perris said, spreading the blanket out neatly on the floor and folding himself into it sleepily.

Theo continued his rant in a lower tone, mindful of whoever was in the next room. "So many squirrels worrying about something they don't even know is real! It's crazy! Magic doesn't exist. Even if it did, once— which I doubt, mind you—it doesn't anymore! They're holding themselves back with all this 'Dark Wanderer' nonsense. It seems sometimes like we're the only ones with some sense."

"Pardon the intrusion, sir, but we *are* following a crooked compass around the land," came the sleepy murmur from next to him, and Theo couldn't think of anything to say to that, which rather took the wind from his sails.

He sat for a while longer on the soft bed, thinking about the events of the past few days, and wondering…but no matter how much he thought he couldn't seem to find a logical, suitable explanation for anything.

"Perris?" Theo whispered into the dark, but the other's breathing had become rhythmic with sleep.

Theo sat a while longer, then flopped back on the bed, staring at the ceiling. There was a draft coming in from somewhere, and he thought he could almost see a star or two through one of the upper cracks in the ceiling. Something moved, cold as the starlight, to spread out through his chest, and Theo realized he was afraid.

The light seemed to wink at him as his eyelids dropped, and there was no explanation for that either. Listening to Perris's soft breathing next to him, and the world of the believers spinning around him in their warm protective bliss, Theo felt more alone than he thought he ever had in his life.

Chapter Six

After making good and sure that the young squirrel hadn't died (Zirreo seemed sure of it), Mae felt herself swept off again in this thing she could not fully grasp or understand. Her anger was still pumping fresh in the back of her mind, but her mind was now elsewhere, thinking of the strange young squirrel, the one who had looked like Flor. Where was he now? Had Callisto already caught up with him, or did he have a sufficient head start?

She shivered as she thought of what it would be like if Callisto had caught up with him, and hoped for the other's sake and her own, that he didn't. She had had too much experience with that incalculable anger, those mad burning eyes.

Would he snap the neck on this one, too?

Zirreo must have seen the look on her face, because his own, which had seemed clouded over with some other sort of business, softened and he pulled back for her to catch up, continuing to go at a good pace along the tree line they were now following. Zirreo seemed to know exactly where he was going now, and Mae was not fool enough to doubt that he did, but she had stopped asking him questions at all and let her bitterness stew. There were other things to worry about, and whatever else she thought of Zirreo, she knew he was good, and whether she liked it or not, it helped her immensely to have him beside her through her journey.

"Mae." Zirreo broke into her thoughts and she jumped a little, almost missing the branch she was headed for. Even though she knew it was stupid and immature, she could not make her mouth answer.

"You said I have not told you everything, and that I ought to be ashamed for it."

Mae ducked her head. "I—

"And you are right. Though I told you no lies back at the night whisperers' lodge, I told you only half of the truth, which is just as bad."

Mae was slowing her pace, listening eagerly in spite of herself.

"You must keep going, as I'm afraid we've no time at the moment to break," Zirreo told her, and she kept pace with him again. "How much do you know about white squirrels?" he asked her.

"Next to nothing." She paused to think. "No, scratch that, nothing,"

"All right then. This may take some explanation. The thing that holds us apart from other squirrels is simply the fact that we are all born with something called pure magic. This does not mean we are all-powerful. Some white squirrels have very little control over or knowledge of their magic. Our most important law lies in that we believe our magic a sacred gift from Astrippa, and to abuse it will have horrible consequences. Because white squirrels have always been fewer in number than any other race, we were always rare, but once there was a time, very long ago, when white squirrels were to be found in a number of places throughout Arborand, albeit almost always alone. We are solitary by nature, and many others are afraid of us. Now. The reason the flying squirrels are so frightened, why they fled so recently in the face of the message threatening a return and why they are so afraid of magic, is believed to be because of something which happened in the Edgewood colony's distant past."

Something strained at the back of Mae's memory.

"They had a run-in with a white squirrel," she said. She had forgotten where she had heard it, but all of a sudden it seemed to fit. "I—someone told me. But I thought it was only a rumor."

Zirreo did not show any surprise at this. "Yes, I thought it likely you might have heard something of it. Unlike most rumors, what you heard is a vestige of the truth. A long time ago, it was said that a traveling white squirrel came to the colony of flying squirrels for rest and recuperation. Being hospitable in nature, they took him in, though you can imagine their surprise that someone had been able to find their carefully hidden location. He may have shown them some of his magic just to show it off, which is another thing that goes against our unspoken law."

Zirreo's voice held traces of annoyance. Mae asked, "Were they afraid, then?"

Zirreo paused. "I can't know for sure. But then, as the story goes, the white squirrel fell in love with a flying squirrel. For a long time it was suspected that he was teaching her magic. And then…"

"They didn't—

"The flying squirrel gave a prophecy. In those times, the flying squirrels, who have always been gifted with the innate magic of the seer, took great pride in grooming the abilities of their young ones. The flying squirrel in question, however, had not shown any signs of power before the white squirrel's coming, which convinced everyone further of their own suspicions. The real problem, however, was how the prophecy chose to come and what it told of."

"What do you mean?"

"It was a prophecy telling of destruction, of the greatest breach of faith and peace between squirrels, all at the hands of a newborn child. The flying squirrels had reason to be afraid, and upset. You can only imagine how the offspring of a white squirrel and a flying squirrel must look. The flying squirrel did not appear to be with child, but that must have done nothing to alleviate their fear. The white squirrel left shortly after, just disappeared. And so the flying squirrels, normally peaceful creatures, could think of no solution but to rid themselves of the baby when and if it came."

Mae was terrified.

"You mean—you can't mean…?"

"Yes, I'm afraid that's how it is told by those flyers who have been around long enough. But they agonized over how to do it, because their conscience would not give them rest. The mother became pregnant long after the white squirrel had left—seasons and seasons, in fact, so it didn't seem possible, and that made everyone afraid. Some among the flyers of Edgewood say to this day that the child was disposed of. Some say that the mother escaped with it. Today, it is not fully known what happened, except perhaps by select members of the colony, the type who hoard away documents of the past from prying eyes. It is known that the mother did leave, though whether she saved the child is not clear. One of the other squirrels in the colony may have tried to divine for the mother, but they could not find her."

"Did they ever divine for the father?"

"The magic of the father was likely too strong for that, being a fully grown white squirrel. And, again Mae, you are not entirely right. I have given this great thought, and it does make sense if you know one more thing about the white squirrels. It is something no one else is supposed to know, and I am going to tell you."

"What?" Mae had been ready to protest; she hadn't expected this last bit from him.

Zirreo smiled. "Oh, yes, I am. We have a place."

"A…place?"

"Yes. We have a place that no one else can find unless they are told about it. Where do you think all the white squirrels disappeared to? They were so ashamed after what happened with the flying squirrels became widely known, that they went back to the Place and haven't come back since. You cannot go there unless you are a white squirrel. It is not a place within Arborand, and it is not entirely a physical sort of thing."

Mae realized her mouth was open just in time to stop from salivating.

"Like…like heaven or something?"

Zirreo laughed. "No. It would not be possible for evil to exist in heaven, don't you think?"

"Are you saying evil exists in the place you go to?"

"Well, now you're hitting upon my theory, Miss Mae. I have come to believe," he stopped moving, and Mae stopped alongside him. "that the reason Kiroba could not divine where the child was, was because the child was in this Place of ours."

"But…how?"

"You may well ask that, and I am not sure. But I believe that the mother squirrel was smarter than they gave her credit for. I believe the father must have told her where the Place was, foolish as he was in all the rest, and that it served her well in this case. She would have gone to the place, and cast a spell to get her child across the hidden barrier. A spell that either required sacrifice, or, as is more likely, killed her in the effort to cast it. And then she sealed the barrier."

"What?"

"She sealed the barrier between the two worlds, so to speak. She made it so her child was safe forever beyond the barrier in the immaterial world of sorts, safe from harm, and so she thought, safe from harming others at the same time. After that, white squirrels were able to cross into the Place of theirs, but they found they could not go back. And that is why there appear to be none of us in Arborand anymore. Rupert thought I was the only white squirrel left living, which is not true. But he also thought I was the only white squirrel left in Arborand, and *that* just may be true."

"So...how did *you* escape the same fate?"

"I was far from the barrier when the other whites started crossing it. So many of them crossed in a rush to get away from the anger against them and to find peace, only to realize too late that they could not get back. There were others, besides me, who did not cross over, of course, who figured out what must have happened in time. But they seem to have died, as I have not been able to seek them out."

"Seek them out?"

"Contact them. Another thing, another important thing we can do, is find each other through our minds. I can figure out where others are, depending on how strong their magic is in relation to mine."

Mae was astonished, and was about to ask a question, but Zirreo answered it neatly for her, getting there first.

"No, we cannot communicate across the barrier. Divining is a power that Kiroba and many of the flyers of the past hold over me. I do not have the power of a seer. So while I could not be certain that the barrier had closed, and that the mutant child had somehow gotten through, my suspicions built over time. Slowly, the few white squirrels left in Arborand died off, or seemed to disappear. I was in contact with no one, so I immersed myself as best I could into life with other squirrels. They never completely trusted me, and I had a rough time of it before I was befriended by a gray squirrel named Ritorren, and later also had the privilege of knowing his family and his son, Floridem and *his* family."

"That's Flor's namesake!"

"Yes. And Rupert's father. I regret that I never told him my suspicions of what had happened and the danger we might be in at any time, but I was displaying a gross weakness—one that many squirrels have, I believe, and sometimes we are unable to escape it, no matter how intelligent we may be otherwise." His face got a little sad around the edges, and Zirreo said, "I was afraid of losing his friendship, that he would believe the superstitions of the others, and so I refrained from speaking much to him about magic, even when…it would have helped a lot."

"What exactly were your suspicions, then?" Mae asked.

"I believed that the flying squirrel mother's prophecy was correct, essentially. I believed that the child born a mutant would bring destruction, just as she said. I hesitate to say anything can be truly evil, can grow up evil, but isolation, even when it might have been meant to protect, can do horrible damage, a damage worse than abuse. In a way, neglect is its own type of abuse."

Zirreo paused for only a moment.

"Time passes slower in the place beyond the barrier. You can come back to Arborand after a time and so much time will have passed that a loved friend in that world could have passed away— yet another reason we don't make a habit of associating with the other races. The child would have grown up slowly. Because it was a mutant, the child would not have been able to get the full benefit of the place it grew up in. It would have been isolated from even the other white squirrels there. I believe we have evidence that the mutant squirrel has abnormally high magical ability. He or she is very angry, deficit of normal emotions which should perhaps have formed in the early stages of life. It is my belief that this mutant has become no less than a monster, and a monster who is trying to break the barrier. To get out again, and in so doing, wreak the destruction that was prophesied so long ago."

"But how…how would they do that?" Mae asked. A sense of terror was curling around her insides, and she was glad they were no longer moving, because the truth was something worse than she had feared, and she no longer trusted her feet to keep her up. She felt dizzy with what she was hearing.

"I believe, perhaps because they are a half-breed themselves, and because they have insanely powerful magical ability, this mutant is able to get into the minds of others *on the other side of the barrier*, possess them if their soul is right, and get them to do his or her will."

"Callisto."

"Yes, and *that* is interesting. The mutant seems to be working chiefly through Callisto, and judging from what you say of him, the mutant must be a female. She appears to be telling him she is Astrippa, and I think it is also clear that she has limited power in that she can only speak to other half breeds."

"Oh." Mae felt ridiculously glad for this, if all it meant was that *she* was not in any danger of getting possessed anytime soon.

"Callisto is power hungry, cut out just right for the job. From the time I lived in Firwood near Rupert, ever since I knew Callisto, in fact, he had been talking to himself."

"Which means he's been possessed a really long time."

"Yes. Which also means that the squirrel beyond the barrier has had her plans moving along uninterrupted for perhaps longer than it is wise to think about. It is a distasteful but honest truth to say that perhaps it is too late."

"But we can't think like that!" Mae began to protest loudly, but Zirreo put a paw up to her face, his expression gentle.

"I don't mean we cannot try. I have thought on this during my time since Venul assumed he could kill me, a useful thing since being dead means one cannot be bothered…"

"Zirreo?"

"Yes?"

They had started to walk again, quick into the setting sun.

"What is this place called, the place beyond the barrier?"

"You're going to have to believe me when I tell you that we forget the name as soon as we leave it. I am not even sure it has one."

His face looked odd in profile, and occasionally she lost sight of it as they leapt from tree to tree, skirting around the occasional houses and towns they saw below.

"You miss it, don't you?"

"Can you miss a place that's hard to remember?"

Unbidden, vague thoughts of Firwood and running through the trees with Flor and that unspoken emotion of something strong and vibrant and young between them came rushing to Mae, and she knew the answer was yes.

Chapter Seven

Theo awoke, in a pattern he was getting used to, with a fear locked tight in his throat.

"*Theo.*"

"Oh, *go away*," he hissed angrily, sitting upright and clenching his paws on the sheets.

"*Theo,*" the voice taunted persistently, as if it were trying to be sweet. "*Come to the gate.*"

In a flash of instinct, Theo fished around the underside of the bed until he found the reassuring bulk in their bag which signaled the compass's presence. It was safe. Brinna had seemed trustworthy, but anyone could seem trustworthy in this day and time, and it was always good to be sure. He paused, then cursed as he realized he had used the same words which chafed at him so often. *This day and time. What* day and time?

Perris's voice coming up from the ground made him jump. "Pardon the intrusion, sir, but you are hearing the voice again, are you not?"

Theo figured lying about talking to himself was not going to come off well, and there was no one within hearing range anyway.

"Yeah, I am. It still doesn't say much. Actually, it's said more than my name now, it's telling me to—but this is all so ridiculous!" Theo closed his eyes tight, opened them, and stared up at the ceiling as if expecting the whole scenario to melt away if he were patient enough.

"Yes, sir? What did the voice say?"

"It told me to… 'come to the gate'. As if I'm doing that, whatever it means. As if I'd do anything some crazy voice tells me to do. You know, I've been thinking, and it really seems to me as if the compass might be…causing the voice. Or the voice *is* the compass. Something screwy like that."

"'Screwy' does seem to fit, sir," Perris said, but Theo could tell he wasn't being disbelieving. "Could I have a question, sir?"

"Er…yeah, I guess."

"Brilliant, sir. Well, let me ask you this: if the compass is talking to you, and telling you to go to the gate, and you are following the compass, are you not also going to this 'gate'? Sir?"

Theo blinked.

"I guess," he said again. Then, feeling rather lame, he added "But it was only a theory. Compasses don't actually talk."

"When I was putting the compass in the pack last night, sir, it did not move for me."

"Wha…?"

"Didn't move. It was frozen on the spot, sir."

Theo felt suddenly uncomfortable, but he gave it to the heat in the room.

"Perris, don't talk about that stuff unless I tell you to," he said.

Perris flung the pack over his back and looked at Theo for a second, eyebrows going all funny. Then he turned around. "Yes, sir," he said demurely.

Theo went as far as the doorway, paused, and turned about, looking at the unmade bed with the extra sheet back on it, folded up neatly. There were words in his mouth but he was afraid, and when he turned back, Perris was started down the stairs across the other room.

He stood there, lost.

Quickly Theo.

Theo took the steps two at a time, passing Perris on the way down. The room adjoining theirs had been empty, and so was the bar with the exception of one particularly drowsy fox squirrel, which was less surprising as it was daytime. But Theo thought of Brinna and of the motionless lump in the bed the night before, and thought that maybe Brinna might be out for a while now too. It left him with a lump of sadness that he hadn't really become accustomed to. There was some payment left on the table, chips of gold and a couple of sweet nuts from those who had come in earlier. Theo told himself that if he had had any payment, he would have put some up there as well. Maybe compasses could be melted for the silver. It wasn't like he'd miss it any.

No more than an hour after Theo's departure, the fox squirrel at the bar perked up his head from where it had been drowsily resting on his paws. Someone else had come in. Turning in his chair, he looked with anticipation at the door. It could be Migg with some sweet stuff from the county store, perhaps that would liven him up, and maybe luckily she had forgot their fight from...

But his thoughts trailed off. It wasn't Migg.

"Oh...oh mercy," he moaned.

The black shadow in the doorway came in out of the bright glare of the morning sun. The white streak across the monstrosity's face had the same effect as a great, bloated scar, corrupting the smile that jerked at the corners of its—*his* mouth for a second only.

The thing spoke, and the voice was reminiscent of a badly timed nightmare.

"Hello, dear John. Would you mind telling us where the little gray one went? I was wanting *so badly* to talk to him." He let out a laugh that was not a laugh at all, and then his face darkened as he leaned close to the frightened fox squirrel. "Unless you haven't *seen* him, which would be such a shame, because *I can smell him.*"

The eyes, Astrippa help me. He's mad. The eyes, don't look at them.

The fox squirrel whose name was not John pointed in the direction he had seen the strange gray leave.

"T-th-they…he went out an hour ago. Or so, yes…" his voice ended in a little shudder, which made the Wanderer crack up again.

"Oho. Useful, usefu-u-u-l!" He turned away, muttering something that sounded like "yes of course," and then turned back quicker than anything should be able to move, and pinned the hapless fox squirrel to the counter.

"Now, dear John, for some night of the soul, hmm? Do you believe in Astrippa?"

"I…um…" the fox squirrel couldn't think with the fear that pounded through his head, and he wasn't sure of the right answer.

Apparently, the Wanderer wasn't in the mood to wait for it.

Migg would come home later that day and wonder why her husband wasn't back from the bar yet, ready to face her with an apology for their latest score of bickering. Males could be so inconsiderate.

Rupert entered Ashwood the same way he had years before. Flor's age, probably, but he tried not to think about that whenever he could summon the power.

Apart from making sure they were staying on course, Rupert had come this way because he knew of a large colony of fox squirrels who lived just beyond the border in the north of Ashwood. He had accidentally run into them before, and he would have had no desire to run into them again if he weren't so desperate. But in a colony their size— if he remembered it correctly— there was bound to be someone who had something useful to tell him.

Rupert could only hope he would not be recognized, and really he doubted that he would. Last time he had come here, it had been with the impudent chickaree Kyan, and they had been shut inside by a nervous fellow named Glimrod. Rupert still didn't understand the actions the seemingly good-natured fox squirrels had taken with he and Kyan to this day, but he knew they would not be fool enough to try and lock him up with a score of armed followers behind him. Things like that could get very messy.

The tree was exactly as Rupert remembered it, except scaled down in size from a time when he had considered it enormously impressive. Still, there was no denying it was large, reaching up, and sloping oddly back down again, thick as five normal trees (and crushing some others on its way down), with the only window visible set in the peak of the slope.

Rupert led his squirrels up a thick, long branch which touched the trunk at what looked like the main entrance. He did not want to look like he was sneaking around. He was purely business here.

Rupert had hammered on the door about four times and counting, so that by the time someone bothered to open it, his paw hurt.

The squirrel staring out at them had wide, bright eyes and was compulsively chewing something that sounded very hard.

Trying to ignore the grinding sound, Rupert posed the usual questions, and the squirrel vanished again without a word. Rupert heard him yelling something to someone farther back, and figured he had taken whatever was in his mouth out. When the young squirrel came back, the rock back in his mouth, he spoke between sucking and chewing.

"Sorry, sir, but Leader Glimrod says we can't answer those questions, on account of other…problems, sir."

Rupert straightened up.

"Glimrod—I know him!" So much for being anonymous. "Could you tell him that the leader of the Firwood grays would like to speak with him?"

The young squirrel looked doubtful. He turned to the side and spit his rock out. "I can ask him sir, but I'm not sure he'll be too keen on the idea."

But the squirrel never came back. Instead, Rupert saw the shadows in front of him stir, and the head of another poked out, a squirrel who was tired and worn looking beyond belief. His face registered no recognition in Rupert, and he knew that last time he had seen this squirrel there had been moons between them. Perhaps they had never belonged to the same world, Rupert thought, torn from thoughts of a time when he was young enough to believe in one big world.

When Glimrod spoke, it was mechanical.

"You cannot possibly want anything from us," Glimrod intoned. He wasn't angry, Rupert realized. But instead of comfort, this just gave Rupert's flutterings of fear more cause to flap harder inside his chest. It was the tone of hopelessness.

"Our leader is gone," Glimrod continued. "We found his head at the base of this tree, his body up on a branch above this one, hanging like some sick flag. He was in correspondence with them, Pernil was. I never knew it. Half of us never knew it, so it fits that I'd be in that half, don't you think?" He gave a dry laugh which wasn't really. "I can't find your children, and in this day and age, you should've made sure they stuck by you all the time, shouldn't you? I'm not judging. I'll tell you one thing. The Dark Wanderer exists, plain and simple. He exists, and he's ruined our lives."

Rupert knew the fox squirrels, hidden in their colony with all their impressive shelves of books and chipmunks to wait on them, were really hiding from the stink of their own cowardice. But he had no idea how to draw them out of it and wasn't entirely sure it was his business to try.

"He's starting an army," the sated Glimrod said, not indicating that he cared whether Rupert was hearing him or not, but more like he was trying to justify his own lack of motives. "They're going to come to him when he needs them."

"An army?" Rupert said, sticking his paw in the way of the door Glimrod was in the process of closing. He was thinking of the misty-eyed squirrel they had met earlier, the way he had been almost in a trance, how he had declared being a part of 'Astrippa's army', the way that had sent chills through he and Dewlim.

"Oh nuts," Dewlim whispered softly behind Rupert, and Rupert knew he had just came to the same thought.

"There's danger for all of us, most of all for those who don't keep out of his way," Glimrod said in a dull voice, and he wrenched the door away from Rupert, closing it with a final clunk.

Rupert stood for a moment behind the closed door, and he could hear Glimrod breathing, waiting for them to leave.

"Should we be going?" One squirrel suggested from the ground. Rupert turned, held up a paw and shook his head. Turning back to the door, he shouted "Fight with us!" He got no reply, which was expected, and kept right on going. "We are going to meet this army the Dark Wanderer has planned. I don't know what they're doing, but whatever it is, it can't be good! We're not going to let him go on with it without any resistance. Claim the pride of your colony back! Fight!"

The breathing behind the door became ragged, and there was a shuffling, scuffling sound.

"I'll fight!" came a voice, and the young bright-eyed squirrel finally forced his way past the door. "I'll do it!" he proclaimed, slightly out of breath.

"Dasmon, no!" Glimrod groaned, attempting to pull the youngster back by his tail, but Dasmon flicked him off irritably. "Dad, don't you see? We've got to do *something*!"

Rupert had expected Glimrod to say something, to fight back against the creeping younger generation with some sort of retort, but he was silent.

"I will get you some others," he said momentarily. "They will bring spears and bows, superior to what you have and light to carry."

Rupert did not acknowledge the insult. "Thank you. But you, Glimrod? Will you not come with us?"

The other's eyes would not meet his own.

"Don't get me wrong, Rupert, I wish you all the best in this, as well as…finding your children, if that is possible now…but I will not walk into death so willingly."

They stared at each other across the moons separating them, from their respective worlds.

"There are worse things than death," Rupert said, so quietly he almost said it to himself, except Glimrod heard it, and shut his door against the words. He did not make another appearance, though soon the troops came out, a good number of squirrels, as promised, and they were ready to go.

As Rupert started away, back on the trail southwest, the young Dasmon caught up with him.

"*You* don't think me foolish, do you...?"

"Rupert. You can call me that way. And no, I don't. There's a great deal of difference between being foolish and being young, but all too often the two do coincide. It's when they don't that a blessing is thrown on the air."

"They're not bad, really," Dasmon said, of the others. "They're just afraid. They've been afraid too long." He stooped to pick up a round, smooth rock and stuck it in his mouth in place of the other from before. "I'm afraid of a lot of things. I'm afraid of war, and the Wanderer, and even thunderstorms. But I'm not afraid to die. It's just how that worries me."

The young squirrel sucked on his stone, and thought, and Rupert looked at him and saw Flor and Mae at once, and had to look away. But he was smiling when he did so, and soon after, he gave the order to take to the trees again.

Chapter Eight

Theo and Perris had been walking in a strange, mystical stream of mist with the sounds of frogs and insects among them for days now. The fog had gotten so thick that it clouded the surface of the compass and made it near impossible for Theo to make anything out, but for once Theo's attention was mainly on the forest around them anyway.

"What *are* these?" he asked, for the second time since they had met the Redwood Forest. "They can't be trees. Whoever heard of a tree this big?" He patted a trunk nervously.

"I don't doubt they're trees, sir. If you would, notice the distinctive bark. It always helps me, sir." Perris was padding close behind, regarding the trees with vague discomfort.

"Well, at least this fog is telling us one thing," Theo said, changing the subject. "It means there's water nearby. And where there's water, an end to our ramblings for sure." He did not hide the complete relief he felt.

"I agree, sir." Perris's voice held the same relief.

Yes.

Theo shook his head angrily, and the voice seemed to back off, because he did not hear it again. He stopped and rubbed his eyes, looked up a redwood, couldn't find the top, and looked down again. This felt like some sort of bizarre dreamscape they had wandered into.

Western Beechwood, never again.

"Pardon the intrusion, sir, but are we going the right way, or can you read the compass yet?"

Theo's consciousness jerked back to the problem at hand, and he started trudging along again immediately.

"Yes, I'm sure."

And he was. For all the trouble it had given him formerly, at least the voice had told him that much.

They muddled on together, two lone forms making their way through the mists.

Although she and her companion had talked rather openly about many of the topics on her mind, Mae was still having trouble bringing up the one thing she worried most over: the subject of her own magic. Was it a lot, or a little? Generally good or bad in the use? Were strengthened intuitive powers all she possessed, or was there more she had yet to tap into?

It was noon when she and Zirreo passed a thatched hut, sheltered in the branches of an elm which had seen better days. At first, Mae made to pass it by completely, but then she noticed the squirrel sitting out on the porch. Old and bent, he was a dark gray in color, suggestive of a rare crossbreeding.

Zirreo stopped completely.

"This is a trading post, if my eyes do not deceive me," he told Mae. "Unless you have any strong objections to the idea, I think you ought to go inside to get us a thing or two."

Mae was poised to ask the question of why Zirreo was not to accompany her, when she realized the obvious truth a bit late and shut her mouth. Zirreo had seemed to know all the least inhabited paths through the trees and on the ground, and she knew this must be because he did not want to draw attention to himself, or be seen at all if they could help it.

"What shall I get?" she asked.

"A bow and arrows might be nice for me, if he has them," said Zirreo, as if he were just now thinking up an inventory. "And whatever you would use in the sad but likely occasion of a violent surprise. Also, I would like some pipe reed, scented thyme."

Mae nodded, and she had already started away when she remembered she had nothing to trade. But when she turned back, Zirreo had gone, melting into the clutter of branches and leaves, and the old squirrel on the porch of the trading post was now looking at her.

Wondering what on earth would be the good of looking around now, Mae continued on her way. As she stepped up to the porch, the old squirrel bowed his head at her. He looked preoccupied with other matters, and Mae happened to look down and see the long, open cut that jagged its way across his right haunch.

Perhaps she had been staring too intently, because the squirrel finally looked her full in the face, and said, "Pretty, in't it?"

Feeling utterly lame and embarrassed for her rudeness, Mae just shrugged, and then because she couldn't help herself she asked, "How did you get it?"

"Red thieves," he grunted, apparently annoyed with the whole story. Then, noticing her look of confusion, "You'd know them as chickarees, maybe. They came, around three of 'em, wanting to know if I'd got something *shiny* for 'em. I said, I don't barter with chickarees. Turn your back, and they'll thieve any gold you got, as well as any supplies what suit 'em." He glared off into the distance for a scowling moment. "Anyway. These chickarees tried to rush past me, like in an organized effort or summat. Of course, if chickarees knew how to be organized enough to work together, maybe they would've been able to get something out of it. As it is…one of 'em rushes past behind me, and another one starts threatening me all garbled like. The other one ignores some sort of order by the first one to take a stab at me with a knife instead. I threw her off, and then she and the other started getting all fighty over 'who was boss' or some nonsense, and they fell off the tree that way, just managed to catch themselves later on, and I think they were too scared to come back up, they'd just let their pal take care of things. Said pal comes rushing out already by the time I remember him, and he's got a pawful of good luck stones, thinking they were genuine rubies, I imagine, and I corner him, and he gets a weapon out of nowhere. He was quick, too. Well, I managed to take back some of what he had, but I got this in return." The old squirrel gestured at his right side. "But you're here to trade for something, not to hear me prattle on about thieving chickarees."

"No, it's okay," Mae assured him, and taking her eyes from the nasty looking cut, she made her way inside, letting her eyes adjust to the dark.

"Whatever you decide upon, bring it out to me!" he called after her, and she nodded, even though she knew he could not see it.

The post was small and modest, with not too much to offer. Mae weaved slowly through the wood shelves, which were old and smelled of rosemary. It was dark and comforting in here, with tallow candles lit to set the mood of a time long past, perhaps even from the keeper's younger days.

Mae found the pipe reed first. She was lucky enough to note that they had thyme in stock, and took a packet for Zirreo, still wondering in the back of her mind how on earth she was going to pay for this.

There were no bows in the shop, but there was a sharp little dagger that looked like someone had carved it with a knife, or even with their own teeth, a skill which is naturally admired anywhere, not to mention rare. It was the only one in stock, and Mae, feeling a want she hadn't anticipated, took it for herself, and after feeling the ridges in the wood in a satisfied manner, carried her selections back outside, where the light made her look down for a time.

"That's a good knife," the keeper commented when she stood in front of him once more. "Chewn." This last confirmed her suspicions.

After standing awkwardly in front of him a bit longer, Mae finally came to the confession.

"I—I'm sorry, you must think me daft, but—

And then he winced, and leaned over with the sudden pain.

"Sorry," he said, through a strained grimace. "Leg acting up."

Mae did not know what made her do it.

"Let me help you with that," she said, and kneeling down, almost on all fours, she slid her paws up to where his cut was, pinching it closed with a murmured apology. Closing her eyes halfway, she reached within her well of intuition, felt her heart thudding vibrantly in her young chest, and got in tune with it, beating ever on, fresh blood in, old blood out. Then, when she was ready, Mae reached out for his beat, and found it, a slower one with a bit of a murmur to it. She matched them, closely, and the sounds filled her head until she felt she was in the womb of her mother once more. A faint humming came to her through the beating, and stayed with her, pursuing her, an electrical buzz.

And then it broke off. Mae's eyes, so heavy moments before, became a rational part of her head again, and she stared around, dazedly. Noticing she was still on the floor, Mae got up.

"I'm…"

She had been about to say sorry for collapsing on his porch in such a way, but the keeper of the shop was staring at her with wide eyes full of awe. Mae, who had never been stared at in such a way in her life, gave him a small smile as her eyes trailed down to his haunch. A jagged, puckered scar, thin and long, was all that was left of the cut. She had made it mend!

When he found his voice again, the keeper said, "I have never..erm, been at such a loss for words. My gratitude is—but how did you learn to do that?"

He did not seem alarmed at the magic, just surprised and grateful, for which Mae was thankful. She knew she had been right about the tallow candles and the older times which he longed for. She almost wished she could leave him with the promise of something else, then, but she knew that was well beyond her or anyone else to do, probably. Not knowing how to answer his question, Mae just picked up her items off the ground and said, "I—

"Paid," the old squirrel said firmly, which made a quick end to her discomfort.

"Well—thank you," she said, stepping off the porch. She realized she felt rather drained for the first time since she had taken the sleep where the colors were a part of the blackness.

"Thank *you*," he whispered back to her. "And good luck, whatever you're about."

When Mae got back to Zirreo, she handed him the pack of pipe reed without a word, and they began an alternate route around the trading post to keep hidden. It would be no good if a white squirrel were spotted in Arborand after the last one was rumored to have died.

While they broke for lunch (food taken from the flying squirrels' domain) Zirreo took some of the long, stiff reed from the pack and held it out to the sun patiently. While he did this, Mae brought up the subject of what had happened at the trading post at last.

"Zirreo, we didn't have anything to pay with. Or I didn't, at least."

"But you did."

Mae took one look at the knowing lift of his eyebrows and said, "Zirreo!" a little exasperatedly. "Why didn't you tell me?"

"I did not know you could do it yet," he said. "I saw the squirrel was in pain from the way he was sitting, and I figured it would be worth it to know."

Mae sat watching as he took the piece of pipe reed, rubbing the hot end between his long, dexterous white paws until smoke appeared. Putting it at an angle between two fingers, he breathed the smoke in through his nose, an expression of contentment coming over his face, before he breathed slowly out again. The scent of fresh thyme drifted over to Mae.

"This," Zirreo said, eyes still closed, an impudent look crossing his face, "Is how I survive confined to Arborand." He settled against a tree, tipping his head back, and took another sniff. "S'not so bad," he said, but once again she sensed he was covering up some deeper sense of sadness.

Mae suddenly realized how famished she was, and set to work gladly on a considerable hunk of oat bread.

Chapter Nine

When Theo came to the water, he was at first not sure if he was dreaming. It was still and the mists off the surface came rolling across the land, making his face damp. For some time now, he and Perris had been walking along a spit of land, the redwoods following them down on one side, guiding them. In their monstrous, looming way, the trees were a comfort, and they stuck close to them, for to their left was a gaping field of fog, and Theo knew without experiment that his feet might hit water if they veered too far off that way. But slowly, surely, the redwoods fell away, and the ground under Theo became damp. He stopped abruptly.

"Perris," he said, his voice a whisper, though he was not sure why he had made it so. "I think we're here."

"Yes, I suppose we are, sir," said the chipmunk from beside him now.

Theo looked out across the water, his eyes playing tricks on themselves. There was nothing here…when he strained his eyes hard enough he thought he could see some lump of land, thin across the water, but it disappeared at intervals, and then the fog got thicker for a moment, rendering his efforts to see altogether futile.

Now that they were here, Theo realized the stupidity of all he had done. It kept trying to catch at his mind, but he persistently pushed the feelings of self-condemnation away. There was simply nothing to find here. He felt half angry, like he wanted to throw the compass in the water and watch it drift out to where it might never come back---how much water was there anyhow? Was Arborand only a speck in this strange, shifting universe?

But another, newer part of Theo, a part he had not noticed there before kept insisting that there *had* to be something. There were signs, and…and yes, *the voice*, as much as he hated to think about *that* more than was absolutely necessary.

He looked over at Perris, and could see his face, patient, maybe pondering, next to him. As lost as he felt, he was glad, all of a sudden, that he was not alone. Watching Perris when he was sure the other was not watching him, he was surprised to see him experiencing doubt. But he was not saying anything, and Theo, in a rush of foolishness also realized that he *wouldn't* say anything.

Because at the heart of things, Perris believed him.

And all at once, the ground seemed to tilt up at an odd angle, and he could smell wet moisture all around, and Perris seemed taller than him, and then he heard something that sounded vaguely like a memory of being held, a soft voice, and the dizziness was over as soon as it had come, leaving him thoroughly disoriented.

"Are you all right, sir?" He was on the ground, and Perris was offering a paw to him. He allowed himself to be held up, and searched around desperately for the other voice he had heard, not the one from his head, but the good one, the soft, comforting one. It was gone, and he was sad for it.

I'm such a fool.

And Perris was telling him that he had fainted.

"Perris!" he said, really loud, and Perris stopped talking to stare at him, bemused. "I need…I need to tell you something…"

Perris waited. The words would not come to Theo, the frightening words that ran against his pride;

something in his mind would not let them. An odd, panicked feeling jumped in his gut. He thought for a moment he had heard something, a distant snapping sound or a cool thud against wood. Evidently Perris must have heard it, too, because he was turning quickly, nervously...

"Face me!" Theo said, loud, harsh, commanding, afraid to death he'd lose what he needed so badly to do, and Perris turned.

The dark shape that came suddenly out of the mist behind him gave Theo no chance to say anything further. It came without warning, and Perris's eyes, still wide on Theo, almost reproachful, fell away from him as Callisto pulled the dagger out of his back, licked it and spat.

"Chipmunk blood," he said, "It is like dirt. Yours, on the other hand, dear boy, will be *much sweeter.*"

Rupert and his band had come a long way in as short a time as possible, and most of them were exhausted. Even though they could not afford to rest for a long time, Rupert knew they must be a bit revitalized in order to face what lay ahead of them, whatever that may be.

Their stopping place was a place of memories for Rupert, a place he had thought he would never see again. And once again, he heard the falls before he saw them. With a fluttering of anticipation in his chest, he wondered if this was where they needed to be, and noticed rather unsurprised, that it had been where he was leading them.

The water fell down in torrents beside them, a solid rock wall on their other side. Squirrels were muttering to each other excitedly, and Rupert clearly heard the young Dasmon exclaim with glee at the dancing

colors in the water. Exactly what he had said was
drowned out by the loud roar of the water all around
them, echoing off the walls. Amid the noise, Rupert
turned around and signaled that they should all take a
breather for a bit, and Dewlim relayed the message to the
end of the line, where an elderly fox squirrel hadn't quite
seemed to get the message, still standing and sniffing
around.

While the rest of his squirrels were taking the
much-needed opportunity for rest, Rupert clambered,
yawning, up the embankment directly above the ledge
they were all seated on.

It is strange the feeling which comes from visiting
an old place, the painful and pleasurable nostalgia that
comes with a place which has changed your life in a
second or two once, quite probably without you knowing
it then. Coming back, there are the haunted, resonant
feelings of a time, the ghost of a self that you feel you
may be able to slip back into, all at once knowing it is
illusion. Words, however, are often, possibly never,
completely sufficient to describe such feelings. Suffice to
say that Rupert had found this sort of place here, and
naturally could not spend the time sleeping until he had
reacquainted himself with whatever it was he had left
behind.

He would remember the next moment forever, if
only because the impossibility of it drove at his stomach,
his mind, and his heart all at once, backing him up a
couple steps, until all he could do was stare.

The ghost of Zirreo stared back at him from its
spot on the ledge above the crashing falls.

Chapter Ten

"It is…quite all right, Rupert."

Rupert backed up a few steps, looking around nervously. The pale apparition in front of him was looking sympathetic.

"If there were a better way to do this, I assure you I would," it stepped closer. "Touch me, Rupert."

Rupert flinched in spite of himself as the figure came closer, reaching out a paw, but he did not move. He stood breathing, a long time just staring at the old white paw stretched out patiently before him. Then he put his paw on the other's, and his eyes came up, sharply, startled.

"Zirreo?"

The old white squirrel smiled, and chuckled deeply.

"Zirreo!" Rupert fell laughing into Zirreo's arms, and there was no need for words for some time after.

"But where have you been?" Rupert asked. They had found a secluded place, hidden by some bramble, on the bank of the river. Rupert was twisting a leaf around his paw over and over. He had told Zirreo about the dreams that had troubled him, and Zirreo had told him so much he could not begin to comprehend it all, about a compass, a possessed squirrel named Callisto, also known as the fabled Dark Wanderer, and a magical barrier to the place of the white squirrels. A barrier that was to be broken for evil to cross into Arborand.

"You disappeared. I thought you were…dead. Everyone thought you were dead," he said, and was surprised to find his tone more than a bit defensive.

"Well, I think *that* at least can be taken from the list of what others suspect of me. I am solid enough. But yes, I did disappear, and for that I am sorry."

Rupert twisted the stem of his leaf so hard it fell off.

"You *disappeared*? Literally or figuratively?"

Zirreo tried to hide a smile at his astonishment. "It was quite literal. I'm afraid Venul did not take it very well. He may well have died of a heart attack as well as vanished immortality."

Rupert stared. "But…but how does that *work*?"

"Now that is an unfair question. I could no more explain it to you than I could explain the existence of the chestnut years ago."

"You really don't know who made it?"

"I have a guess."

"You think it was the same squirrel who's possessing Callisto?"

A pause. "I don't know what to think. But if that is true, the implications are very disturbing. If she could magic something like that up, and then get it to Arborand from where she is, then she must know what she is doing to get herself out. And she must have been planning it a long time. I suppose in the time of the chestnut, the immortal black squirrels were to be her army. And again, under the name of Astrippa, who supposedly gave them that immortality."

His voice was harsh at this last, and Rupert could tell it got on Zirreo's nerves that the force they were up against was so blasphemous as to persistently pose as Astrippa in each new strategy. Rupert was unnerved by it too, if for a different reason. To him it meant that the enemy was showing no respect or even fear of the goddess, if they would use her name so freely to achieve their means.

"Zirreo?" he asked again, thinking immediately of something else, something he had pondered over for years. "Who moved the chestnut? Who put it here, under the falls?"

For some reason this question seemed to make Zirreo almost happy for a moment.

"No one," he said, taking out a stalk of pipe reed from the pack next to him, "knows *that*."

Rupert waited for more, but Zirreo was busy channeling heat towards the reed, and it did not look like he had anything more to say on the subject. Rupert was puzzled, but he changed his tack.

"What's it like to disappear? I mean, where do you go?"

"You go," Zirreo said "Invisible."

"Others can go through you?" Rupert asked, interested. He threw the leaf he had been fooling with into the water, and it floated away, cupping the water that flooded into it until it could not hold anymore, and was tugged under by the pulsing rapids.

"I thought we had been through this, my boy," Zirreo said, like he was going to laugh. "I was always quite solid. I lay there a while, letting Venul think he could get the better of me, and then when he was about to take my head very messily from my shoulders, I went invisible, slid out from under him, and watched his reaction to my heart's content." There was a glint of mischief in his eye.

Something had occurred to Rupert and his heart pounded in anticipation of the answer. "How long did you stay around after that?"

"Oh, not long."

Rupert's heart sank, but Zirreo continued. "I did not want to be run into while the black squirrels were milling about, the older ones dying on the spot from their outlived lives and all that. So I went back to my home, which was a rather brainless move on my part, for of course they had had it deconstructed while I was imprisoned. I took a trip over the border to Pinewood, seeing as most of the black squirrels had origins in Oakwood, and so were heading back that way. I waited in Pinewood for a week or so, occasionally walking out to look for your return. I saw the speech you made to everyone, the way you tamed their wild fears and brought them together."

Rupert looked up, wide eyed, and Zirreo met his gaze steadily.

"Never in my life have I been so proud of anyone."

Rupert looked away, embarrassed. "I wasn't—

"You would have done your father Floridem proud, as well. I wish—

But he trailed off in a way that was so unlike Zirreo that Rupert looked up at him once more, questing. This time Zirreo didn't meet his gaze, but threw the pipe reed in the water still smoking and lay silent for a while. Then he said, "You were looking for your children."

Rupert jumped up real quick. "You knew? Where are they, do you know?"

Zirreo held up a paw. He looked sorrier than ever.

"I do not know how to tell you this, Rupert—

And then, through the fear that had clenched up around Rupert's middle and the burning that drove at his eyes, came another voice.

"I will tell him. I-I should."

Mae stood at the top of the trail down to where they sat, her face rigid with the mix of emotions that had driven her to speak.

There was an intensity then, on the air between the two who had lost each other, and Zirreo knew he was no longer a part of their world for the time being.

Getting up, the old squirrel moved around them silently, to go down to Rupert's squirrels where they laughed and talked, under the falls. They needed another night, and Zirreo knew it was all they could afford.

Once, he turned and looked behind him, to where he knew Rupert was suffering in some bittersweet way.

Floridem would have been so proud he couldn't see straight. Wish you were mine.

He wondered what Flor had been like, this blood of Rupert's that had frozen young. What it would be like to lose a child, he could not guess.

"That sometimes it is necessary, I cannot comprehend," Zirreo mumbled to himself, wishing he had not thrown his pipe reed away so quickly. "Astrippa help me. Help us all."

And then, strong again as ever, he straightened and looked ahead. The squirrels here would not question another night's rest, would not worry overly about it. In their minds still, they had nothing to lose.

Rupert and Mae did not come down to the campsite that night.

And here I suppose there is something to be said for crying oneself to sleep. When it is done alone, loneliness settles heavy in the chest, and there is nothing to hold onto. But the two who lay twined together that night never let go of each other, crying when they had to cry so that their tears mingled, creating something like hope.

Chapter Eleven

Theo wanted to move, wanted to fight, to call for help, to do *something*, but the big black hulk of a squirrel was making it impossible for him to utter a word or complete a movement. His mind was frozen in place. Everything he had tried so hard to deny, everything he would not believe in was upon him at once, choking the life out of him. And he would not look at Perris.

Didn't die, that didn't happen, there was something I had to say, did not DIE.

The Dark Wanderer— for there was no use pretending anymore, *The Dark Wanderer*— reached out for Theo and he backed up clumsily, a move he hadn't thought himself capable of. His feet sunk into the wet ground behind him and he almost fell over, almost threw up.

With a horrid squelching sound, the Wanderer made it easily out to Theo this time and grabbed him by the arm. There was no way he was getting out of a grip like that, Theo thought at the same time as he struggled. And then the Wanderer pulled him up against himself, wrenching the compass from his grip and flinging it onto the sand next to them where it froze, motionless.

"You'll have no need for that anymore."

Theo could smell his scent; it smelled like death, and now his struggles were dying down and he felt drugged. He turned toward the water, unable to see his captor. But he could smell him. He could always smell him. That smell would haunt Theo forever.

A bright, hot light flashed through his mind, knifing through his body and Theo writhed back from the Wanderer, almost pulling free in his agony. A warm flow trickled down Theo's front, and he knew he had been cut, cut deeply, cut across the chest.

"Now there's nowhere to go, Theo," the voice, the grating, nightmarish voice reminded him. Then, "That didn't hurt much, did it? And you're done for now, you just have to lie there. They're coming, ever closer. All thanks to you, Theo. Hold still. There's nowhere to go after all. You've got no one."

No, no one. Not anymore.

Theo opened his eyes. He hadn't realized they were closed, but now there were spots in his vision. His mind felt fuzzy. He could see the Wanderer holding the compass in one paw, and in the other something that looked like paper, paper with writing on it, and blood

Whose blood? A faint trace of alarm, but it died away quickly.

The Wanderer wasn't talking anymore, just standing with his eyes closed, looking almost in pain, in concentration.

Goodbye then, he thought. There was sand beneath him, and in the dull corners of his mind, nothing had changed, and he was younger, irresistibly tired, and being carried to his room, laid on the bed, the blankets coming over him in the warmth which spilled down his chest, all around him now.

"Thank you, Perris." The words he'd been choking on came out real, whispered and ragged.

And the lights went out in his room. From somewhere, he thought he heard a yell, but he paid it no mind. It was high time for sleep…

Chapter Twelve

When the redwoods ended, Rupert saw them, far out on a spit of land. The Wanderer, Callisto as Zirreo had called him, was standing, an ominous shadow cutting into the fog. The young squirrel appeared to be lying on the ground, motionless.

Dead?

They could not have come all this way to be too late. They *would* not.

Rupert broke into a run.

Callisto turned to see them coming, a whole group of them. At first he had thought they were the army, who shouldn't be much longer after all. But no, you had to have those who needed to meddle, even after the fact. He cast a quick look at the ground, and noted to his satisfaction, that the sacrifice was weakening, almost unconscious. The young ones bled quick and long.

You see, Callisto?

Yes, I see.

Mae had been of aid. She had not been able to work the compass, and wouldn't work as a sacrifice, but with time she had led him to the perfect candidate. Astrippa had been right. All she had said had come to pass, and he was ready to reap the benefits.

Mae, who had practiced running with Flor long weeks which felt like years (*had it only been weeks?*) ago, knew how to run. She was even with Rupert, keeping pace until she saw the squirrel, stretched out and dying, dying or dead, *please don't let him be dead,* on the ground by the water. Then she broke ahead of Rupert and ran straight for the still form.

Rupert, watching her streak up the beach, let her go with much difficulty.

Dewlim came up beside him, panting rather heavily, and Rupert could tell that he had come from the very back of their ranks.

"There…are…squirrels…others…behind us. Pos—

But he was grabbed from behind, and Rupert had nearly run into the solitary figure of Callisto, smiling crazily at them all. Rupert made to move towards the big black squirrel, but someone was restraining him from behind.

Turning, he noticed with horror that he was being held back, his whole band was being held back by a mass of squirrels, all misty eyed and staring in the same manner as the squirrel they had seen on their way here.

Astrippa's army.

No, he corrected himself firmly. *Callisto's army.*

Rage burned through him, and he noticed Mae up ahead. She had not been restrained, and as she ran out to the form of the young squirrel on the ground, he felt real, live fear leap within him as well.

Don't you touch her, he thought at Callisto, and a low growl escaped his throat.

This was the squirrel who had killed his son.

The force of his thought seemed enough that Callisto actually turned to look directly at him.

And then Rupert recognized him. He had never actually seen this squirrel, but he remembered from a story, a story told to him by a friend of his father's once. A half breed squirrel with white twisting his otherwise dark face, making him look like some sort of devil, younger then. Lifting a stone spear high…

This was the squirrel who had killed his father.

And Rupert came to believe that he had not known true hatred until then.

Callisto turned from the squirrel, the gray one in the front of the mass. There was something in his eyes that...

You're scared. Why are you scared, Callisto? I am coming.

Coming. Yes. There was no need, indeed, to be afraid, for he would reap his reward.

Callisto noticed that Mae had come running over to Theo, but he hardly paid it any mind. Let her cry over him, the boy was good as dead. His blood was already floating out on the water, calling her. He had done the spell, and now it would not be long. The army would wait. He had handed them over to her.

Theo heard something dimly, murmurs, then someone touching his face. Putting up a paw, he swatted weakly at whatever was around him, but whatever it was persisted, saying things, asking him questions.

I don't know. Please go away. I need to rest. I don't know where my parents are, Perris put me to bed after I heard the noises. I don't know. Please go away.

A female's voice, soft and soothing, then, like the time he had stood staring across the water, before things fell apart.

Mother?

Something better, the voice answered, but it was a different voice, the voice he kept hoping he would never hear again. Would this be the last thing he would hear before he died?

Your creator. He tried to block it out, push it down, the paws above him touched his chest and he felt a numbing pain spread throughout his body. He could not stop it. Something was wrong. Something was terribly wrong.

YES.

Theo screamed.

Mae started from where she was trying to get a good grip on the young gray squirrel. He was struggling so much now, twitching, and she knew he was dying.

She tried to get herself together, tried to think about healing.

I need to make him better.

She had seen him across the land, knelt down beside him, and then he had ceased to be a stranger anymore. He was Flor.

He was Flor, he was dying, and this time she needed to save him. She could reverse what had happened if only she could save him. Mae tried to close her eyes, tried again to concentrate, but she kept having fears that the damage was too deep, that her magic would not be strong enough.

And Flor kept bleeding in her head.

The young squirrel beneath her screamed, something terrible again, and the formerly calm water slapped one, strong, breathtaking angry wave against the shore, coming up and over the injured squirrel, driving sand and water into his wound, and then the surface went still again.

Mae felt a sense of dread, so terrible that she was forced to look up and across the water, and she saw it before anyone else. A shape, some sort of creature was walking across the water toward them, getting ever closer. She did not feel its presence as anything akin to her at all, and she was afraid. The young gray that looked like Flor went still beneath her, not before murmuring something very quietly, weakly. Mae leaned close so she could hear, but she could not make sense of what she heard at all.

"The gate has opened."

\---

Rupert saw the shape coming across, as did the squirrel holding him captive, who was strong but strangely blank as he stared with those milky eyes, waiting for an order, perhaps.

This thing controls them, he thought suddenly. He looked at Callisto, who was riveted to the spot, oblivious to anything except the approaching form. *Controls them all.*

From behind him, he heard a scuffle, and managed to turn around to see one of the enemy army looking confused and angry.

"We've lost..." came a hiss.

"Shh…" another hissed at the one who had spoken.

"But the white squirrel—

"Really."

The second squirrel slit the throat of the first. Warm flecks of blood hit Rupert's cheek, and the crowd behind him was silent once more.

Zirreo. Where did Zirreo go?

But the form of the squirrel coming across the water was clear now. For it *was* a squirrel, but Rupert could hardly have recognized it as such for its freakishness. Albino, it's eyes a gleaming red, wing-like structures stretching like webs between its front and hind legs. It was quite young looking, an effect of the place from which it had come. The squirrel stood, not touching a foot to the ground, staring out at them all with those burning red tinted eyes, and there was anger coming from those eyes, real, tangible, sickening anger. Rupert understood everyone's fear. Most squirrels hated while all the time wishing they had no reason to. This squirrel thrived on the hate, worked on perfecting it. And it had been successful.

A javelin came soaring out of the crowd. One of the squirrels from Rupert's army had broken free from her restraints and aimed straight at the mutant squirrel, standing seemingly so large on the water's edge. The mutant didn't even attempt to move aside, and the javelin stopped in midair, close to her face, falling to the ground. The air around the mutant crackled, and all Rupert could think was *oh, Astrippa, help us all, she's maintaining some sort of invisible force field.* And at once he knew, almost as if the mutant wanted him to know, had sent the thought over, that she was maintaining it out of hate, hate and pure power, and the anonymity of every face staring back at her out of the crowd.

Then the mutant stretched out her paws, the fingers bending at an odd angle, and narrowed her eyes. Someone screamed, and Rupert turned as much as possible in the arms of his captor. He wished he hadn't. The squirrel who had rose so bravely up against their doom was hung suspended a few inches from the ground, screaming and screaming like her insides were on fire. A sickening, cracking noise came from the area of her head, and the victim slumped, lifeless, to the ground, blood flowing from her nose and eyes.

We're nothing. We're doomed.

And then the mutant spoke.

"I would think you would be more inclined to give a better greeting to your goddess. But I have come. And I will judge. Callisto," she said, and her voice was softer.

Callisto looked up from where he was lying huddled in a deep bow on the sand.

"Yes, Astrippa?"

"You have done your job well. Delayed," She said, and a slight snarl curled the side of her face, "but well." She then turned her burning eyes to the crowd and appeared now to be addressing her army.

"Kill the nonbelievers."

Chapter Thirteen

Rupert was knocked to the ground hard, and felt a lump already beginning to rise where he had been hit. The squirrel who had been holding him was bearing down on him now, his milky white eyes seeming not to see Rupert at all, but Rupert knew better.

Stumbling over himself, crawling away, he was grabbed by someone else, felt a knife at his throat, cool hard metal ready to crush his life out of him...

"Ugh!" his attacker crumbled behind him, as Dewlim gave him an axe to the head. Shakily the other smiled at him, but there was no time for words. They were swept up in the escalating battle and its deafening noise. Dodging and weaving his way through the melee, Rupert was caught more than once in combat with another, and more than once he slid his knife—a fine piece of work that Mae had given him tearfully the night before— cleanly through their ribs, darting away before they could get a final lunge at him.

He did not pause to consider that his enemies were under the workings of a spell, because to do this would only make it harder for him to fight. Rupert had never been one for war, but now his mind was on one thing only.

He would find Callisto, and he would kill him.

Through the crowd, he thought he caught sight of a flash of black, but it turned out to just be another squirrel, one of the mutant's army. He turned quickly, saw Callisto this time, off separated from the rest. He had a younger squirrel by the ruff of the neck, and had slammed him up against the trunk of a redwood. Rupert sped in their direction, dodging when he could, and chopping down anyone who refused to budge. The young squirrel cried out in pain, and Rupert recognized the voice.

Dasmon.

Mae knelt over the gray who reminded her of Flor, still trying desperately to heal his wounds, but every time she would start to ease herself into the place where she worked best, the young squirrel would twitch and jerk away from her paws before going limp again. To attempt to soothe him, she had tried to talk to him.

"Sssh, I'm only trying to help you. Can you hear me? My name is Mae. I'm trying to heal you, but you need to hold still so it can work. Can you hear me?"

Theo could almost see sometimes through the mist that was clouding his thoughts and vision. Someone was leaning over him, talking to him, but he didn't know what they wanted. It wasn't the voice, but it wasn't his mother either.

Heal, he heard, and felt something warm spread through him. He jerked away instantly.

No.

No, that was bad. He couldn't heal, it would make the gate close. And then they would all die.

"No."

Rupert reached Callisto, just as Dasmon gave another scream, which quickly turned to a whimper as he collapsed near the trunk of the tree, breathing hard.

"Dasmon," Rupert said, making to bend down, but Callisto struck out at him, and Rupert felt his claws rip across his cheek. He reached up to touch the wound, and his paw was slippery with blood. Callisto went again for young Dasmon, who was beginning to crawl for his dropped weapon, and Rupert noticed that he sported a deep cut in his side. So Dasmon had gotten a hit in.

As Callisto went to inflict more pain, his face curled in a snarl, Rupert stepped between the black squirrel and Dasmon, readying his own knife. Callisto seemed to hesitate for a split second, and Rupert drove himself at the bigger squirrel, knocking him off balance. Callisto snarled close in his ear, something about death, but Rupert thought of Flor, his only son, and of his father, the father he had never known, and did not answer. He was pure concentration. This was a fight he did not intend to lose.

Mae propped Theo up slowly, leaning him against her as she worked. She had managed to begin healing the gash on his chest, despite his struggling and protesting. She could not understand his reluctance to heal, but thought it perhaps had to do with his delirium. There was chaos roaring all around them, and the presence of the mutant squirrel, the one with the burning eyes was very close by, watching with satisfaction. As if it was all a show. And yet no one was bothering them, almost as if they did not exist here on the edge of the water, and Mae was confused over this.

"Theo," the squirrel breathed to her, "Theo."

His name. She had it at last, and it could not have fit more perfectly, she found herself thinking.

"Look, Theo," Mae said, with an intake of breath, her eyes roving out across the water.

Theo was starting to see through the mists again, and he heard her voice as if from behind a door.

Look, Theo, his mother agreed, distant, leaving. *Look, darling.*

Wait!

But she did not. Theo's vision was coming back. And then he saw them. Out across the water, there were shapes in the air, far away and distant, back where he had imagined seeing an island before, only now they were squirrels. Shy, sad, faces peered at them, almost made of clouds, only to disappear again behind the fog before he could get a good look at them. Something in the faces calmed him, and for a second he forgot about the gate, forgot how he was not supposed to let himself be healed. He leaned up against Mae, felt her heartbeat against his spine, and willed it to give him strength. One of the squirrels in the distant sky seemed to smile.

Then the mutant spoke, and everything slid to a stop. Theo almost lost consciousness again, for he could hear her voice, loud and clear, vibrating through his head, setting his nerves on fire. If she stayed here much longer, he would die anyway. And she would stay here. There was no way to get her back.

"Now," the mutant squirrel said, lifting her paws. The air around her crackled with intensity, reflecting the sparks in the red eyes. She lifted her paws, and the wing structures, so similar and yet so different to a flying squirrel's, appeared transparent in her ghostliness, so that everyone on shore could see the red of the veins shooting through them. It wasn't natural, and it made Rupert shiver, from where he had paused, locked in combat with Callisto. Callisto moved a bit to the right, waiting for word from his mistress, and Rupert noticed that he was wincing, as if her voice were a million times louder than it actually was. He should have taken advantage of the opportunity then, but it seemed the mutant's eyes were fixed on his, and it seemed she had the same effect on everyone else, for everything went deadly silent and everyone paused in their actions, focus gravitating toward the flaming red eyes as if they could not look away.

Perhaps they couldn't, Rupert thought. He looked out among the other squirrels gathered there, and was shocked to find that most of those lying strewn across the beach were his own. It filled him with an empty lead feeling of guilt and sadness. Sadness that things should ever have to come to this, that life should take such a turn.

And then, as if brushing his sad thoughts aside as inconsequential, the mutant raised her paws high again, began to speak. But another voice had come from somewhere in the crowd, and despite its softness, Rupert was able to hear it clear as day. It was a voice he knew well.

"Nebula."

Zirreo stood off to the side, as though he had come from nowhere, a polished bow of white wood with an arrow notched in it in one paw. He was staring directly at the mutant, who had turned at the word, looking startled, unprepared for the first time. Their eyes met and held for a time, and Rupert had no way of knowing what had passed between them, but in that instant he knew. He remembered Zirreo telling him the story of how the mutant had come into being, of the mother who had most likely sacrificed herself bringing her offspring here, and of the missing father. His eyes found Mae's for a second across the beach, and he saw that she knew as well.

The arrow found its mark, drove itself deep into Nebula's chest. Her force field had been down for an instant, and an instant was all it took. Looking down at it, she brought her paw to her chest as if unable to register what she found there. Then she looked up again, and the fire went out in the burning eyes as her body arched backward, and she fell slowly, soundlessly to the ground.

A muted, waiting silence held onto the crowd like magic, and no one moved. No one except Zirreo.

Moving forward slowly but deliberately, he approached the prone form of Nebula, looking down for a moment, face turned away from them. Then he lifted her up, easily, with a strength no one would have expected from a squirrel of his age, and began to walk across the water away from them all. He went slowly, but he did not look back.

Chapter Fourteen

Theo had gone limp in Mae's arms, all the blood drained away from his face. When finally Zirreo's resolute form disappeared beyond her line of vision, she was able to break her gaze away from the horizon, and then she feared she was too late. Still, Mae put her paws again on Theo's half-knitted wound, and a strength came humming up from within her, from her very core. She listened closely to the rhythm of her own heartbeat, and then quested out to Theo and found what she was looking for. His own heart was growing weaker, beating ever slower, making his blood sluggish. But Mae caught up to it, and clung to it with her own, bringing it up to speed until all that existed were their two hearts, thumping in unison, and a world of black. When next she opened her eyes, Theo's wound was closed, leaving an ugly scar across his chest, but still the young gray did not move. A jolt came across the water, as suddenly as Theo had been healed, and a cold wave came crashing over Mae, leaving her soaking and uncomfortable.

The gate had closed.

Rupert, too, found himself entranced by Zirreo, watched him leave, watched him walk across the water away from him until he couldn't see anything at all and the distant horizon blurred with his tears.

Will I ever see him again? He thought to himself, and was not surprised to find he was not at all sure of the answer. What was this place Zirreo went to, even? Zirreo had been like a father to him, and he wanted to go, pull him back or come along, but even before trying he knew that he would not be able to cross over no matter how he wished it, that Zirreo was beyond him now, no longer a father to anyone.

The squirrels of the so called army of Astrippa were waking from their spell-induced slumbers, looking troubled or frightened as they blinked around at each other. Rupert realized they had no idea where they were, and when one of them tripped over a body of someone he had possibly slain himself, he let out a little scream.

Callisto was not in shock. Nebula's death, the snapping of the line which had been hooked into his mind for so long had merely rocked him back on his feet, causing him to lose his orientation for a few minutes. But now he was back to himself, lost, questing out in his mind and coming back with nothing. Nothing, except that he had some unfinished business to attend to with the gray standing dumbly next to him.

Theo opened his eyes. Glancing around dazedly, he attempted to turn and look at whoever was holding him.

"Mae," she said.

The name had a familiar ring to it.

"Theo."

"I know."

Theo was silent. There were a thousand different things he could have said, over half of them painful, and none of them would change a thing. On sudden inspiration, Theo looked about for the compass, but could not find it.

"Where did…?"

"I think it got washed out to sea," Mae answered him. "It's a good thing, really. There's no need for it. All the white squirrels are…back where they were,

only…well, this time I don't think they can come back."
She didn't know why she thought it, but she did. "You
know, I think he gave it to her. I think he made that
compass and gave it to his wife, the flying squirrel. So she
could find this place."

Theo noticed that she was talking more to herself
than him when she said it, so he didn't ask what she
meant. Something new had dawned on him.

"You…how do you know about the compass?
Did you—were you---the one who—

"Left it with you, yeah." Mae looked away from
him. "I'm sorry. It's hard to explain. I was told by
someone that I had magic, mostly really strong intuition,
and that intuition told me to go to you, and…well, leave
it with you."

Theo might once have been angry; but that was a
long time ago, when he had been a different squirrel, the
cynical orphan who had come here without purpose, with
only fear and a need to escape it.

"I died, for a while," he whispered, not knowing
whether Mae would believe it or not, but feeling
somehow that it needed to be said. She said nothing to it.
She believed him, then. Theo knew this was something he
needed.

"Your chipmunk saw me," Mae said, after a while.
"I thought maybe he would have remembered, told you
he saw me with the compass."

A burst of buried pain. "Perris."

"Hmm?"

"Perris. That's his name."

At first he did not even register the tears, wet
against his cheek, and then Mae was tightening her hold
on him.

"I didn't get to say thank you. I didn't even get to say good bye. I didn't know my parents. He was all I really…"

"I know," said Mae, thinking of a journey she had taken once. "It's okay, I know…"

Rupert turned at the pain he felt in his side, looked down and saw the knife too late, sticking out below his ribs at an angle. Deep. It had gone deep. How could he have been so stupid as to leave Callisto unguarded? He drove himself madly at the other squirrel, clicking his teeth in rage.

Callisto, formerly ready for the attack, did something odd. It could be said that perhaps it was then that he realized the full extent of what he had lost. For the first time he could remember in years, Callisto ran. He ran out to the water and kept running, even as Rupert's dagger lodged itself in his back.

As the water swallowed him up, pounding in his ears, beating an eternal drum against his mind, and the scent of his own waterlogged blood filled his nostrils, only one thought drifted through his mind, heavy and useless, unanswered from an irrelevant childhood.

Astrippa?

Astrippa, where are you?

Back on shore, Rupert finally gave in to the pain, and leaned over, falling backwards onto the ground. He propped himself up against the redwood nearby, breathing heavily.

"Rupert?"

It was young Dasmon, lying motionless in the sand nearby, where he had fallen before.

"Are you going to die too, Rupert?"

"I don't know, Dasmon," he said honestly.

"Oh. Well," he said, and his voice quivered. "I hope Astrippa comes real soon."

What exactly happened next was up to anyone's speculation. Some said it was widespread jubilation at the fall of a dangerous enemy. Others said it was the effects of the salt and the fog finally settling on a gathering of so many. But still others would say that Astrippa indeed had come at last.

Chapter Fifteen

Rupert felt Dasmon's young life leave his body warm and turned, looking at the small form lying on the sand beside him. Rising, he buried it in what seemed a matter of minutes, tenderly, without pain. Someone moved next to him, within him, and it was another squirrel, and he loved the other squirrel if just for that fact alone, and there were so many of them all here together. It was wonderful, he thought like a child.

Rupert stared down at the knife in his side, pulled it out. For a moment there was pain, and then the pain ceased to matter. Mae came up the beach toward him, mud covering a good deal of her, the young gray squirrel supported at her side. She exclaimed over his wound, but he said *It's all right*, and could hear his words repeated up and down the beach.

> *It's all right.*
> *It's all right.*
> *It's all right.*

Theo, leaning up against Mae, felt close to her in a way that made his chest hurt, and it was wonderful. There was something in the air, the same as after a thunderstorm perhaps, when the world goes quiet, or after someone says *I love you*, and he knew he had felt this before, a thousand little places in his life. Perhaps he had always been so sad because somehow he had looked past it, looked past this because it was so simple, like being, and it was so *good*.

Mae turned to him, and she was saying *come back with us*.

Yes. Theo gave it no hesitation; she left his side and he stood, and thought *some things are no good describing*. The air smelled wonderful, and every second was a new second and the youngest he would ever be. It didn't scare him. He wondered why it ever should. A squirrel next to him screamed in rejoicing at finding someone she knew alive in the crowd, and Theo rejoiced with her.

Thank you Thank you Thank you.

He wondered why the words had ever seemed awkward on his tongue, why they had been frightening. After all, they were just words, and words were not nearly enough.

But perhaps they're the best we have. The best we can do.

Mae came back over to Theo, and she smiled at him, letting him know she was with him here. Then she took his paw and they left, all of them, every last soul on the beach. They cried, and that was okay, and they laughed, and that was also okay.

They were going home.

Epilogue

Moments so pure as the one on the beach, whatever you would say it was, pass, of course, and truth goes back to assuming elusiveness as the mind takes everything under its wing again. But an attempt can be made at preservation, and whatever they might have thought of it, the squirrels in the group traveling that day had felt a bond that they did not wish to discard.

And so they did not. Traveling together on their way to different places, making new friends even as they went, and sharing food, the large troupe of squirrels was quite a spectacle for the towns it crossed through on the way home.

Gradually, their group would get smaller as its members lived scattered across Arborand. Their journey was easy, uneventful, and they did not rush. Leaving behind the redwoods and the spit of land near the water felt almost like leaving another land, a land which almost seemed fictional in looking back.

Rupert had had the wound below his ribs looked at by a healer, a knowledgeable black squirrel from Oakwood, who had proclaimed that he had been lucky. The dagger, in going in at an odd angle, had just missed puncturing his lung. He would live, with no years taken off his life. However, Mae was able to heal him only after the healer removed his lower rib, which had been damaged irreparably due to his constant movement after the injury. The only consequence being that he would likely have to use a walking stick, Rupert was in a good mood, and took the healer's advice on medication without a spot of bitterness, though it was painful to have to resign himself to the ground while others ran about the trees freely.

Mae and Theo had found a lot to talk about, and got to know each other well in a very short time. They were a strange pair, for apart from being orphans, neither of them had much in common at all. But perhaps it was this very thing that drew them together, each needing something they found in the other. At first only together from what each felt as some sort of obligation, restless, adventurous Mae, and sensible, grounded Theo grew to be close friends on the journey home to Firwood, a place Mae looked forward to with mixed feelings, and to which Theo was coming for the first time.

Rupert, watching the two walking up ahead of him, thought of the future of Firwood when he would be gone and dead, not with morbidity but with simple wonder. Realizing the idea in his head, he ducked it shamefully but could not keep the smile from spreading full across his face.

We shall see.

Indeed. They would all see. For what was the future now, but a mellow, butter-melted sun on an imagined horizon?

Rupert closed his eyes, let the breeze play on his face, and went toward it, knowing the journey would never end.